I0653099

English Ivy

The Late Bloomers Series (Book 2)

By Betsy Talbot

Website: www.BetsyTalbot.com

Copyright © 2015 by Betsy Talbot

All rights reserved. This book or any portion thereof may not be reproduced or used in any manner whatsoever without the express written permission of the publisher except for the use of brief quotations in a book review.

ISBN-13: 978-0-9862697-6-9

ABOUT THE LATE BLOOMERS

After a lifetime of friendship bordering on sisterhood, five forty-something women from Arizona each embark on their own adventures in love, travel, and discovery around the globe. Knowing themselves far better than they did in their twenties and thirties, these seasoned women are ready to take on the world.

If forty is the new twenty, then these women are just getting started.

Find out more about The Late Bloomers Series at www.BetsyTalbot.com. Sign up for the email list and get details on the private (and free!) Late Bloomers Facebook Group, where women from all over the world share their wisdom, experience, and humor about life after forty.

Because why should Ivy and friends have all the fun?

CHAPTER ONE

Ivy mentally ran through the plan one more time as the Secretary of State gave the speech. First, she'd fake an upset stomach to her colleague Ben, touching her abdomen and nodding gravely before slipping quietly out the door. Then a firm nod to the Secret Service agents situated outside, secure in her clearance badge as a senior US Embassy employee to move freely about the building.

The carpet would muffle the sound of her high heels as she quickly walked down the empty hallway, and then she'd slip into her office and close the door. The press conference was mandatory for all staff, so Ivy would have the entire building to herself. But all she'd need was in her office. A few quick strokes to enter her password on her laptop, and then she would open the draft of the email she'd been perfecting for weeks. One click to send.

Ivy would take one last look around the office she'd occupied for the last five years, half her total stay in London—the functional, government-issued desk covered with manila folders; the dark blue carpet whose only selling point was the ability to hide stains; and the stand by the door, home to the umbrella she carried to work most days.

She'd shrug on her trench coat, wrap her Hermès scarf movie-star style around her long red hair, and take the elevator down to the lobby. At the top of the steps outside, she would pause, taking in this view for one last time—Grosvenor Square ahead with Dwight D. Eisenhower's statue greeting visitors, a giant gold eagle above her head proclaiming demurely that the Embassy belonged to the United States.

One final goodbye to Sal and Chester, the guards at the gate, and Ivy would be free. Walking away from Hyde Park, she'd look up into the uncommonly sunny sky, cover her sparkling green eyes with oversized sunglasses, and head for the Piccadilly Circus tube station. An hour later she'd emerge at Heathrow Airport.

Once on board, Ivy would settle into first class, order a glass of champagne from the flight attendant, and look out the window into the fading daylight sky as the plane taxied down the runway full speed ahead to her exciting new life. She wouldn't even bring a suitcase, leaving all the baggage of her current life behind. Everything from that point forward would be new—new job, new clothes, new country. Maybe even a new man, one who didn't even own a suit. Her mouth curled into a slow smile, feeling the rush of takeoff. She gripped the arms of her chair just as she would on a real plane.

"You can't be that excited about trade agreements," Ben whispered, elbowing her in the side.

Ivy snapped out of her fantasy, instantly transported from champagne in first class to bottled water in the conference room. The Secretary of State stood at the podium up front, outlining the latest link in the ongoing chain of economic cooperation between the United States and Great Britain. Reporters from the *Financial Times*, BBC, and Sky News were there, raising their hands to ask questions and scribbling furiously in their notebooks like actors in a political drama.

Ivy sighed, feeling the weight of her nine millionth press conference, the Groundhog Day cycle of repetitive, microscopic advances at work that were undone and then redone by whoever won the last election.

Ivy looked over at Ben and shrugged. "I was compiling my grocery list."

"The curry takeout queen of London? I doubt that." Ben grinned, waiting for Ivy to pounce back as usual.

"I'm slipping out. Cover for me if Sylvia comes by?" Ivy patted his arm and then stood up, not waiting for an answer. She was glad she'd taken the seat at the end of the row.

Outside the door, she took a deep breath and replayed the first part of her fantasy, all the way into her office. Instead of sending the resignation email that she'd typed up weeks ago, she sat in her chair and surveyed her surroundings. The walls were closing in daily, and if she didn't leave soon, she'd be crushed inside her shrinking life.

The one bright spot in her office was the silver frame, a

photo of Ivy with her best friends together in New York. She remembered the wine, the food and the laughter around the table that night. Since then her friends had all made big life changes. Rose was moving to Australia with the man of her dreams, Daisy was heading to France soon to be a judge on a cooking show, Violet's jewelry line was being sold at Barney's, and Lily was bouncing back from her divorce. Only Ivy was the same now as she was when she posed for that photo.

She touched each face on the photo, full of love for these women who were her closest friends. Ivy wasn't jealous. Who wouldn't want their friends to find success and happiness? But she wanted the same for herself. Surely that didn't make her a bad person.

Ivy put the frame down and took a drink from her water bottle, glancing at the forlorn plant on the edge of her desk. She doused it with the remaining water in her bottle.

"Little ivy, we need to find a place where we can grow. This place is killing us." She pulled the crunchy brown edges off the leaves and dropped them into the pot to decompose.

Her friends in the US thought her life was glamorous, and a few years ago it was. But now, ten years into her life in London and five years in the same position at the Embassy, she had to face the truth. Ivy was in a rut, stuck in her job and with a non-existent love life. She was about as wild on the weekends as her elderly neighbor Mrs. Bingham.

The formerly adventurous Ivy Cross, breaker of rules and hearts, had crossed the threshold of middle age and lost her spark.

She was on a mission to get it back.

# # #

"For a guy starting a new life, you sure are bringing a lot of your old life with you." Ruben grunted as he carried the last heavy box into the living room of Mateo's nearly empty flat. He looked around, wondering why Alejandro wasn't helping them.

"It's more like a new version than a total reboot. I need to keep the basic operating system." Mateo wiped his forehead with the back of his hand as he smiled.

"I appreciate you speaking my language," Ruben countered. "Is it time for *cerveza* yet?"

They were packing up the last of Mateo's belongings before his move. Never again would Ruben crash on Mateo's couch after a late night out. Never again would the three of them watch *fútbol* together in this place. And all those fun weekends on Lake Como were over now that they'd sold their restaurant.

Known as the Three Amigos, they were inseparable since childhood. Now Alejandro had kids and a busy law practice in Madrid, and Mateo was marrying Rose and moving to

Australia. Only Ruben still lived the same life he'd had since just after university, something that had never bothered him until now.

Alejandro came into the room, holding three bottles of Mahou. "While you guys sweated in here, I cleaned out the refrigerator. This is all that's left." He gave each man a bottle of beer.

"Always taking the toughest jobs, aren't you? We appreciate your sacrifice," Ruben said with a grin as he grabbed his bottle.

"My strongest muscle is up here," Alejandro said as he tapped his head with his finger. "You should try working your brain as much as you do your biceps." Alejandro avoided the gym like the plague, and it showed.

Ruben's energy had always been high, and if it weren't for the gym and his sadist of a trainer, he'd explode. Those relentless hours of punishing workouts not only kept him hard and lean, they alleviated the pressure continually building in his body. Without an intense workout every day, he couldn't function. Alejandro, on the other hand, was happily growing soft with middle age. He'd always been the thinker of the three, a good trait for a lawyer.

"We only need one set of brains for this team," Ruben joked, even though all three of them earned the highest marks at university. But only Alejandro was known for it. Throughout their lives, Ruben usually suggested the ideas that got them into trouble. Alejandro was the planner who tried to reason with him to find safer alternatives. And angel-faced Mateo was always the one who begged forgiveness if they got caught. Ruben thought it was an effective strategy, and he wondered how he'd fare now that he had to do most of it by himself.

Ruben raised his beer in mock seriousness. "To Mateo, a good man who was tragically taken from us far too soon."

"May he rest in peace—every night after shagging the brains out of the beautiful Rose," Alejandro chimed in.

The three men laughed as they clinked bottles and drank, the icy cold beer a welcome reward for their work.

"I still can't believe you're getting on a plane tonight. Even when you lived in Italy, you were just a couple of hours away. Now I'll have to plan a holiday just to hang out with you." Ruben couldn't help but mourn the loss of his good friend, even though he was happy for him. He pointed his thumb toward Alejandro. "And this one is always too busy with work and the kids to hang out with me."

"Ruben, I'm a happily married man. I'm not going clubbing with you. You know you're always welcome to hang out at my house." Alejandro trotted out the familiar lines, used to Ruben's complaints about his tame lifestyle.

"But the only beautiful woman there is already taken."

"Do you ever get tired of being on the prowl?" Mateo asked with a laugh.

Ruben felt the sting of his words in a way he wouldn't have in the past. "You make it sound like I'm some wild animal. And no, it doesn't get old," Ruben said, lying through his teeth.

"Wild animal? More like a house cat chasing its tail," Alejandro said with a laugh, clinking bottles with Mateo.

"You guys are just jealous. You're stuck with the same woman forever, and I still have variety." Ruben smirked.

Mateo shook his head and set his empty bottle down on top of a box. "I'll tell you what a wise old man said to me: 'It's easy to be a good lover for one night. The real challenge is to keep it hot with the same person for years.'"

"That is the best closing argument I've heard in years. You guys ready for some food?" Alejandro gathered their empty bottles and put them in the recycling bin, Mateo following behind to get the last bag of trash. Ruben watched them, two men comfortable in their relationships and decisions. They were so calm and contented, something he'd never been able to feel with one person. Ruben always felt like a shark, in constant motion just to keep breathing.

Maybe the monogamous life was right for them, but he couldn't see it for himself. He was still a man of conquests, and he didn't think he'd ever find a woman to change his mind. Ruben was wired this way, and no amount of convincing from his friends would change him.

"You can ask your sweet Rose what kind of lover I am after I blow her friend Ivy's mind," Ruben said, cocky swagger back in place.

"Ivy Cross? She'll never go out with you," Mateo said. "Not only is she not into you, she's not into anybody."

"You underestimate my charm," Ruben replied. "Besides, she lost a bet and owes me a date. And I plan to collect later this week in London."

"It's been nice knowing you, Ruben." Mateo embraced him in a big bear hug. "I'm on the plane to Australia tonight, so I won't be able to come back for the funeral."

"Don't worry. We'll make it a good service. I hear they can do a lot with makeup these days to cover up the trauma." Alejandro joined in on the ribbing.

"I wonder if all his ex-girlfriends will show up?" Mateo asked, pretending Ruben wasn't even in the room.

"Just send one invitation to the twelve-step group they all join when he dumps them," Alejandro said.

"Joke all you want, my friends. But there is no woman who can withstand my charms. Not even the prickly Ivy Cross."

Alejandro looked at Mateo. "I've never met her, but after the stories I've heard after the fiasco with you and Rose, I think Ruben should buy dinner tonight. He won't be around to pay his credit card bill next month, and I'm in the mood for some expensive wine." The three men laughed as they locked the door and headed out for their last night in Madrid as the Three

Amigos.

CHAPTER TWO

Ivy wasn't looking for permission. She never did. But she did want to know what her friends thought of her idea to change jobs, change locations, change everything she could to regain her spark. Ivy picked up her phone to send a group message.

Send to Group: Late_Bloomers

Ivy_Cross: Quitting my job. Shaking things up. Crazy, or crazy smart?

LilyL: Probably both. What's up?

Ivy_Cross: Feeling stuck, gotta move.

RoseGarden: Staying in London?

Ivy_Cross: Not sure. Not sure of anything except need a change.

VioletStackDesign: Did something happen?

Ivy_Cross: That's the problem, nothing is happening. I'm cruising into a boring middle age.

LilyL: Watch your mouth, sister. We're the same age as you.

Ivy_Cross: Can't help it. I feel old. Stale. Routine.

VioletStackDesign: I'm wearing comfortable shoes.

Daisy_Eats: This is interfering with my nap.

LilyL: Time for me to take my fiber pills.

RoseGarden: I think I just pulled a muscle typing.

Ivy_Cross: You guys are jerks.

RoseGarden: Shaking things up in your love life, too?

VioletStackDesign: Ooh, good idea. "Faster! Faster! Faster!" than getting a new job.

LilyL: No vesting schedule for "benefits."

Daisy_Eats: You can apply for a variety of "positions" in a single interview.

RoseGarden: He can "show you the ropes."

Ivy_Cross: Okay, pervs. Thanks for the "penetrating" analysis of my situation. Will keep you posted. XOXO

The Late Bloomers got her in a way no one else did. She didn't have to look far to figure out why—she didn't allow anyone else the opportunity.

Even after all her years in London, Ivy still chatted almost daily with the four women she'd grown up with in Arizona: Violet, Rose, Daisy, and Lily. Most people found it funny to discover that Ivy's mother was a hippie and she came very close to growing up in a commune. Thankfully her mom and her friends were so terrible with money that they lost the farm before Ivy was born, or else she'd would be macramé-ing and composting her way through life right now.

Mom and a few of her friends moved to tiny Hobart, Arizona to regroup. While they became a little more conventional over the years, they still believed in sharing parenting duties. Ivy grew up with four sister-like friends who all lived in the same neighborhood. They were in and out of each other's houses from day one, permanent fixtures in each other's lives. Their schoolmates nicknamed them The Bloomers, a name as unfashionable as they felt. The girls bonded even more tightly over the teasing. Their garden-themed names were a throwback to the flower child days of their mothers, an unwelcome inheritance in a middle school populated by kids wearing preppy clothes and listening to Walkman cassette players.

The girls hated it at first, just like any kids who wanted to blend in. But they stuck together through the storm of puberty and finally embraced the nickname, going so far as to call themselves The Late Bloomers in their late twenties. Now over forty, the name was starting to carry some meaning, possibly even a premonition of things to come.

# # #

Since none of the Late Bloomers had voiced a good reason why she shouldn't change jobs, Ivy felt more confident in her decision to make a move. She liked to pretend she didn't need anyone's help, but the truth was that her friends served as a sounding board, able to talk her down from ideas that were too crazy. Ivy liked to push boundaries, but even she had to admit sometimes she went too far.

Like the time the five of them went to Las Vegas together right after college, a celebratory trip for entering adulthood. None of them had much money back then, but they combined their cash and bought a package deal for a hotel suite with a free breakfast buffet every morning. The plan was to sit by the pool and relax, drink fruity beverages, and work on their tans.

As usual, Ivy had a scheme in mind, something to make the trip more exciting. "More" was her guiding principle in those days, no matter what the situation.

Ivy read a book on how to count cards on the flight and told the others she was going to win big and take them all out for steak and lobster after. The others laughed at first. But as Ivy went on, explaining what she'd learned about blackjack and counting cards and how she was going to pull it off, they tried to talk her out of it.

"There is no law against counting cards. I checked," Ivy said in response to their worries.

"Even if that's true, they still have a right to kick you out if you break house rules. And if they kick you out, they kick us all out, Ivy," Rose said. "The room is in your name."

"Don't make me lose this swimming pool," Daisy whined. "I move to Portland next week, and I'll probably never see the sun again."

"One hour max is all I need. And it's probably better if you guys aren't around watching. Less suspicious." Ivy calculated the winnings in her head. "If you each give me $50 to play, then I can make some serious money, maybe even upgrade us to first class on the flight home."

"Why don't we each use $50 to buy our own steak dinners?" Violet's logic was a thorn in Ivy's side. "Then we'll stay up all night before we leave and sleep on the plane. No need for first class."

"Because I can make us enough money for a proper vacation! Why get an economics degree if I can't use it to make life better for us?" Ivy was frustrated with her friends for not sharing her enthusiasm or their dollars. Maybe it was because they hadn't read the same book to see how easy it was.

That night, they went out for a cheap buffet before playing

quarter slots and then dancing. When the four others decided to go back to the suite at three a.m., Ivy stayed in the casino. She took a cash advance against her new credit card, bought $250 worth of chips, and sat at the blackjack table. She played for an hour, surprised to discover her strategies weren't working. The chips pile dwindled. Ivy knew it took money to make money, so she withdrew another $250 from her credit card. Lady Luck worked against her all night, which infuriated the logical side of her brain. Without her friends to rein her in, Ivy kept at it, sleep-deprived and determined to win.

By the time the girls came downstairs in their swimsuits at ten o'clock in the morning, Ivy was down $2,000, the maximum allowed on her new credit card. The rest of them dug into their meager funds to pay Ivy's share of the bill and her steak dinner that night. Thankfully, they didn't scold her then, knowing her embarrassment and loss were punishment enough. But they didn't hesitate to mention it every time Ivy came up with a crazy new idea.

But not this time. One of them always warned her that her idea was too wild or risky to work, usually Rose. The fact that they didn't made her even madder at herself. If she couldn't shock them with her behavior anymore, she really was slowing down.

CHAPTER THREE

Ivy should have been helping Sylvia prep for the upcoming Berlin conference, but she had more important things to do. She sent another résumé off to a headhunter, spreading her job search further around the world. Ivy was up to four countries now, and she imagined what her life would look like in each one. Australia would be the furthest away, and she'd have summer when everyone else she knew was in winter. In Scotland, she'd have whisky and men in kilts, and she might even discover what Scotsmen wore underneath the plaid. Washington, D.C. would be full of power players, not too different from London in that respect, but she'd be closer to her friends. Hong Kong was the wildcard, an exotic destination without any frame of reference.

As she thought about pork buns and learning to eat with chopsticks, her phone rang. She picked it up without looking at the caller ID.

"American Woman. I've missed your sharp tongue and sexy insults. Have you missed me?" Ruben's English carried a slight Spanish accent and an unmistakable flirty edge. Ivy cradled the phone against her shoulder and rotated her chair away from the open door of her London office for privacy.

"I would have to live a thousand years without companionship of any kind before you would ever cross my mind," Ivy replied smoothly, continuing the game they'd been playing for weeks over phone and email. "Besides, with you in Madrid, the chance of us seeing each other again is slim." She paused before continuing. "Probably good news for you, though. I'd break you within twenty-four hours."

Ruben growled softly in response, and Ivy felt a shiver go down her spine. She never could predict what he was going to do next, and he delighted her just about as often as he aggravated her.

"This sounds like the opening offer of a new bet," he said. "But first, you have to pay up on the original. You owe me." Ruben enunciated those last three words slowly, and Ivy pictured his lips curling around every syllable, then spreading into a grin framed by dimples. Most women couldn't resist his single-minded focus, quick wit, and good looks. But Ivy Cross wasn't most women. There was no way on earth she'd let this man near her heart. Correction–there was no way she'd let *any* man near her heart again.

Ruben hummed a few bars of "American Woman," and Ivy pictured him bobbing his head and strumming an air guitar as he did it. She'd never admit it to him, but she liked his playful nature. Most of the men she knew lost their sense of fun about the same time they started losing their hair. Maybe there was a connection; he still had a thick brown pelt covering his hard head. Ruben was handsome, no doubt, his deep brown eyes and broad shoulders exactly what Ivy liked in a man. He even smelled good, a musky, manly odor that didn't come from a bottle.

It would be easy to have a short fling with him before she left London for good—and she was definitely leaving London soon. But he was off-limits, too close for comfort to her friend Rose. When Ivy eventually dumped him, like she had done with every man since Zach, it would complicate her friendship. And if there was one thing in life Ivy guarded like a lion, it was her friendships.

"Don't you have better things to do than chase after a woman who lives in another country?" Ivy asked.

"It is sweet of you to be concerned about my schedule. It shows you care," Ruben replied, dodging her question.

"Care? That's the least of it. I'm trying to find a way out of our date. This can't be the first time that's ever happened to you. I'd imagine the regret factor is high in women who say yes to you." Ivy aimed to wound his pride and worried for a second that she'd gone too far. She was known for being a bit caustic, but she wasn't a total bitch. Or at least she tried not to be. No worries on that front, though; Ruben was armor-coated when it came to her digs.

"American Woman, I am a man in demand. Or a demanding man, I can't remember which. But I must insist that you honor our bet. There will be shame upon your house if you don't."

Ivy's eyes narrowed at his sly reference to her favorite series, *Game of Thrones*. How did he know that? Probably from Rose, the source of the bet that got Ivy's smart mouth into this situation in the first place. Rose adored Ruben like a brother, and Ivy suspected she was encouraging this silly infatuation. Wouldn't Rose love to have her fiancé's best friend as Ivy's new boyfriend? One big happy family. The idea was as appealing to Ivy as chickenpox.

"The only shame is in you asking Rose and Mateo to help you score a date. What else did they tell you about me?"

"I don't need any help to get a date. You already owe me one. Unless your mouth wrote a check your body can't cash. Isn't that what you Americans say?"

"You've been watching bad seventies movies, Ruben. No one says that."

"You bet me Rose and Mateo wouldn't get back together after their big fight, and now they are moving to Australia, happily ever after, the end. I was so right about them it makes your head spin." Ruben clucked like a chicken, egging her on. "And now you have to pay up. Unless you're scared of what might happen." He clucked again for emphasis, the cockiest cock on the block.

Ivy wondered if Rose had told him about her competitive nature, too. She couldn't resist a challenge.

"We have nothing in common but Rose and Mateo, and they are moving halfway around the world. We aren't going to double date on Friday nights and go on vacation with them. This non-relationship is going nowhere, Ruben. And by nowhere, I mean no sex."

Ivy clicked her email icon on her laptop and began scrolling, trying to distract herself from thinking about his bare skin rubbing against hers.

"We're already at phone sex? You move fast. I'll try to keep up." She couldn't hold back a smile and was grateful he couldn't see it. Ivy felt a little guilty about her lusty thoughts, but only a little.

"You were right about Rose and Mateo, and he's lucky she didn't throw him in the river before he could explain. But Rose doesn't have the upper-body strength I do, and you might not be so lucky." Ivy relished the thought of throwing him in the river, if only to see him climb out all wet, button-down shirt sticking to his abs and chest and drops of water dripping from his dark lashes over his brown eyes. She shook her head to remove the image. "Dinner would be a waste of time."

"I agree. Let's go dancing instead. I'll pick you up at eight o'clock."

"Wait, tonight? You're in London?"

"I'm in London all the time for business. Didn't I mention that?" Ruben's laugh was low. "Wear something sexy to torture me. Please." The phone disconnected and Ivy tried hard to be mad, but her smile wouldn't let her.

# # #

The technology conference was an excuse to get to London. As CEO, Ruben typically sent Tomas to this kind of thing to network in the industry and recruit more business for Alegre Data. But in the weeks since Ruben had met the fiery Ivy Cross, he hadn't been able to shake her from his mind. This tall, redheaded American invaded his mind during business meetings, cast a shadow over his dates in the evenings, and settled in his loins as he went to sleep at night. Her green eyes dared him to make a move. He had to have her if only to cure himself of this obsession.

"Ivy is too much woman for you, Ruben," Mateo had said on more than one occasion. "I think she's too much for any man." His words were like throwing fuel on a fire.

Now that Mateo was getting married, he considered himself an expert on women. Hadn't it been Ruben who saved the day when Mateo had almost lost Rose? How short his memory was on the things that mattered. Just because Ruben didn't choose to have a relationship didn't mean he didn't know anything about women. The last woman who'd stormed out of his life had sent him a book titled *Outliers*. She highlighted the first passage about the Ten-Thousand-Hour Rule, meaning most people became experts after ten thousand hours of practice at a particular skill. In the margin, she scribbled *Player*, underlined three times. He didn't think she meant it as a compliment.

But with all the practice he'd had in his life, he should be considered an expert. Why deny it?

Ruben made his way downstairs to the meeting room, taking the stairs instead of the elevator. Even after his strenuous workout in the hotel gym after his flight, he was still amped. He had a feeling he'd be wired until he got Ivy out of his system.

Her confidence turned him on in ways he didn't even know were possible. He felt centered around her, less manic than usual. Having one conversation with her was equal to the effect of a strenuous workout, and he couldn't imagine what sex with her would do for him. Were all forty-something women like this, or just this one? Ruben had nothing for comparison. And he certainly wasn't going to risk the ridicule of asking Mateo. Even so, he had to play this one carefully so as not to upset Rose and Mateo. But Ivy didn't seem like the fragile type, and he thought they could both be adults about it. He just needed one date to let the chemistry between them ignite and then fizzle out.

Ruben walked in the door to the hotel conference room and made a beeline for the coffee bar at the end of the lunch buffet, glad to see a proper espresso machine and barista. Caffeine had the opposite effect on him than it had on most people. It was the only thing that tamped down his energy, other than the workouts, and he drank it several times a day.

His phone buzzed. Tomas.

"Hey, boss. How goes the conference?"

"Dull so far. But I have a date tonight, so ask me again in the morning." Ruben walked over to the side of the room to avoid the buzz of conversation from the conference attendees.

"As if I need to know where you tuck your little boss in at night." Tomas was his right-hand man, the one he was grooming to take over one day. Savvy and book-smart, Tomas had only one flaw. He was as moody as a teenager sometimes, melting down over the smallest problems. "I have some bad news, but the good news is that it's bad news for everyone," Tomas said, as only he could. The trick was to know when something was a real disaster and when something was just a Tomas tantrum. Ruben didn't have enough information yet to make a judgment.

"Give it to me straight," Ruben replied.

"We have the option to file an addendum to the bid, which is a good thing," Tomas started.

"Don't butter me up. What's the problem?" Ruben prodded.

"We can't meet our original bid on the servers. The supplier we were using just went out of business, and the others are too expensive for us to make a profit."

Ruben ran his hand over his face. "You said this was bad news for everyone. What do you mean by that?" Ruben asked.

"Well, Brandt's company used the same supplier, so he's in the same bind. And Lars's company has their own supply, but they are not as financially secure as us or Brandt. ConStead won't trust them with a deal of this size and length of time if they're not stable. Our real competition here is with Christof Brandt, and we'd better hope he doesn't find a solution to the problem before we do." Tomas paused, waiting for Ruben's response.

"Thanks for the heads-up, Tomas. Give me some time to think about it." Ruben pocketed his phone and looked around the room for Christof Brandt, his lips curling in distaste when he saw him saunter into the room like a movie star. A lackey trailed behind him, fetching his lunch while Christof scanned the room for power brokers. Men like Christof didn't waste time with small talk unless it was for a bigger purpose. He made a beeline for Ruben.

"Don't tell me, mine was the first face you thought of when you woke up this morning," Ruben said by way of greeting. "Your obsession with me is getting out of hand."

Christof smirked, his high cheekbones slicing the air around him. "You always joke, Ruben. And yet I never laugh." Christof's green eyes were cold and shallow.

"Then why do you keep coming back for more? Doesn't make you look very smart." Ruben took the final sip of his coffee and set it on a nearby table. Time to go.

"One question," Christof said as he held up his finger. "You know about the, ah, disruption to the ConStead deal for all of us."

"What do you want from me, Christof? Besides my brain, good looks, and human heart?" Ruben replied, ready to leave this conversation before it even got started.

"I want to know what you're doing about it because I can find another vendor and take a loss on this deal. You can't." Christof's thin smile was anything but friendly. He often beat his competition with enormous reserves of money. More accurately, he beat them with his father's money, but he didn't like to advertise that fact. Most of the time, he behaved like an overgrown school bully, and people were either suck-ups or scaredy-cats around him. Ruben was neither.

"For the last time, Christof. I don't want to be your friend. We're not going to eat lunch together in the cafeteria or ride bikes after school. We're not going to share secret handshakes. I'm just not into you." Ruben turned to walk away, done with this conversation.

"We'll see how friendly you get when ConStead comes to me and you're out looking for a job. Again." Christof laughed as he pulled out a chair and sat down, his lackey arriving just in time with his meal.

Ruben's blood boiled, but he wouldn't give Christof the satisfaction of knowing it. One day he'd knock the smug grin off his aristocratic face.

He mentally rearranged his afternoon schedule to fit in

another workout. This time, he'd use the punching bag.

CHAPTER FOUR

Ivy would never forget the expression on Ruben's face when he picked her up. For once, the man was speechless. Her green silk halter dress draped over every curve. A delicate gold chain fell almost to her waist, tracing a path through her cleavage. Ivy's red hair was loose, the waves falling to her shoulder blades and highlighting her broad shoulders. Her smoky eyes were lined and smudged to seduce without words, her lips a glossy nude that begged for color from vigorous kissing.

Ruben may have controlled the conversation today, but Ivy planned to control the actions tonight.

He chastely kissed her on the cheeks in a typical European greeting, lingering after the second kiss to whisper, "I surrender. Let's just stay here."

"If you think it's going to be that easy, then perhaps you're not worthy of the prize." Ivy's voice was soft and breathy as she gently pushed him back.

"You're right. I asked you to torture me with a sexy dress, and you have. I like it when you follow my orders," Ruben said with a sexy smirk, knowing how to push her buttons. Before she could respond, he put his hand on her back and ushered her into the waiting black cab.

He sat beside her, his leg casually crossed to reveal his low-rise black boots. The leather was buttery soft, and Ivy guessed his shoes easily cost as much as hers. A man who took care of his shoes was a man who paid attention to detail in everything. Ivy liked a thorough man.

His fitted pants revealed not an ounce of fat on his frame, not even a little pudge at the waist from sitting down. Ivy wondered if he had a six-pack underneath his button-down shirt. She had an overwhelming urge to burrow underneath a button with her fingers to find out.

Ruben directed the driver to a familiar street.

Ivy raised an eyebrow at him. "You can't be serious."

"I want what you Americans call a do-over." Ruben grinned.

The cab stopped in front of Ibérica, the Spanish restaurant where they first met.

"The last time I was here, you ruined my appetite," Ivy said.

"Then let me make it up to you. This time I promise you'll leave satisfied."

Ivy remembered the cocky man who'd approached her

table that day, asking for advice for his lovelorn friend as an excuse to chat her up. She didn't know who he was, and he didn't know who she was, at least not at first.

She was already in a mood that day, angry with the callous bastard who had hurt her friend Rose. Any other day and she might have been receptive to a man who approached her in such a confident manner. But that day, it just fed her need for revenge. He would have been the recipient of her wrath no matter what, and even more so when she discovered who he was.

"After last time, the management might have our pictures posted by the hostess stand. Do not allow these crazy people to enter." She smiled at him, the unexpected charm of the do-over at Ibérica softening her outer shell just a little.

Ruben grinned, reaching down to the bag at his feet. "I came prepared," he said, pulling out two cardboard masks on wooden sticks. Ivy's cool demeanor broke when she saw the faces—William and Kate, the Duke and Duchess of Cambridge.

Ivy laughed from deep in her belly, forgetting his attractive face for a moment as she reveled in his sly sense of humor. She hadn't laughed like that in a long time.

"You think we can pass as royalty, eh? You are an arrogant one," she said, her laughter dying down.

"Would you like to be Kate or Wills? I think I can pull off either one, so the choice is yours." Ruben held up each mask to his face, the cab driver looking at him through the rearview mirror and laughing. "See, he agreed with me!"

"Let's try to be ourselves first, but if we run into trouble you can be Wills, and I'll be Kate." Ivy couldn't believe they were taking the masks into the restaurant with them.

Ruben paid the cabbie and offered her his arm to walk into the restaurant, where the maître d' greeted him personally at the door. This man was full of surprises.

"Señor Alegre, we are happy to see you again. Your table is ready."

Ivy looked at Ruben with eyebrows raised as they followed the maître d' into the restaurant, stopping at the very table she sat at last time.

Ivy sat down, wondering what else Ruben had in store for the evening. She placed her mask on the table. "I'm keeping this close in case you get out of hand," she warned. "I'd hate to get blacklisted from this restaurant before I ever get to eat the food."

"I said you'd be satisfied, and I meant it. We're going to burn a lot of calories tonight, so eat more than you think you need to," Ruben said.

"I thought I told you we wouldn't be having sex, Ruben." As Ivy said it, she felt her resolve weaken.

"Why do you keep bringing it back to sex, Ivy? I was

talking about dancing. But now I know what you're thinking about," he said with a wink. "Such a fast girl."

The waiter arrived with their wine, and over the course of the next two hours he continued to bring a variety of Spanish tapas—tender meatballs, nutty Manchego cheese, tasty chorizo, sautéed almonds, and of course the famous Ibérico ham made from specially bred, acorn-fed pigs. The only olives Ivy had ever eaten were on the cocktail stick of a martini. Tonight she feasted on an assortment of olives lightly coated with oil and spices, a far better use of olives than a martini, in her opinion. The Spanish tortilla, far different than the flour and corn ones she ate growing up, was a fat little omelet made from eggs, potatoes, and onion. Tiny little croquettes filled with salted cod were an elegant version of the battered fish sold at every chippy on every London street.

As the food kept coming, stylishly displayed on small plates, they began their first real conversation. Ivy delighted in the explanations of the food, the stories behind them, and tales from life in Madrid. He fed her curiosity and never tired of her questions. Food was safe, and it allowed them to become comfortable with each other and move on to deeper subjects. Now that they were face to face, acting out the roles of the tenacious playboy and the disdainful dominatrix felt inappropriate, like wearing a bathing suit to the grocery store.

Ivy shared stories about the Late Bloomers and some of her adventures in London while Ruben talked of his friends Alejandro and Mateo and the years he'd spent building his company, Alegre Data. It was a true first-date conversation, awkward only in that they'd acted shallowly with each other for weeks before finally revealing some depth. Ivy laughed more than she had in months, and when she talked with Ruben, she felt her old spark coming back. He was pulling her to him, breaking through the shell she'd allowed to form over herself.

Ivy thought that if all relationships worked backward, maybe they'd have one where the breakup was already done and it could only get better as they worked back to the first flirtation, a Benjamin Button sort of relationship. If only she weren't leaving London, of course.

# # #

Ruben was mesmerized by her laugh, and he found himself trying to coax it from her lips. He wished it were his full-time job to please her, his paycheck the sound of her delight. He could only hope that her satisfaction with the night matched his own. She couldn't fake a laugh like that.

"You're not like what I thought you'd be," Ruben said, taking the last of the mussels in tomato vinaigrette. He found himself wanting to stay at the table, to keep talking with Ivy instead of taking her to bed. Well, he still wanted to do that, of course, but it wasn't the only thing.

"And what did you think I'd be like? All horns and pitchforks?" She smiled and it lit the room, tiny wrinkles like rays of light escaping from the corners of her sparkling green eyes. She'd lined them with dark kohl, a sophisticated look that still couldn't hide the mischief of the small-town girl from the American Southwest. Her stories of growing up—defending her friends from bullies and pushing boundaries—surprised him. Ivy Cross was a woman of many layers.

"I thought you'd be more like an icy and tart margarita, but instead you're a warm glass of brandy." Ruben often spoke without thinking, and it usually got him into trouble. But this time, he was glad he didn't have a filter. She was full-bodied and ripe for consumption, and he wanted her to know it.

"Most people don't see me as a warm person," Ivy replied, squirming a little in her seat. Was she uncomfortable with what he'd said? "Saves me a lot of trouble to let them think I'm not."

"They should see the view from where I'm sitting," he replied. Ruben was falling, and it wasn't until that very moment that he understood why.

The tightly wound coil inside him gently released. He felt calm, measured, in control. The yearning he had in his regular life to always seek something else, some immeasurable thing, was fulfilled. For once, his energy was at a moderate hum, a pleasant vibration instead of a jarring pulse. Ivy Cross had managed to accomplish in one night what he'd been trying all his life to do—and he didn't even think she realized it.

He didn't know how to tell Ivy what just happened, or to find out if she felt the same way.

The waiter brought espressos to the table, and he could feel Ivy changing gears. Ruben sensed a little panic emanating from her and wondered if he'd said the wrong thing. His sense of calm began unraveling.

Ivy dumped a spoonful of sugar into her small cup and stirred, sloshing a bit over the edge. He'd never seen her nervous before. The warm feeling they'd shared over dinner diminished, and Ruben didn't know how to reclaim it. So he fell back to his role as the playboy, stoking the fires of the competitive game that was not nearly as hot as the genuine conversation they'd just had.

"Are you ready to dance? I should have you sign a waiver, because I can't be responsible for what happens after you see me move this," he said, motioning to his body. His face grinned, but inside he burned with the disappointment of being locked outside her ivy-covered walls again.

# # #

The club had a dance lesson starting at eleven p.m., a way to loosen up the crowd. Ivy watched an impossibly hot guy with tight orange pants, a dark gray T-shirt hugging his muscular chest, and black-and-white oxford shoes bend and sway at the front of the room while everyone followed. His hips moved in ways that should be illegal, and Ivy would have liked to be the one to arrest him.

The Latin music pounded in her ears, a sea of sweaty bodies around her gyrating to the music. The rhythm permeated her pores, breathing in and out of her body with each beat, stretching like vines between her and every other dancer in the room. Ivy felt a dizzying mix of physical freedom and connectedness. A warning bell went off in her brain, aware of the risk of being with Ruben when even the air oozed sex. She'd already felt the live wire connection at dinner, an uncomfortably close moment where he veered too close to her heart. Her reflexes were fast, honed over years of practice. Now that she'd shut it down, she had to keep it that way. Ivy would have preferred sitting at a table, drink in hand, and just watching the instructor, but Ruben pulled her to the dance floor.

"This is the basic step," Orange Pants called out. "*Básico! Básico!*" he shouted over the music.

Ivy felt the rhythm, swaying her hips and stepping forward and backward. As long as they kept it to solo dancing, she'd be okay.

Ruben stepped over and placed his hands on her hips. From behind, he said, "Do you need help loosening up?" He squeezed gently, his pelvis perfectly surrounding the curve of her rear end.

"If I showed you how limber I am, you'd never leave," Ivy said, narrowing her eyes. "But since you asked for it, I will show no mercy." She quickly turned and put her index finger against his chest, flicking him back to his position.

The music started again, and Ivy kept her eyes on Orange Pants at the front, the way his body melted into the music. She matched her moves to his, hips swaying, back twisting, and shoulders turning. The music ran through her like a waterfall, seeping into her ears and drenching every cell in her body. When he commanded them to turn and start dancing with a partner, she connected with Ruben almost without thinking.

He pulled her close, their hips aligned, eyes locked on each other. Ivy's breath caught in her throat as his leg went between hers, his steps rubbing the silk of her green dress against her inner thighs. She felt her nipples rise in response. Ruben's firm grip on her upper back told her he knew how to handle a woman. *He's had a lot of practice*, she reminded herself.

Ivy had her share of encounters over the years, mostly men who were as career-conscious as her with no desire for a serious relationship. The sex was hard and fast, something to fit in around a busy schedule. Dancing with Ruben for just these few short moments was already hotter than most of the sex she'd ever had.

The justifications for breaking her rules started without prompting. Maybe being with him just once wouldn't hurt. They could both be adults about it, never breathing a word to Rose and Mateo. It wouldn't complicate her life in the least, and she was leaving soon. How deep could it get? She'd proven at dinner how she could deflect any emotional connections.

She pressed closer to Ruben's body, the fit of their legs and hips together a sexy preview of how good they'd be together in bed. All her restrictions on why they couldn't enjoy at least one night of passion were fading far into the background of her mind.

"*Cambio!*" Orange Pants gave the signal to change partners, hand in the air making a circle. A curvy blonde in a tight dress shimmied her way into Ivy's spot, delighted to pair with a handsome man like Ruben.

"I've got this, luv," she said to Ivy, barely even glancing at her. Ruben embraced her like a pro, dismissing Ivy with a slight shrug.

Ivy looked right and saw her next partner was a balding man who was hopping from side to side, out of rhythm to the music. He held out his hand expectantly, waiting for her. Ivy plastered a smile on her face and joined him, wincing every time he stepped on her feet. Front and back, side to side, twirling in his arms, Ivy felt the lack of heat between them, their mechanical movements a mockery of the sensual music. When Orange Pants signaled another change, Ivy was glad to move on, wishing the curvy blonde woman behind her a broken toe from dancing with the rhythm killer.

She circled the dance floor for almost an hour, changing partners and never finding the rhythm she had with Ruben. Tall men, short men, fat men, skinny men, young men, old men–no one fit her like Ruben. She looked around the dance floor to see how many more changes until she got back to him. Ten, nine, eight. He was smiling too much with a raven-haired woman in a red dress. Seven, six, five. A short-haired woman with an impossibly small waist and wide, curvy hips looked like a professional dancer, moving in tune with Ruben in a way that made Ivy green with envy. This woman looked how Ivy felt when dancing with him though there was no way Ivy was that coordinated.

Ivy didn't do jealousy, or at least she hadn't until tonight. And she did not like the way it made her feel. Her current dance partner was a young guy, probably barely in his twenties, with a thin, hipster-looking build. She stared at his oversized black glasses and close-cropped hair and forced herself to be into him, to feel the rhythm in the same way she felt it with Ruben. To make Ruben jealous, too.

Hipster Guy was into it. He was a superb dancer, and Ivy could barely keep up. But his was a technical precision, a dance instructor way of moving that felt less sensual on the inside than it probably looked from the outside. Ivy wondered if Ruben was watching, irritated that she even cared.

Four, three, two. Next to him now, she could see the sparkle in his eyes. He was having a good time—without her! A woman with curly brown hair was in his arms, laughing at whatever he'd just whispered in her ear. Ivy's partner was a tall, thin man with an unkempt beard, a professor type loosening up outside of class. He was surprisingly light on his feet, a fun partner with soulful eyes who probably wrote poetry in his spare time. Men like that were perfect for Ivy's flighty friend Daisy, maybe even her artistic friend Vi, but not for the hard-charging and slightly abrasive personality of Ivy Cross.

"Cambio!" Orange Pants called, finally delivering Ivy back to Ruben. She'd make him pay for his wandering eye, show him exactly how much fire she had in her belly. Ivy put on her best lusty look and moved toward him, vindicated when he took her hand and pulled her close to him. She was ready to show him what she'd learned, to make him forget about those other women. Ivy felt her full sexual power humming through her body, ready to pounce on her prey.

"Let's get a drink," he said, oblivious to her powers of seduction. Without waiting for a response, he grabbed her hand and dragged her off the dance floor toward the bar.

Ruben ordered two cocktails from the waitress who smiled at him a bit too long. His default personality was to flirt, and Ivy felt less special with every passing moment.

"Having fun?" Ivy asked, left eyebrow raised.

"You can move one eyebrow at a time?" he responded.

"I can do a lot of things with my body," Ivy said. "But you didn't answer my question."

"I'm always fascinated by people who want to control themselves like that," Ruben said as the waitress returned with their drinks. She placed Ruben's down first, her finger casually pointing to the phone number scrawled on his napkin. She put Ivy's glass on the table without even looking at her. "Me? I don't have that kind of self-control." He took a drink, folding the napkin and placing it in his pocket. Right in front of her! "And I don't want it, either."

While she wanted to have an affair with no strings attached, her pride demanded that he be more into her than she was into him. Who was he to chase her down like this and then act like being with her was no big deal? She was doing him a favor to go out with him!

"Do you think we've settled the terms of the bet now?" Ivy asked, a deep freeze descending over her loins.

"So soon? The night is still young!" Ruben's grin was like that of a kid at an amusement park. But Ivy was closing her rides for the night, shuttering the ticket booth, and turning out the lights.

"You had your chance, Ruben. You didn't convince me of anything except that I like salsa dancing. And since they have clubs all over the world, I'll be sure to find one when I get settled into my new job. So for that, I thank you." Ivy looked into her slinky purse for her lip balm, no longer needing the lipstick, perfume, or other tools of seduction.

"What new job is this?" Ruben asked, finally showing he was paying attention.

"Well, I don't have it yet, but it is only a matter of time. I've got interviews scheduled in several cities." Ivy felt her keys in her bag as she put the lip balm back, thinking of her warm and cozy bed at her flat in the trendy Marylebone section of London. The one she'd be sleeping in alone in less than an hour.

"Why would you leave London when it's the easiest place to see me?" Ruben's confusion was sincere. "Well, besides Madrid," he added.

"The world doesn't revolve around you. At least my world doesn't." Ivy stood. "I'm going home now. Alone."

Ruben stood, throwing a few pounds on the table for the drinks. "I'll take you back."

"Not a chance," Ivy said.

"One last thing, promise." Ruben reached out and put his hand on her bare arm, the warmth of him sending a tingle down her spine. "I brought you a gift. It's in my hotel room, and it will just take a minute to get it."

"You must think I'm an idiot to go to your hotel room. But nice try," she said, momentarily forgetting that she was the idiot who had wanted to go to his hotel room a few moments before.

"No, really. I have a gift, and you don't have to come up. Besides, the hotel is on the way to your flat. And if you still want a cab, I'll call you one from there." He placed his hand over his heart. "No seduction. I promise."

"One stop in the lobby for five minutes and then I'm out of there." Ivy was already thinking of her claw-foot tub at home and the nice long soak she was going to have to wash away the memory of this evening. Ivy didn't demand long-term relationships, but she did demand to be the center of someone's world for the brief time they were together. Ruben broke that rule on the first date.

Correction—the only date.

# # #

Ruben did most of the talking as the cab drove them back to his hotel. Ivy briefly wondered if his conference was in her neighborhood of Marylebone or if he'd purposefully stayed there just to be close to her. She didn't want to know.

Once inside the lobby, Ruben directed her to the bar area in the corner, seating her in a plush chair and ordering a glass of wine. "I'll be right back," he said, practically sprinting toward the elevator.

The bartender brought her drink over along with a bowl of Twiglets. These Marmite-flavored crackers were an acquired taste, for sure, but one of the things she'd learned to love during her time in London. Once she left, though, she'd probably never eat this odd snack again. So many things in her life were temporary, a fit for a time, and then discarded when she moved on—people, places, things. Ivy had a hard time looking at anything as permanent, which is why her long tenure at the Embassy was such a surprise to her. Tonight was a lesson in getting out before the damage started.

As she doodled on her napkin and thought about snack food, she saw a fuzzy face peering up at her from the floor. Ivy reached down to pet the dog, letting him approve her scent by sniffing her hand first. The dog was a miniature schnauzer, a handsome little fellow. His front legs were soon on her lap, and she quickly grabbed his paws so he wouldn't snag her dress.

"No, no!"

"For the longest time, he thought that was his name." The man leaned down to leash the dog, and all Ivy could see was the top of his wool newsboy cap. When he looked up, his hazel eyes met hers, and Ivy's voice caught in her throat. His reddish-brown hair curled out from under his hat, and his big smile revealed a row of perfect teeth. His English was fluent but not native, and she guessed he was either Dutch or German.

"What is his name?" she asked, scratching behind his ear.

"This is Fritz, my right-hand man and keeper of the secrets." He knelt down on the ground to pet Fritz, positioning his body closer to Ivy. His hand moved to the dog's back, his big hands and long fingers easily touching her own. Ivy pulled her hand away and put it in her lap.

"So you're a man with many secrets, eh? What happens if someone interrogates Fritz here with a big slab of steak? I don't know that he'd hold out for long. He looks like a pushover to me."

"Ah, but Fritz is a spoiled dog, eating only a special diet prepared for him by a chef I know. He wouldn't even know what to do with a raw steak. I think my secrets are safe with this little guy." He ruffled Fritz's back with his enormous hands. "My name is Christof, by the way. Are you in London on business, too?"

"My name is Ivy, and I live here. Well, not here in the hotel. But here in London. I'm waiting for a friend who is upstairs." Ivy was intrigued by this tall gentleman who kept his eyes on her and no one else.

"An American in London, on purpose? I thought they would have tried keeping you colonists away from the mother country after your insubordination. These Brits have a long memory, you know." His mouth curled up on one side.

"Well, I work for the US Embassy, so I guess you could say I spend my workday on US sovereign land and only venture into the hostile land of the mother country after hours. It's much safer that way, for them and me," Ivy said, enjoying the repartee with Christof.

"What is all this on your napkin? A secret code from the Embassy? Wait, you wouldn't tell me anyway, would you?" His eyes twinkled as he teased her, making her think for a brief moment that he might be a spy. Not that she had anything secret to share, but still. It was a little thrill.

"I doodle when I think. Helps clear the cobwebs." Ivy put her hand over the napkin, a little embarrassed at her goofy dragon curving around the edges.

"A woman with something on her mind, who might be a US spy, coding secret messages on napkins, and who is loitering in my hotel lobby. I am lucky to have Fritz on hand to protect my secrets from the likes of you." Christof looked down at Fritz, who was glad to be remembered and barked in appreciation.

"Looks like someone is done with the social time and ready to explore. It's been a pleasure talking with you, Ivy." Christof stood and looked toward the elevators, and Ivy saw his expression cloud over.

Ruben strolled over, and Ivy felt the temperature drop by ten degrees. He was clearly not happy to see her talking with Christof. Well, guess what? That's how she'd felt all night at the salsa club, waiting in line for Ruben's attention.

Christof seemed to sense the tension, too. What was it with men? They were no better than little Fritz in that way. Maybe all three of them could go outside and pee on the same streetlight.

"Christof." Ruben said it as a word, not a greeting.

"Ruben." Christof returned the non-greeting with the same lack of enthusiasm.

"You two know each other?" Ivy was confused.

Christof smiled. "Of course. I bought the company where

Ruben used to work. I guess you could say I am his former boss."

"Get over yourself, Christof. I'd never work for you." Ruben's tone was even, with the least amount of emotion Ivy had ever heard from him. Somehow, that was more disturbing than if he'd yelled.

"Oh, Ruben. I didn't know you carried such a grudge. It's just business, you know." Christof gave Fritz a quiet command in German to stay still, and the dog sat on his haunches in obedience.

"It looks like we caught you on your way out with your dog. Have a good evening, Christof." Ruben's dismissive tone was a tiny little thrill for Ivy, a dark side of him she'd never seen before. There was some deep resentment here, and she wanted to find out what could get Ruben so fired up, especially from a guy who did not seem like the devil. How could Satan have such a cute dog? Or such a warm sense of humor? Ivy was very glad she'd stopped by the hotel on the way home. Ruben might have just regained her attention, at least long enough to find out what that was all about.

"Ah, it looks like I'm being dismissed. Well, I can see why you'd want to have Ivy all to yourself, Ruben." Christof's cocky grin turned into a charming smile when he turned toward Ivy. "If that is your real name," he said with a wink. "I wish you the best of luck in the spy game." Christof then walked out into the London night air with Fritz happily trotting by his side.

Ivy and Ruben were silent for a moment, then he walked

over to the bar to order a drink and came back to sit down. In the short time away, there was a reset in his personality. The old Ruben was back, shoulders relaxed, an easy smile on his face, and ready to talk. *Odd.* It was like two different people. She wondered how much effort it took to regain his easygoing manner and if it was a regular thing. Or was his relaxed manner something he only showed to her? She was beginning to wonder which was the real Ruben.

Ruben put the box on the table, a black and brown box with a white grosgrain ribbon. The label read, *Cacao Sampaka.*

"Is this what I think it is?" Ivy raised her eyebrows in anticipation.

"Well, if you're expecting a key to my flat, then no. I think you should come stay the weekend with me first, take things slow. Don't rush me, Ivy." His eyes crinkled at the corners when he smiled, the heaviness of just a few minutes ago completely gone. The playboy Ruben was back.

"Nice try." Ivy reached over to the ribbon and paused. "Can I open it?"

She didn't wait for an answer before untying the ribbon and lifting the lid. The chocolates were little masterpieces, neatly arranged on tissue paper. She picked the one in the center, her choice to always go to the heart of the matter. The chocolate melted in her mouth.

"I bought these at the best chocolate shop in Madrid." Ruben leaned back in the upholstered chair, arms stretched out to his sides. He looked like David Beckham in his stylish clothes, and his fit body and flat stomach were the envy of men half his age. She wondered if Ruben could pose in underwear as well as Beckham could, too. An image of her favorite H&M billboard starring the famous *fútbol* player popped into her mind. Ivy put Ruben's face on his body.

I knew you'd enjoy them, but I had no idea how much I'd enjoy watching you eat them," Ruben said, his voice full of longing.

She held her hand up to prevent him from speaking. "I'm gonna need a moment," she said, letting the dark chocolate and orange flavors melt on her tongue. Ruben shifted uncomfortably in his seat.

"The shop is near my flat in Malasaña. When you come to visit, we can go there and buy whatever you like." He grinned, taking pleasure in hers.

"You didn't think the chocolate would distract me from what just happened, did you? I'm an economist. It's my job to ask questions and find out what makes the world tick so I can make predictions." Ivy picked up another chocolate and held it aloft between them. "Usually it taints the results to pay people for their opinions, but you seem like a hard case. Tell me your story and I'll give you a chocolate."

"So you're basically a fortune teller? Then you should be able to know how this is going to end between us, Ivy," Ruben said, avoiding the question. He took a bite of the crackers instead and scowled. "This is disgusting," he said as he spit it into his napkin.

"I could have predicted that reaction, you know. Now stop wasting time and answer my question," Ivy commanded.

"There isn't much to tell. Christof is in the same kind of business as me. I don't like him, and I don't want to give him any more attention. You'll never see him again, and even though I probably will, it will be short and sweet, just like tonight." Ruben leaned forward and took the chocolate from her hand, popping it into his mouth. "Mmmm. Now let's get back to what we were discussing before I went upstairs. You want to change jobs. Why?"

"I'll get my answers later," Ivy said, popping another chocolate into her mouth. His eyes watched her every move. "I always do."

"I can't wait for the interrogation," Ruben said, holding his wrists up for handcuffing. Their flirtation was dangerously close to reversing her opinion on him, and she wasn't going to make that mistake again. Not after her humiliation at the dance club. It was time to wrap up this date with some very unsexy talk.

"Time for me to go, Ruben. I have job interviews to line up tomorrow morning." Ivy folded the paper back in the box and stood.

"You still haven't told me why you're looking for a new job," Ruben said.

"Simple, it's time to move on. I want to do something more exciting than working for bureaucrats who will just change every election cycle and tear all my work apart so they can put it back together again with their name on it." Ivy shook her head, putting her fork down on the plate. "I should have left a few years ago. And if I'm being honest, which I hate to do, I'm worried that I waited too long to find something better."

"Why would you hate to be honest in front of me?" Ruben asked.

"I just shared my fear of making a job change too late and the only response you have is how it affects you? Might want to rethink your future as a therapist, Ruben." Ivy's green eyes flashed with irritation. She'd let him get too close again. Stupid, stupid, stupid. "Listen, this night was a mistake, and we both know it. But the debt is paid, and there is no need for us to torment each other anymore."

A slow smile spread on Ruben's face. "I torment you? That sounds like progress to me."

Ruben stood and walked Ivy outside to hail a cab, settling her in the back like she hadn't just told him this was a mistake. Ivy admired his confidence, but it didn't change the facts. That was their first and last date.

CHAPTER FIVE

"Hey, Dorothy. How's Oz?" Ivy asked. For once she was glad her friend Rose was now living in Australia, the nine-hour time difference making it possible for a video chat so late at night.

"Well, the yellow brick road is actually a sandy beach, and I've hardly moved my butt off it since I got here," Rose said with a laugh. Ivy could picture her sitting under an umbrella in Australia, book in her lap, sipping a cold cocktail. After all those years of running her own business and raising a daughter alone, Rose deserved some relaxation.

"What? I thought you'd be sexing it up twenty-four-seven with Mateo," Ivy replied.

"He just arrived from Spain. I think I'll give him one night to sleep off the jet lag before I attack him." Rose's laugh was music to Ivy's ears. "And there's still the logistics of life, you know. I'm in the middle of registering our new design firm, and we're going to scout locations with the agent later this week. Too bad we still have to make a living, you know?"

"The poets say you can live on love alone, but if that were

true their books would be free."

"Always the economist, Ivy. Just wait until love knocks you on your butt." Rose's voice was warm as the sunshine, her power more like a constant glow compared to Ivy's flickering hot flame. Ivy missed her.

"I'm in the Wonder Woman stance at all times. Don't you worry your pretty little head about my balance, Rosie," Ivy said with a chuckle.

"Even with Ruben?" Rose asked. "You two are so much alike."

Ivy rolled her eyes. "Especially with Ruben. And no, we are not," she said emphatically.

"Remember who you're talking to, Ivy. I know you better than you know yourself."

Ivy used her authoritative voice when she most wanted to bluster her way through a situation. It worked well at the Embassy, but not so well with her friends. Rose had been able to see through her bluff since they were kids.

"I kind of hoped you two would hit it off. Is that selfish of me?" Rose asked.

"I love you, babe, but double dating is not my thing. Besides, you've already got your man. You don't need me to date his best friend to help you seal the deal. Mateo is mad for you," Ivy said, remembering the look of desperation in his eyes when he thought he was going to lose Rose. Ivy hadn't always been a fan of Mateo, but she'd changed her mind when she saw them together. They were right for each other, and no amount of pigheadedness or miscommunication could keep them apart.

"There's no attraction to Ruben at all? Because that's not what I saw when we were in London."

"Your vision was clouded by your situation with Mateo. I can't blame you if you saw something that wasn't there," Ivy said, comfortable with stretching the truth. Rose didn't need any more ammunition for this matchmaking nonsense.

"So this big change you're looking for is only about work," Rose said. "Sounded more dramatic in your message."

"I'm a dramatic person," Ivy said, flipping her hair back for show. She couldn't hold the serious look long before she broke character, erupting in a full-body laugh that went from her hair to her fingertips to her toes.

"Your red hair and green eyes may get all the compliments, but nothing compares to the way you laugh, Ivy. You bring your whole self into it, just like a kid. I've missed hearing it." Rose was one of the few who got to see her unfiltered personality, and it felt good to just let go.

"I haven't had anything to laugh about lately. But that's all about to change."

"So what's the plan? Where do you go next?" Rose asked.

Ivy took a sip of water, still feeling the dehydration of dancing the night away with every man except the one she wanted.

"I'm casting a wide net. I kind of like not knowing at this stage, imagining what my life would look like in each new country."

"Then it is about more than just work. Maybe you should consider Madrid." Rose's evil grin lit the screen, an odd fit on her sweet face. The problem with Rose knowing her this well was that there was no chance of keeping secrets. "You speak Spanish, and you already know someone there," she added, clearing her throat.

"He told you we went out, didn't he?"

The pregnant pause that followed was the first sign of Ivy's mistake.

"You went on a date with Ruben?" Rose's eyebrows leaped up in surprise. Ivy kicked herself for letting the cat out of the bag. Rose's smile spread across her face while she waited for Ivy to explain her way out of it.

"Only to pay off the bet we had over you and Mateo getting back together. I can't believe he held me to it." Ivy drew an image of a cat eating a canary. Feathers floated in the air while the cat tried to look nonchalant.

"The Ivy I know doesn't do anything she doesn't want to," Rose countered.

"Look, I did this because we had a bet. There was no fooling around, and there will be no second date. Over before it even started. Case closed."

"Doth she protest too much?" Rose was having too much fun with this. Ivy decided to change the subject.

"So now I just need to find a new job, move to a new city, and start my life all over again. Maybe even start the manhunt again."

"I'll be sure to alert the authorities," Rose said drily. "I can't let you loose on an unsuspecting populace."

"That ruins all the fun. Harder to break a guarded heart, you know."

"You would know better than anyone," Rose said softly. Ivy felt the sting of truth in her words. "I love you, Ivy, and I want you to be happy. Don't you think it's time to start letting someone get close? Let me help you the way you helped me with Mateo."

"I appreciate the thought, Rose, but I don't want anyone else close. I'm not giving up my independence for a man. No offense." Ivy felt like a jerk, even though she meant what she said. Rose wasn't trying to hurt her, and she'd never do anything to hurt Rose, at least not on purpose.

"You think a partnership means giving up your independence?" Rose laughed. "You can't learn about real love from books and movies, Ivy. You have to get your hands dirty."

Rose softened her voice, shaking Ivy from the past. "Zach was a long time ago."

# # #

When Ivy thought of Zach, she always pictured the sun. He was a powerhouse of energy. Zach's blond hair radiated the beam of his personality, and people wanted to be close to him. Ivy loved him from the moment she saw him on the university campus, throwing a Frisbee to his friends and laughing without a care in the world. He was active and athletic, always moving. Ivy recognized a kindred spirit, a fellow seeker of all the world had to offer. He was the first one she'd ever met.

Her first days at college were like learning to breathe for the first time. Growing up as a fiery redhead in tiny Hobart, Arizona was stifling. Everyone in town knew her business and told her what she could and couldn't do. Teachers, neighbors, and coaches told her to stop speaking out, act like a young lady, and mind her manners. Ivy chafed under the restraint, living as a shadow of herself until the day after high school graduation. That's when Ivy moved to New York City to go to Columbia University and study economics. No one there cared what she did, who she was, or what she thought. For the first time, Ivy was free to be herself.

That in and of itself was enough to make her heart soar, but to find another wanderer, a man who had exploration and adventure in his DNA, was a gift too good to be true.

Ivy remembered the phone calls back to her friends. "Zach is the one," she told them. "We're going to climb every mountain, eat every food, and swim every sea. We'll go everywhere and do everything together."

Her friends oohed and aahed over her new love, happy that Ivy had finally found someone to match her drive. They begged her to bring him for a visit on the summer break after freshman year. Ivy didn't want to break the spell, to infect her newfound happiness with claustrophobic memories from her past, so she and Zach spent the first summer apart. When they returned to school in the fall, stronger and more in love than ever, Ivy convinced herself that keeping him from Hobart was the right thing. The second summer, she got a job as a barista and told Zach she'd be too busy for him to visit.

Neither of them was good at writing letters back in the days before mobile phones and texting, but they did talk long-distance once a week. Ivy lived for those Friday-night phone calls. They dreamed of what they'd do after graduation, the kinds of jobs they'd take that would fund their discoveries. They'd go on an archeological dig, snorkel in the Great Barrier Reef, learn Mandarin, and work as researchers in Antarctica. Life would never be dull.

In August, Zach went on a sailing trip with his family to Cape Cod. He wouldn't be able to call her again before they got back to school, but they made plans to see each other on campus the first day back. They'd meet at their favorite pizza place at six o'clock, chowing down on their staple food before returning to her dorm to celebrate their reunion in a more intimate way.

Ivy showed up at the restaurant on time, wearing his favorite shirt and bursting with excitement. They were halfway through school, so close to starting their life together, Ivy could almost taste it. So many plans to make! She waited at their corner table for over an hour, finally ordering when the waiter told her she had to leave if she wasn't eating. Ivy waited another hour, slowly chewing her pizza as the tables around her filled with noisy students returning from break. Was he chatting with his new roommate? Stuck in traffic? Every time the bell on the door jingled, Ivy hoped it was him. At nine o'clock she asked for a box and paid her bill, taking her pizza back to her dorm room. Ivy would not be one of those girls who chased her boyfriend around campus.

She cried herself to sleep that night, probably freaking out her new roommate. Ivy didn't even know her name yet.

The next morning, she looked at her puffy eyes in the mirror and felt the anger. How could Zach have bailed on their date? Had he gone out with his friends? Forgot? She was mad at herself for acting like a typical lovelorn girl, the very thing she said she'd never be. She thought their relationship was different, more mature. She wondered what could have happened to weaken Zach's bond with her. Nothing in his phone calls hinted at a problem.

Ivy marched over to his frat house to give him a piece of

her mind, forgetting her vow to not be one of those girls. As she stormed across campus, various insults and arguments popped into her head. She had the moral high ground here, and she was going to use it to her advantage.

When she arrived at the gate at the frat house, she saw Todd Nelson walking out.

"Hey, Todd. Have you seen Zach?"

He looked at her and blinked, a look of alarm passing over his face. Ivy suspected the worst, that Zach was inside hiding from her. Her fury increased.

"Ivy," was all he said. Then he reached out and put his hand on her shoulder. His silence unnerved her.

"What the hell is going on, Todd?"

"Ivy, I don't know how to tell you this."

"Tell me what, Todd?" Ivy asked through gritted teeth. Zach must have done something outrageous, and his brothers were rallying to protect him. She clenched her fists at her sides, digging her fingernails into her palms.

Todd's voice was barely above a whisper. "Zach died, Ivy. I'm so sorry." His eyes were glassy, and he blinked a few times to clear them.

The air whooshed in her ears. A tornado of confusion clouded her brain, quickly washing away with a shower of anger.

"Todd, that is a sick joke." Ivy pushed his hand off her shoulder and took a step back, filled with disgust. "What kind of person says things like that?" Her heart pounded in her chest so loudly she could hear it echoing in her ears.

"Ivy, I'm not joking. I'm so sorry to have to tell you. You should have known before now." The look of pity on Todd's face compounded her misery. "Zach fell off the boat while sailing with his parents a couple of weeks ago. He hit his head and drowned before they could rescue him. I'm so sorry." Todd stepped forward to brace Ivy as she started swaying.

"No. Zach is a strong swimmer. You're lying!"

"Ivy, he hit his head on the boat when he fell over. He was unconscious. The coroner said he didn't suffer at all." Todd's words were meant to comfort her, but they did the opposite.

"I'm supposed to be happy he didn't have any control over his body while he drowned? Is that what you're saying?" Ivy began to hyperventilate as her mind filled with images of her beautiful Zach falling into the water, sinking to the bottom without a struggle. It was an unworthy death for such a vibrant person.

"Ivy, get hold of yourself," Todd said. He probably hadn't imagined being the one to tell Zach's girlfriend about his death. Zach and Todd weren't even that close.

"I have to see him. Show me!" Ivy demanded, not

recognizing the gravelly voice coming from her mouth.

"The funeral was last week in Connecticut. I'm so sorry."

"Stop telling me how sorry you are!" Ivy screamed. She turned and ran back to her dorm, burying her head in the pillow that was still damp from her tears the night before. It was the last time she ever cried over a man.

# # #

Ivy sighed, the memory of Zach's death like an old familiar scar now. The wound healed long ago but remained prominent, something she saw almost every day. The forty-two-year-old Ivy knew that she and Zach would likely have grown apart after college and gone their separate ways. She was practical about those kinds of things now. But she vowed never to tie her goals and adventures in life with another man again. Ivy shared her body and experiences selectively with what she called "a few good men," but never her heart or her dreams. There was too much risk.

Those years after college sent her on a path of professional achievement, working harder and longer than anyone else. She still had her few adventures, but she never did any of the things she planned to do with Zach. Those places were drenched with memories of what she'd lost.

"You can't let what happened stop you from interacting with half the population."

"Rose, I'm not a nun. Before you met Mateo, my *interacting*, as you call it, was more vigorous than yours." Ivy frowned, unwilling to talk about Zach.

"I'm not talking about sex, Ivy. I'm talking about relationships and all the stuff that happens when your clothes are on. Ever since Zach, you've built a wall around your heart. I'm lucky to have gotten in before you started construction, but everyone you've met since college doesn't get a chance to know the real you. And as someone who thinks you're terrific, that's a real shame." Rose wore her heart on her sleeve, and Ivy didn't know how she could stand baring her emotions so freely.

Ivy blinked to keep the water in her eyes from turning into tears. "Allergies," was all she could say as she sniffed, quickly dabbing her eyes with her fingertips.

The Late Bloomers had helped her make it through Zach's death without falling apart. They took turns calling her every week, visiting at least once every semester to ensure she didn't sink into her pain too deeply. But they didn't realize she was walling herself off from everyone else because they still had full access. By the time they noticed her solo tendencies, Ivy was closed off to new people, a situation that hadn't changed in twenty years.

"Don't let a one-time event change your actions for a lifetime, Ivy. You don't have to guard your heart. You're a strong woman. You can manage a little risk." Rose kissed her finger and placed it over the camera lens on her computer, their standard "I love you" when chatting by video. Deep down, Ivy knew Rose was right. But she'd been this way for so long it was just too hard to change.

Ivy took a big breath and plastered a smile on her face. "Speaking of independence, I am going to have my own room at the seaside mansion you book for your wedding, right?"

"All right, Ms. Avoidance of Intimacy, I'll let the subject go…this time. But don't think you've escaped this conversation forever. As for the wedding, since you're my closest family, isn't it up to you to pay for this shindig? Because I do have a particular mansion in mind, and it's not cheap."

"Oh, right," Ivy drawled. "Change of plans. I'm thinking more about a casual beach wedding with beer and burgers for the reception. The poets say love is all you need, so who am I to argue?"

"Spoken like an economist," Rose said with a laugh. "But you know I don't care. Mateo can marry me on the beach, in a mansion, or not at all, as long as we wake up together every day. Sappy, but true."

"You scare me, Rose. Truly, you do. But I can hear how happy you are, so I'll just chalk it up to momentary insanity. Plus I get a great vacation out of it."

"And you get a second date with Ruben. Nicely played,

Ivy." Rose laughed as she blew a kiss goodbye.

CHAPTER SIX

One date was supposed to cure Ruben of this infatuation, but he wanted Ivy more now than ever. It killed him to put her in the back of the cab, to watch her drive away into the night without a guarantee they'd see each other again. All he could do was sit at the almost empty hotel bar nursing his drink, wishing he was upstairs in his hotel room with Ivy using their fiery chemistry for something more enjoyable than what had just happened.

Salsa dancing was a bad idea, or at least salsa dancing with a group lesson. He should have known they'd switch partners and spend much of the night with other people. Ruben had thought if Ivy saw him in demand she'd want him more, but the whole thing backfired.

Back when he was at university, he had a routine with all the women he dated. The same first date, the same romantic gestures over time, and even the same sexual experience. Step one, step two, step three, and so on. The method was reliable, and he followed it like a script, patting himself on the back every time he got through to the end. But Paz Gallegos threw cold water on his success when she told him he was too predictable to date.

Too predictable? But he was Ruben Alegre, lover of women, charming man about campus!

Paz had laughed at his outrage, before outlining his moves by counting on her fingers. "First, you'll take me to the Egyptian monument for sunset. You'll put your arm around me and then tell me I'm the only one you've ever taken there. Then we'll go to a bar in La Latina where your friend works and you get two-for-one drinks with tapas. You'll tell me you've never been there with anyone else. And on the way back you'll stop to kiss me and shove your tongue down my throat to show your passion. Should I keep going?" Paz's laughter killed his confidence, but then she saved him by revealing the best lesson he'd ever learned about women. "Where did you learn to do all that?" she asked.

Ruben remembered his stuttering response, face red-hot with embarrassment. "The guys. We all talk about what works, and I memorize the best moves."

Paz nudged him with her elbow, face screwed up in confusion. "Why would you ask other men how to please women? Or even other women? Why not ask the one you're with? We're all different, you know." Paz said it like it was the most logical thing in the world, and Ruben slowly realized it was. He was trying a cookie-cutter approach to custom chocolates.

Ever since then, he'd worked hard to pick up cues from the

women he was with, anticipating what they'd like, asking when he didn't know, and making sure they left satisfied. Ruben was now legitimately good at attracting women and making them happy. He just wasn't good at staying in those relationships long enough to let them get to know him.

He'd misjudged Ivy, used some of his old tricks to inspire jealousy because he didn't know how to draw her to him after their dinner conversation stalled. From now on, he'd have to pay better attention. He had no intention of this being their last date, not while she still occupied so many of his waking thoughts.

Ruben motioned to the bartender for the bill, and he signed his name and room number. He should have hit the gym instead of the bar. When his energy was this tightly coiled, the only way to safely release it was with vigorous sex or a grueling, torturous workout. Tonight he'd had neither.

He stood up just as Christof walked back in the bar, minus the little dog. Ruben smirked.

"Did you lose the prop dog? It must go over really well in charming the ladies so they don't realize what a jerk you are right away." Ruben put on his jacket.

"You dislike me because you lost, not because I am a jerk," Christof said. "I think the word you're looking for is *winner*. C'mon. Be a good sport. Let me buy you a drink." Christof held up a finger to the bartender, ordering his usual without a word. What a smug bastard. He looked at Ruben, waiting for a response.

"You're only trying to get information for the ConStead deal. Unlike people who've just met you, I know how you operate." Ruben turned to walk away.

"Why would I talk about ConStead when we can talk about Ivy? She's quite a woman. You wouldn't mind if I gave her a call, would you? She said you were just friends." Christof's smile was cold, and Ruben didn't want to show that he'd hit him where it hurt. What had Christof and Ivy talked about before he got there?

"I doubt Ivy would take the call of a guy like you, but you're welcome to try. Her jerk meter is finely tuned. I'm surprised it didn't shake the building when she met you." Ruben had to get away from this guy before he exploded.

"Why do you have to be so harsh, Ruben? You're letting a little bit of past business get in the way of a possible partnership. We could do some incredible things together, make a lot of money. ConStead is just the start." The bartender placed Christof's Scotch whisky in front of him, no doubt the twelve-year-old single malt variety.

"I don't play with men like you, Christof. You break and burn everything you touch, all for the sake of winning. And one day that is going to backfire on you. I just hope I'm there to watch. If I'm lucky, I'll get to light the fuse." Ruben nodded his head one last time and walked toward the elevator. He barely stopped his gait when Christof called out to him.

"That's why I win and you lose, Ruben. I don't depend on luck."

CHAPTER SEVEN

Ivy hit the snooze button one too many times. Four hours of sleep, and no makeup in the world could add back in the rest she didn't get. She rushed through her morning routine and walked out her door, waving to her neighbor as she locked up. Mrs. Bingham was sweeping her front porch and humming to herself, as usual. Her chubby cheeks were pink from the crisp morning weather, making her look like a storybook grandma with her white bun and floral apron.

"Good morning, Mrs. B! If you're interested, I have half a box of specialty chocolates from Madrid that a friend gave me. You'd be doing me a huge favor to take them."

"Well, if it will help you, I'm happy to take them, Ivy." Mrs. Bingham loved sweets. Ivy usually donated her goodies to Mrs. B, but she'd learned years ago that she had to position it as a favor. Otherwise, Mrs. Bingham would say no and talk about her latest diet or health regime.

"I'll drop them at your door when I come back from work. Thanks for the help, Mrs. B!"

Ivy enjoyed her daily walk to work. Those few minutes between home and office were like what being on an airplane used to be—no Internet, no phone, no distraction. It was a pause button on everything, an in-between space that made no demands on her. Instead of reading a trashy novel like she would on a plane, Ivy focused on the little mom-and-pop shops in her neighborhood, the foliage level on the trees, and where the sky rated on the spectrum of blue to gray. She felt like a guard on patrol, monitoring the neighborhood for change.

The doors on the buildings on her block were all painted black to stand out against the white stone. The gold doorknockers were a posh touch. Little gardens of well-tended grass and potted flowers adorned the street. Young moms with strollers, older people walking small dogs, and a postman with a rolling carrier bag were her usual sidewalk companions on her daily commute. If one were looking for a postcard of a great neighborhood to live inside of London, this would be it.

Ivy walked double-time to work, thankful for the short commute since she'd overslept. She hated being late, appearing as if she didn't have control of herself. After the usual slog through security, she entered the elevator. She was now in work mode.

Ivy scanned her emails on her phone as the elevator rose. The only one she opened was her quote of the day email, something to help her focus on the task of self-improvement. The ritual was a new one, only a few days old, and so far she hadn't experienced any ah-hah moments. Still, change didn't happen overnight. Ivy was predicting a month to overhaul her life, a lifetime for an impatient woman like herself.

This quote resonated: "The secret of change is to focus all of your energy, not on fighting the old, but building the new."

The quote was attributed to a gas station attendant named Socrates, a character in a popular book. It wasn't the ancient philosopher Socrates. No matter. The message resonated with her, and whether her guide wore flowing white robes or a blue shirt with an embroidered nametag, she didn't care.

He was right. She wouldn't worry about the mistakes from last night with Ruben or even oversleeping this morning. For letting herself become complacent in her life and career. Or even for her misbehaving waistline. Today was the start of all things new—new job, new life, new health regime.

When she stepped off the elevator, Ivy discovered she wasn't the only one thinking about change that morning.

# # #

Before she made it to her office, Ivy heard the news from four different people. Her boss Sylvia resigned. She was forced out. There was a power struggle. There was a scandal. The stories were mostly guesswork, but there was no denying that her office was cleaned out and she was gone. No one knew for sure why Sylvia left. The quick exit was suspicious, as was the generic announcement from Sylvia's boss, Jack Shelton. No one leaves for "family reasons."

Sylvia was a woman Ivy had thought would be a lifer at the Embassy, quietly working her way to retirement. She ran a pretty tight ship, but she never bucked for advancement or acted like she wanted anything else. If she hadn't been the boss, Ivy would have likely never even noticed her.

Socrates whispered in her brain—*build the new*. For a dead and/or fictional guy, his voice was pretty active in her head. And he was right. No more worry about Sylvia or the Embassy or even Ruben, for that matter. Today, Ivy was going to find a new job and jumpstart her life.

Ben popped his head through her door. "Got a sec?"

"If you're here to gossip about Sylvia, I don't know anything." Ivy turned back to her laptop, waiting for him to turn on his heels and leave.

"This gossip is about someone you actually like. Rare species, as you know." Ben's eyes twinkled.

"I don't like anyone here, Ben, including you. And you'll never get into my good graces if you don't come bearing gifts. You have sugar on your upper lip, and you didn't bring me even a small nibble of whatever you've been eating." Ivy shook her head in mock disdain. "I'm just saying, Ben, this is a serious misstep in advancing your career." Ivy returned to reading her email.

"Mea culpa, mea culpa. But once I tell you the news, you'll forgive me for not sharing the donut stash from the breakroom." Ben's thin body bounced on the balls of his feet, dying to share his news.

Ivy looked over at Ben, giving in to her curiosity despite the stern look Socrates was giving her inside her head.

"Spill it, Ben. Who do I like and what have they done now?"

"The gossip is about you, Ivy. The word in the office is that they want you for Sylvia's job." Ben beamed, waiting for a pat on his blond head from Ivy for his prompt delivery.

"Ben, there are two people ahead of me in seniority, and you know that's how it works around here. They'll get first dibs on the job, and one of them will take it. The job will never even come close to me, and I don't care." Ivy hated to burst his bubble, but she couldn't get drawn into the office politics and gossip. Now that she had a plan, this kind of stuff was just a distraction, a wasted use of her time.

"I don't know, Ivy. I got it from pretty high up the chain." Ben leaned on her desk, coffee cup in hand.

"Oh, so you're schmoozing with the ambassador now? Discussing staffing changes over drinks at the club? I doubt that, Ben. And get your butt off my desk. I don't know where that thing has been." Ivy swatted him with a manila folder, smiling as he jumped just out of her reach.

"This is Grade-A American beef, Ivy. The English love it and treat it with far more respect than you do." Ben started backing out the door. "So when you become even more of my boss than you are, you're finally going to treat me like a professional, right?" Ben smirked.

"You'd better hope not, Ben. Otherwise, you'd probably be fired. Now get out of here." Ivy's words were harsh, but her tone was like a big sister to a little brother. She liked Ben, but he was a colleague, not someone she'd trust with her new plan. Friendly but with distance was her new strategy at work. Okay, maybe not quite friendly, or people would think something was up. Ivy did have a reputation to maintain.

Her phone beeped, and Ivy picked it up, a trained response.

RubenAlegre: Last night didn't go as planned.

Ivy_Cross: No doubt.

RubenAlegre: Take two?

Ivy_Cross: Are you a masochist?

RubenAlegre: What?

Ivy_Cross: Trying to make this work when it can't. Beating your head against the wall.

RubenAlegre: How do you know it won't work? We haven't even tried.

Ivy_Cross: You live in Madrid. I live in London. Logistics.

RubenAlegre: Stay in London. I'll always come to you.

Ivy_Cross: You say that now.

RubenAlegre: Can we talk?

Ivy put her phone on the desk, crossed her arms, and leaned back in her chair. No matter how good his leg felt between hers, the way his arms held her and pulled her tight against him, he was still a complication in her life, a distraction to her goal of changing jobs and shaking things up. And he was too close for comfort. When it didn't work out, and she knew it wouldn't, there would be hell to pay in her social life. She would not let a silly fling complicate her friendship with Rose. He was sexy, but he was sexy with baggage, and that she didn't need right now.

Ivy_Cross: Not necessary. I sort of like you Ruben, but you are logistically undesirable.

RubenAlegre: Planes. Phones. Email. Get with the times, American Woman.

Ivy_Cross: I'm tired of fixing what's not right. Better to just look for right at the start.

RubenAlegre: Life doesn't work that way, *chica.*

Ivy frowned. Breaking up via chat wasn't going to work. She'd have to see him again to finalize it, especially since she'd have to see him at least one more time at Rose and Mateo's wedding. Why did he have to be friends with Mateo? He'd never be completely out of her life, showing up on vacations and big life events. Ivy imagined seeing him on the beach in Australia, a twenty-something tart in a bikini as his date, laughing at all his jokes. A tart who lived in Madrid.

I can't hate her just because she looks good in a bikini. Or because she doesn't exist, Socrates prompted her. *Get back to building the new.*

Ivy_Cross: Gotta get back to work. Will call later.

Or not. Ivy would figure out a goodbye strategy. Now she had more important things to do.

Ivy spent the next two hours working through her list of contacts by phone and email, trying to forget the present and work on her future. The US contacts were still in bed, but she wanted them to see her emails and listen to her voicemails first thing. She wasn't sure she was ready to go back to the US, but being in New York City wouldn't be a bad gig. Lily lived there when she wasn't on assignment, and Vi was moving there now that her jewelry line was taking off. A mini reunion after so many years of living apart would be a good thing.

A knock on the door interrupted her flow.

"Come in!" she barked without looking up.

"Delivery for you." The mail clerk dropped a single envelope on her desk before walking out.

Thick, creamy stationery drew her attention. Also, no stamp. The envelope was messengered over from within London. The address was written in messy script with quality ink. Probably a fountain pen. Ivy's usual mail consisted of cheap envelopes run through postage meters, or re-used manila envelopes sent over by diplomatic pouch from the US. Nothing this elegant ever came across her desk.

She stroked the outside of the envelope, feeling the slightly bumpy texture of the paper underneath her fingertips. She placed it under her nose, the scent of wealth unmistakable. Ivy reached into her desk drawer for the letter opener. One quick slice and she saw the matching stationery inside, a single folded piece of paper.

Ivy, It was a pleasure to meet you at the hotel last night. I have to confess to doing some research on you afterward. You are a very smart and accomplished woman, and I think there is an opportunity to do some business together. I'll be dining at Chiltern Firehouse today at 1:00 p.m. Please join me.

~ Christof

Chiltern Firehouse was the latest hotspot in London, and reservations even for famous people were hard to get. Ivy wouldn't be surprised to see Daniel Craig or Dame Judy Dench eating there. And now she was getting a last-minute invitation to go? To dine with a handsome and successful businessman? If Christof was trying to impress her, he'd succeeded.

Ivy wondered what kind of business he had in mind. If this were a lame attempt at a date, then she would let him down easy after she tried the famous food. Ivy didn't mix business with pleasure—too risky. She felt only slightly guilty that she would give Christof an in-person brush-off when they had no history together, but she'd tried to break off with Ruben over chat. Still, Ruben wasn't offering an exclusive lunch at a place she'd never get into on her own.

Ivy traced the outline of his name on the top of the paper— Christof Brandt. And she was right; he was German. The address on the envelope was simply The Werks in Berlin, no street or postal code. Ivy imagined some exclusive development with a trendy name.

She checked the time. Still plenty of time to research Christof Brandt and come into this meeting prepared.

Ivy googled Christof Brandt and learned that he was the son of a wealthy investment banker father and socialite mother. Instead of going into the family business after a ridiculously expensive and exclusive education, he gravitated to the technology world. He lived and worked in Berlin, one of the centerpieces of the startup world in Europe. Christof managed a portfolio of companies out of a large suite in The Werks, an old building renovated as a high-end co-working space for startups. That explained the name on the stationery.

That must be part of the bad blood between him and Ruben. He'd bought a company where Ruben used to work. But if he hadn't, Ruben wouldn't have gone out on his own and built a successful business. There were probably messy details in there, but on the surface Ivy couldn't see why Ruben would be so cold to Christof other than their competitive natures. Men like that always wanted to win, to be the top dog.

Well, so did Ivy. But she didn't feel the need to shove other people out of the way on her way up. It would be better if the crowd parted voluntarily out of respect.

The whole article sounded a little slick to Ivy, one of those shiny profiles that didn't even pretend to be objective. When you're filthy rich, you can probably commission as many puff pieces as you want about yourself.

But why would this guy go from sailing yachts and living in mansions to hanging out in a converted factory with people who made apps and games and looked like they got dressed in the dark? He obviously didn't have to work, and even if he wanted to, she would have expected him to go into the family business. She was curious to learn more, to find out the story behind the hype.

And to spot James Bond sipping a martini at Chiltern Firehouse.

CHAPTER EIGHT

"I won't confirm or deny who the final three are, but our needs are particular. A lot of these requests get padded with a bunch of inconsequential stuff and nice-to-haves, but there's not a lot of fat on this one. No extra ingredients in this recipe. We need it all, and for the price we're willing to pay, we should get it." Susan crossed her arms and leaned against the wall.

Ruben leaned in, his voice near her ear. "Thanks for your help, Susan. I knew I could count on you."

"Ah, but I didn't help you. That's not allowed, even though I'm not on the selection committee." Susan reached up and straightened his collar. "You're a good guy, Ruben. I hope this works out for you. I'd love to see you around more." She ducked under his arm and walked down the hall, an extra sway in her step. She looked back to make sure Ruben noticed. He did.

Ruben didn't seek out Susan just because she was one of the few women at the conference. She was his inside source at ConStead, a woman he'd met at a similar industry event a few years before. Back then, he'd wanted to get her in bed, but now he was glad it didn't happen. That would have made it harder to get the information he needed today. Ruben wasn't so good at goodbyes, and women had a tendency to remember that.

He walked back into the sterile conference hall, a room that could be in any mid-priced business hotel or conference center in the world. He wondered if hotel organizers around the world got together to see what they could do to prevent homesickness in weary business travelers. They decided to make everything look the same, whether it was in St. Petersburg or London or Beijing. His favorite was the uninspiring inspirational art on the walls. What businessperson stuck in a conference room wanted to look at other people climbing mountains or paragliding in the great outdoors? Ruben thought it cruel to taunt people that way, but maybe it was reverse psychology. *Act like this and you'll get to live this life.*

This poster was titled Commitment, and Ruben stopped to consider the man kayaking down a raging river, water splashing in his face. Once you started down that watery path, you were committed. No choice but to find a way to make it to calmer water—or, better yet, to shore.

Was he committed enough to win this deal? Would he do what it took? Ruben wondered. So far, he'd been thinking about it logically, like the guy who studies whitewater rafting and knows all the specs and maneuvers but never tests himself in a live situation. Commitment was throwing yourself in the craft and working out your knowledge and instinct in real time.

If Ruben was looking for a thrill ride, a way to test his

accumulated knowledge in life, he could dive in with Ivy. He couldn't shake the memory from last night, the connection they'd had at the restaurant before she got scared. That's what it was, of course. He got too close, going from playful banter to soulful confessions too quickly. His attraction to her was growing exponentially, her fire and confidence like a drug. But if he wanted any chance of having her, even for just one night, he'd have to go slow. But not too slow. She was looking for another job, and it might not be in London.

Christof walked over and stood next to him, hands in pockets while looking at the poster. "Looking for some inspiration, Ruben? Personally, I like photos of me rafting down rivers, climbing mountains and sailing the ocean. Got them all over my office. It's an excellent reminder of how much I win at life already." He laughed and patted Ruben on the shoulder. "By the way, I'm skipping out on the lunch presentations, so don't save me a seat. I've got a much more attractive date." With a smirk, Christof walked over to the conference display tables, talking to a few vendors who treated him like a king. Everyone knew Christof, mainly because he had money to spend at a time when many companies were pulling back. Being the son of a billionaire had its advantages.

It was just like Christof to duck out of an industry conference for a date. While everyone else was networking and building their businesses, he was cruising through life, secure that people would always answer his calls and listen to his proposals because he was Christof Brandt, son of Hans Brandt. It was a double-edged sword, though. Without the money to back him up, Christof didn't have much to offer. He surrounded himself with smart people—the best money could buy—but his own instincts were crap. At least that's what Ruben told himself. *Let's see Christof build a business from the ground up on his own, no help from Daddy. Like I did.*

Ruben pulled out his phone to call Ivy. She probably wouldn't see him tonight, but he wanted to hear her voice at least. Tomorrow he was on a plane back to Madrid.

"Ivy Cross." Her curt manner was like a splash of cold water.

"Ruben Alegre." He parroted her sharp response back to her, waiting to see what she'd say.

"You are a hard man to shake," Ivy said. Ruben heard the sound of traffic in the background.

"So stop trying." Ruben smiled, even though she couldn't see it. "Where are you off to?"

"Meeting someone for lunch. I have a job interview." Ivy's voice hummed with excitement, and Ruben was impressed that she got an interview so quickly.

"Nice work. I knew you'd get a lot of attention as soon as you put the word out that you were looking." Ruben was glad she couldn't see his selfish grin. If she was meeting someone for a job interview in London, the job must be in London. There was still a chance to explore a relationship if she stayed here. He thought of the kayaker again, imagining a smooth drift down a calm river.

"That's what is so weird. The call came out of the blue. I still haven't heard from any of the contacts I made myself. So we'll see what happens." Ivy was chatty, more comfortable talking about her career than their relationship, however premature he might be in calling it that.

"Well, good luck today. Will you call me later and let me know how it went?" Ruben was grateful to have one conversation without snark, especially given how tense things got last night.

"Sure, Ruben. Besides, I have you to thank for it. I'm meeting with your colleague Christof," Ivy said.

Ruben felt the floor drop beneath him. Anyone but Christof. Satan himself, even. But not Christof Brandt.

"Is this a joke?" Ruben stiffened and narrowed his eyes at the wall in front of him, imagining it was Ivy.

"Why would it be a joke? I'm a senior economist with an impressive track record. Who wouldn't want me on their team?" Ivy's voice lost some of the exuberance from earlier, and Ruben knew he'd have to play this carefully.

"Ivy, you are way too good for him." Ruben tried to stay calm, to not sound like a crazy person on the subject of Christof Brandt.

"Ruben, I am way too good for every single man I've ever met, including you." Ivy tried to resume their normal banter, to make the conversation go away, but Ruben couldn't let that happen.

"I'm serious, Ivy. Christof is interviewing you to get back at me. He always has an ulterior motive, and you'll never learn what it is until it is too late." Ruben thought back to his past dealings with Christof and couldn't help but curl his lip into a snarl.

"Well, that's awfully narcissistic of you. The only reason in the world Christof has to interview me is to get back at you for some vague business deal that didn't go your way years ago? If he won back then, why does he need to get back at you now? Get over yourself, Ruben."

"Ivy, I'm not going to hash out everything that happened. I'm telling you what I think of the guy, and it's up to you to decide if I'm right or not. I'm not going to beg, but you should also realize that I'm not the kind of man who plays games. Do what you want." Ruben had to grit his teeth to keep from screaming with oblivious and hardheaded Ivy on the phone and smug Christof just across the room. He thought his head was going to explode.

"Thanks for the permission to do what I want, which I don't need from you or anyone else. Player." As Ivy disconnected, Ruben felt the surprise wave from the side come rushing into his kayak, turning him upside down, and leaving him to drown in the river.

He looked over at Christof, who was gathering his jacket to leave. Christof winked at Ruben, aware that he knew about the lunch plans and enjoying the tense moment even more because of it.

The conference tech guy came in to connect the microphone for the lunchtime presentation. He bumped up against the wall with his backpack, knocking the Commitment poster to the ground. The glass cracked when it hit the floor, shattering right next to Ruben's feet.

CHAPTER NINE

Ivy planned to memorize every detail of this interview at Chiltern Firehouse. First, because she'd likely never go back, and second, so she could rub it in Ruben's face to show him how wrong he was. His attitude annoyed her, the idea that Christof would only be interested in her because of Ruben. She would have never considered that before, and now it was all she could think about.

The cab pulled up to the building, a historic firehouse recently converted to a hotel and restaurant. The door led to the world of celebrities, top politicians, and people who could trace their lineage back to before the US was even a country. Ivy shivered a little, then pulled her hair back and put on her game face. She paid the driver and stepped out onto the sidewalk, looking up at the grand, red brick building. She took a deep breath and let her stress fall away, not caring how she looked outside the doors. What mattered was how Ivy behaved once inside, and she wouldn't carry this ball of tension on her back like a well-dressed mule.

She swept into the lobby, putting on the air of someone

who belonged here. Before the hostess could speak, she said firmly, "I'm meeting Christof Brandt. Can you show me to our table?"

"Of course, Ms. Cross. Right this way." The hostess began walking, and Ivy followed, impressed at the kind of restaurant that called people by name. Her nerves were working overtime, doubts nibbling away at her brain thanks to Ruben. Ivy shook her head once, clearing the negative thoughts and cursing him again. She belonged here.

Christof sat in a rounded corner booth with leather button upholstery. In the warm light of the restaurant, Christof was even more striking than last night. His reddish-blond hair was wavy and just the right amount of unruly to keep him on the near side of the line of professionalism. Green eyes held steady as she approached. Christof stood as she reached the table.

"Thanks, Marta. You can tell Pablo to send our lunch out when he's ready. I'll pour." The hostess blushed as Christof touched her shoulder in thanks. He knew how to turn on the charm. She took Ivy's coat and walked away.

"Ivy, thank you for coming on such short notice." He reached out to shake her hand when she was fully expecting the usual two-kiss greeting. The action threw her, especially after this warm interaction with the hostess. "I am only in London one more night and couldn't wait to share my idea with you." Christof motioned for her to sit, sliding back into his side of the banquette. Ivy scooted her way around, not nearly as graceful as she wanted to be in her tight skirt. "Running into you in the hotel last night was a stroke of luck." He pulled the bottle of wine from the cooler, pouring her a glass without asking. Christof then filled his. "To new acquaintances and new opportunities."

Ivy lifted her glass to toast, remembering the quote from Socrates. This conversation, this person, this was all new. The restaurant was certainly new for her. And she was excited to hear Christof's offer, something that wasn't even on her radar yesterday. Christof was all business, no messy flirtation to screw up her life. He was everything Ruben was not—polite, professional, and detached.

"When you told me you worked at the US Embassy, it fired an idea in my mind. And then I did a little research on you— you don't mind that I googled you, do you?" Christof paused briefly for Ivy's forgiveness, which she gave with a shake of her head. "When I discovered that you were a respected economist and had a track record for accurately predicting long-term results of government projects, I knew you were right for the job."

"How would you have access to my job performance details? That's all behind closed doors, and my name is usually not publicized." Ivy traced a small circle with her glass on the white tablecloth. She wondered if he was just playing to her ego.

"You'll find there aren't very many doors closed to me, Ivy," Christof said simply. *Well, that answers that.*

The server arrived with their starters, a cornbread with

chipotle maple butter and steak tartare with a hot sauce containing pine nuts and chipotle. For a moment, Ivy thought she was back in Arizona, or at least the most gourmet version of Arizona that ever existed.

"I haven't had cornbread in years!" She smiled, thinking back to the black cast-iron skillet her mom used to make cornbread every week.

"I read that you grew up in the Wild West. London must be a very different experience for you." Christof's eyes followed her as she picked up the fancy cornbread stick and add a pat of butter, popping it in her mouth and tasting home.

"Home is wherever I am, and I've always been that way. But it doesn't mean I don't like to remember my favorite parts of the places I've lived." Ivy put the bread on her plate, aware that she was making too much of such a simple thing in front of a billionaire's son.

"What would you miss from London if you moved?" Christof asked.

Good question. Ivy'd thought for so long about leaving, all the things she hated about her job and her life in London, that she'd never stopped to consider what she'd be giving up— Indira's curry, for one thing. If she left, Indira's profits would take a hit. What else? Friday night exhibits at the Tate, random conversations on a variety of subjects with opinionated taxi drivers, Sunday roast at the corner pub in the winter, a refreshing Pimm's in the summer, running in Hyde Park. Oh, and her flat. She'd miss her little zone of eclectic comfort, lovingly decorated over the years with finds from flea markets and showrooms.

She realized with a start that she hadn't answered his question out loud. Christof wouldn't care about all that. Her answer should be more polished, professional.

"I'd miss being in the center of everything. Every flight seems to route through Heathrow, and everyone comes to London eventually. We just don't always stay." Ivy smiled politely, waiting for him to continue.

"What would you say to an offer of coming to work for me in Berlin? I think Berlin easily competes with London for access to everything you'd ever want, and the tech market there is hotter than Silicon Valley."

"Technology? I don't see how an economist will fit in the tech world, but I'm interested enough to want to hear more. What do you have in mind?" Ivy took another sip of wine to hide her confusion and appear more confident than she felt.

"I want to expand my data services to government agencies, and you have the right contacts and credentials to get me into every country in Europe. You can explain to them in government language how it would benefit them to overhaul their systems and be my customers."

"You want me to get you in the door? That would be my entire job?" Ivy furrowed her brow and tilted her head, not liking the turn of this conversation. She took a bite of the steak tartare, making sure to leave this meeting with at least something juicy to remember.

"My apologies. I speak fluent English, but sometimes I still get tripped up in the nuances of your language. German is more direct, plain-spoken." Christof smiled, an act Ivy was sure he did a lot to smooth over difficulties in his life. And he should, because his smile was magnetic.

"You understand the needs of government agencies, and you understand the economic benefits of certain infrastructure and system improvements, and you are an expert at explaining these situations to officials. What I want is for you to learn our products and services inside out and then research how we can best fulfill the needs of every single country in Europe, to start."

"What you're talking about sounds like the makings of a monopoly." Ivy took another bite of her cornbread, relishing the reminder of her simple start in life on the table in front of her. Was it a sign that this was the right path for her, a nod to her ambition to move forward? Or was it a warning that she should go back to her roots, to something easier to recognize?

Christof chuckled. "It is about as far from a monopoly as you can imagine since I currently don't have a single government client yet." He held his hands out at the side, a "who me?" type of gesture that didn't work on such a sophisticated man. He probably always got what he wanted, which would work out well for her if they were on the same team.

"So you want me in at the start of this dastardly plan?" Ivy said, signaling she was at least considering the job. She could see Christof's face visibly relax, confident he was going to win her over.

"Not only that, I want you to orchestrate it." Christof put his elbow on the table and leaned in toward her, speaking softly. "I'm surprised Ruben didn't already offer you a job, but I guess that would be complicated to work with your lover." Christof looked up as the server approached with their food. "Oh, I think you're going to like this."

Ivy's stomach dropped at the casual mention of her personal life. She was grateful for the distraction of the food because it gave her time to think. How would she respond? Ruben wasn't her lover, and if she left London, he never would be. But they weren't friends, either. And she knew there was a bad vibe between Ruben and Christof, probably one of those stupid macho things. In any other job interview, she'd refused to talk about her personal life. But this one was weird because Ruben was there when they met. Time to tread carefully.

"I don't know much about Ruben's business. We know each other through mutual friends. Last night was the first time we've been out together." Ivy felt like a traitor, downplaying her sort-of relationship with Ruben. But why would she share her personal life with Christof? It was none of his business. Besides, she couldn't explain their situation even to herself.

"Ah, well that makes sense. Maybe he was buttering you up slowly, waiting to make the offer. And then I swooped in, spotted your talent right away and made the move. That's

Ruben's problem, you know. He's too slow, never seizing what he wants until it's too late. Smart, but not ruthless enough to win." Christof smiled as if they were talking about the weather. "Please eat; I'm keeping you from your food."

Ivy looked down to find a glazed salmon while Christof was eating duck confit. She wondered when she became the kind of woman to let a man order for her, and then she realized he never even gave her the choice. The meal was set before she arrived, before he even knew if she was going to show up. She was uneasy with the idea of being a foregone conclusion to anyone.

"I like smart and non-ruthless friends." Ivy decided to back away from the subject of Ruben. Talking about him with Christof felt like a betrayal. She could see how Christof's manner would irritate Ruben, especially if they'd been on opposite sides of a deal in the past.

Christof sliced into his duck, obviously unconcerned about his cholesterol. Ivy wondered if he ate this way all the time and how he stayed in such great shape. Then she wondered if this was a special treat for him, too. She hoped so, that he was pulling out all the stops to impress her. Ivy cut into her salmon, the maple glaze giving it a touch of sweetness.

"Very kind of you, Ivy. I hope you'll be there to comfort him when he loses the ConStead deal to me later this month." Christof smiled as he picked up his wine glass. "Ruthless always wins."

# # #

No one seemed to notice Ivy's long absence except Ben, who popped his head in the door right after she took off her purple trench coat.

"You took a cab to lunch," Ben said.

"Cabs are forms of transportation that people take every day to get where they want to go, Ben. Do you want me to explain how they work?" Ivy hung her coat on the rack by the door and then walked to her desk, unwinding the scarf from her neck as she stood to look at him.

"Something's up, and you're not telling me." Ben crossed his hand over his chest, clutching a small stack of files.

"Of course I'm not telling you, Ben. You are the worst gossip in the building. Now get out of here. I have work to do." Ivy sat down, emphasizing her order.

"You really should trust me more, Ivy. I see things that you don't. Like the fact that Jack is going to ask you to apply for Sylvia's job. Today." Ben raised his eyebrows and then backed out the door, a total diva move. Ivy had to admit the gossip was worthy of drama, but still, it was gossip. Until Jack showed up at her door, she wouldn't worry about it.

Ivy waited only ten minutes before Jack Shelton turned up

at her door. He knocked lightly on the doorframe as if his mere presence in front of her desk wouldn't alert her he was there.

Jack was wearing a navy blue suit with pinstripes, a classic look obviously tailored to fit his tall, thin frame. His dark-framed glasses were trendy, but his balding-but-not-bald head was not. Jack was all about work, and Ivy had never seen him crack a smile. If you were looking in the dictionary for the "unnamed senior official" always quoted in anonymous leaks to the news, Jack's photo would be there. The rumor was that Jack Shelton was running for US Senate in the next election. Some said he wanted to be president someday, an image Ivy couldn't even imagine. Jack lacked the vision to be truly great. He was a bureaucrat through and through.

"Ivy, do you have a moment?" Jack asked, even though as her boss's boss he didn't have to.

"Sure, Jack, I mean, Mr. Shelton." Ivy stood, motioning to the chair in front of her desk. She'd talked about him for so long by his first name that she assumed a level of friendliness that wasn't there.

"It's fine. You can call me Jack." He unbuttoned his jacket and sat down, crossing his legs and exposing black socks and black leather wingtip shoes.

"With Sylvia leaving, we have a hole in a vital role in this department, and I'd like you to fill it." Jack didn't waste time with the social niceties. No fancy lunch to woo her, no sweet talk over her qualifications. Ivy wondered how happy Mrs.

Shelton was with that kind of approach.

"I appreciate your confidence, Jack. Are you also having this conversation with Alice and Javier? They both have more seniority than me, and the US government is pretty strict about pecking order." Ivy's voice was steady as she wondered how in the hell Ben got his information. Was he recruiting her because he wanted her or to pressure Alice or Javier in some way? Ivy had never trusted the "by the book unless no one is looking" Jack, and she wouldn't start today.

"The application process is open, as you know. But no, I'm not making a personal visit to Javier or Alice though I have no doubt they will both apply." Jack waited for her next move, elbows on the armrests and fingers clasped at his waist. Even in the little guest chair, he acted like this was his office.

"I'm curious as to why you would select me as your favored candidate. Choosing me will ruffle feathers for you." His face froze, and she knew he was unused to being questioned. Ivy shrugged her shoulders and smiled. "Sorry, hazards of the job. I can't help but analyze the situation."

Ivy leaned forward on her elbows, looking Jack directly in the eye, challenging him to break protocol and admit favoritism. It happened all the time, of course, but no one ever acknowledged it.

"You are the smartest, most ambitious person in this department. And it makes sense that you should run it as an example to the people who work for you. The ambassador has some big plans for the future, and he needs capable and innovative people to lead the charge. One of those people is you." Jack had to know she'd be impressed that she'd been the subject of a conversation with the ambassador, if that were even true. But was it enough to turn down a job offer from Christof?

"I appreciate your vote of confidence, Jack." Ivy tested him with her government doublespeak, appearing to say yes without actually doing it. He heard what he wanted to, same as everyone else.

"It will be a pleasure working with you, Ivy." Jack reached across the desk and shook her hand, a little surprise on his face when her firm grip matched his own. He nodded his head once and then turned to walk out the door.

I can't be the same woman who complained just a few days ago that life was too boring. From a boring job to two new offers, and two handsome and intriguing men in her life. Ivy knew only one option would win out, but for a moment she just wanted to bask in the glow of possibility, watching her life play out in different scenarios.

Her training made this reaction second nature, a way of following events to their logical conclusions.

The bigger office down the hall could be hers, a level of recognition so far denied to her. Five or ten years of steady work in that role, and she'd be in a prime position for lucrative consulting work. She could see herself at fifty, working part-time, traveling extensively, and enjoying a comfortable bank balance.

Or she could go to Berlin, make a lot more money now, be privy to deals and opportunities that were currently off-limits, and see and do more than she ever imagined. It would be risky, but she would never be bored again. She'd learn from the best, broker major deals, and have a completely different lifestyle than the one she had now. She'd never sleep with Christof, but the idea of working with a smart, handsome, and charismatic man had appeal.

Ruben didn't so easily fit into either of those plans, considering he lived in Madrid. But maybe he was sent into her life as a parting gift, a way to celebrate her good turn of fortune. She'd felt more kindly toward Ruben before she learned he had competing business with Christof for ConStead, a little detail he neglected to tell her when he accused Christof of using her to get even with him.

Ivy looked up to see Ben standing at her door, flowers covering his face. The vase in his hands was tall, and the wildflowers spilling over the top and sides were surrounded by ivy.

Ben walked in and set it on the desk, waiting for her to read the card. After giving her the heads-up on Jack's intentions, Ivy felt like she owed him this one, though she wouldn't tell him who Christof was. She opened the card, looking for the telltale ink from what was undoubtedly Christof's fancy pen.

Everyone wants you, but no one as much as me. Sorry for being a jerk. Dinner tonight? ~ Ruben

The surprise must have shown on her face because Ben's eyebrows went up.

"From an admirer." Ivy slid the card underneath the blotter on her desk, out of the reach of Ben's snatching fingers.

"Is this the same admirer you met for lunch today? Or is that another bit of drama you're hiding from me?" Ben pouted, pushing his luck with her generosity.

"Ben, there is nothing to hide. I have an ordinary life outside of work, just like you do." Ivy reached forward and touched the ivy, tracing the outline of the leaves with her fingertips.

"People who have something to hide always say they have nothing to hide. Spycraft 101, Ivy. Read the manual." Ben leaned against the doorframe. "So, did Jack come by yet?"

"Ben, we aren't spies. You watch too many movies. And yes, Jack did stop by." Ivy counted at least ten types of flowers in this arrangement.

"You and I might not be spies, but there are spies among us. As secretive as you are, you probably are a spy."

"Accusing someone else of being a spy is a great cover for

an actual spy. Did you think of that, Ben?"

"Touché, Ms. Cross. I will leave you with your mystery man flowers and the swirl of political intrigue around you. But I expect to be kept in the loop from now on."

"You should write a book, Ben. Such imagination. Now get out of here." Ivy turned her chair toward the window. The clouds gathering in the afternoon sky promised rain for tonight. Maybe she should give Ruben another chance. She was feeling benevolent after the successful interview and Jack's offer. She had already refuted Ruben's claim that she wasn't enough for Christof, that the interview was all to get back at him. With a likely move to Berlin in front of her, it would be easy to make the break before things got messy. And didn't she deserve to have a little fun?

Ivy_Cross: Dinner at my place at eight. Pick up the order at Indira's place on the corner. Cocktails will be waiting.

RubenAlegre: Such an old-fashioned girl. See you then.

CHAPTER TEN

Ruben held the plastic bag in front of his face. "My safety shield. I knew you wouldn't attack me if there was a danger of hurting your curry." Ruben lowered the bag slightly and wiggled his eyebrows suggestively.

"Smart man to protect yourself like that, but I can't guarantee your safety once the curry is gone," Ivy said, standing at the door in a dark blue sweater and jeans. Her hair was in a ponytail, making her look younger, almost like a college student. Ruben briefly thought of his college friend Paz and silently thanked her for the lesson he couldn't learn inside a classroom.

"I've also taped garlic naan all over my body as a backup measure." He dropped the bag to show his whole face. "It will either pad your attack or tempt you to devour me." Ruben grinned, waiting at the door for permission to enter.

She cracked a smile, considering the options. "Come in, I have cocktails ready to pour." Ivy stepped aside so Ruben could enter and then shut the heavy black door behind him.

Ruben studied her surroundings as she took the food and his coat. This place was a museum to the personality of Ivy. Solid construction, functional and no-frills appliances, but touches of luxury and eccentricity all around. The old wooden floors held a dark stain, covered with antique rugs in dark colors. Moroccan? Indian? Ruben didn't know, but he liked the contrast. The red couch was velvety, and a mirrored chest accompanied the brown leather chair to the side. An exposed brick wall behind the sofa bordered Ivy's desk, bare except for her laptop and a vase of flowers. Not his flowers, though. He supposed she'd left those at work.

Ivy ushered him into the living room and onto the couch while she made drinks and plated their takeout on white plates that screamed luxury by design, not embellishment. Nothing in Ivy's house looked accidental, and even though it didn't all go together, it belonged together. Ruben liked the way she curated her home to reflect her personality. Most people weren't that in tune with themselves.

"Thank you for the flowers today. Nice touch to send me ivy. I don't think anyone has ever done that before." Ivy turned to the old-fashioned refrigerator and pulled the long handle to retrieve the tonic for their drinks.

"I tried to find poison ivy, but none of the florists had it in stock. So you got the more conventional English kind." Ruben got the feeling she liked the possibly dangerous nature of her name and personality, and he wanted her to know that he did, too.

"I am not here to be liked. I'm here to be respected and appreciated. Those are very different things." Ruben thought that might be the truest thing she'd ever said.

"Don't I know it," Ruben said.

Ivy arched her eyebrow at him as she put their food and drinks on the table and settled onto the couch. She curled one leg underneath, a casual look he'd never seen before. Ruben imagined her curled up like this on his couch in Madrid, talking after work. Would he want something like that after they had sex, or would he lose interest like he always did? He hoped to find out.

Ivy looked him in the eye, hands crossed over her chest. "Why do you keep trying to force this thing between us? We both know it's not going anywhere. I don't even like you most of the time!" Ivy threw her hands up in the air. "Your life is in Madrid. My life is here. Or somewhere else. I don't know."

"Are we going to eat first? Because I'm starving." Ruben picked up the drinks and handed one to Ivy. "Here's to spicy food, hot chemistry, and impossible situations. May things never be easy or boring between us." Ruben clinked glasses and drank, enjoying the confused look on Ivy's face. "If you expected me to come here and argue the facts of the situation, you were wrong. I can see it as clearly as you. I just don't think it's a deal-breaker." Ruben reached over to the plates and began scooping biryani and spicy vindaloo onto his plate, a dash of cucumber raita sauce on the side to cool his tongue.

A worried look crossed her face. "Sure you can handle that

much spice?" Ivy looked at Ruben's plate with pursed lips, challenging him. "Indira makes it extra hot for me." Ivy was warming to him, no doubt.

"If you love it, I want to try it. And if I can't eat it, then you'll have to put me in the tub and pour milk all over me." He grinned, taking the first bite of vindaloo.

"Mmm-hmm. Go ahead, then." Ivy challenged him.

The fire started slowly, an arsonist setting flame to his taste buds in several locations at once, fanning them individually until they all joined forces in the middle. The blaze in his mouth burned out of control, and he felt his lips start to numb. Ruben's eyes watered, but he kept chewing. Beads of sweat gathered at his hairline, threatening to fall down his forehead and into his eyes.

"Delicious," he croaked. He reached for a piece of naan, hoping the soft bread would soak up some of the heat. A slow smile spread across Ivy's face. Ruben set his plate back on the table and cleared his throat. "Think I'll just savor that first bite for a while."

Ivy walked over to the refrigerator and poured him a big glass of milk. His mouth watered for it.

"Here you go, you crazy fool." While he drank, Ivy continued. "Why did you eat that, Ruben?"

He set the empty glass down on the table, relieved to downgrade the raging fires of hell to a mere bonfire.

"I'll do just about anything to get what I want. And I want you." Ruben didn't know how to say it any clearer than that.

"Trying curry is a lot different from trying a relationship." Ivy wasn't making this easy. Ruben had thought the food example was going to take him a lot further than this.

"Ivy, you keep bringing up the location as the one reason we shouldn't see where this leads. But what about all the reasons we should?" Ruben scooted closer to her on the couch and picked up her hand. "Number one is that I have yet to kiss a single freckle on your body. A tragedy." He kissed the small grouping of freckles on her wrist. "Number two is that we are the most fascinating people we know. There is no one who occupies my thoughts as much as you, and even though you might not admit it, you feel the same way as me. If you don't have me, you'll drive yourself crazy. And I can't allow that to happen." Ruben grinned, moving closer.

"You're forgetting about our conversation today, my job interview with Christof, and the fact that I'm probably leaving London." For such a fiery woman, Ivy was surprisingly good at cooling things down.

Ruben forged ahead. "You've made a pro-and-con list about us, I can tell. But all I've heard so far are the cons. Let's make tonight an exploration of the pros."

Ivy's face softened, and the shield fell away.

"This is only going to end badly for you," she said in a hoarse whisper. "I will break your heart." Ivy's words were harsh, but the challenge only excited him. "And we won't live happily ever after. At least not together." Ivy leaned her forehead against his, closing her eyes as she gave her final warning. "You know this going in, and you still want to move forward?"

Ruben curled his fingers through her thick ponytail. "I can't wait to prove you wrong."

Ruben tilted her head and pulled her lips to his, feeling a different kind of fire in his mouth than before. They kissed cautiously at first, like two wild animals circling each other before mating. Then Ivy became more aggressive, scooting forward on the couch to straddle Ruben.

"I've wanted to kiss you from the moment I first saw you," Ruben said when their lips parted.

"Then shut up and do it," Ivy growled, pushing him back on the couch and unfastening her long red hair, which formed a curtain around their faces. In the shadow, he could only see her green eyes above him, challenging him to resist her. He couldn't.

Ruben sat forward and picked Ivy up, hands gripping her ass, and dropped her back on the couch. Then he leaned over her and whispered in her ear. "I know you'd like to be in charge right now, but that's not going to happen." Ruben gently tugged on her ear with his teeth, then nuzzled her neck, inhaling the fresh scent of her.

His arms were braced to hold him above her, and Ivy

reached forward to caress his upper arms. Ivy's eyes grew wide as she felt his biceps and triceps.

"You've been hiding things from me, Ruben," Ivy breathed.

"You have no idea, Ivy Cross. But tonight you'll discover everything." Ruben leaned back and unbuttoned his shirt slowly, watching Ivy's expression change as his rock-hard abs were revealed. She brought her hand forward and traced the outline of the six-pack on his stomach, then pulled herself up on one elbow while she traveled up his chest to his lean and hard pecs. Ruben stayed in place, watching her explore him with his shirt unbuttoned.

"Take it off," Ivy said, her whispered command vying for control.

"What did I say? I'm in charge right now. And I say that you have to take it off for me." Ruben grew hard at the thought of commanding Ivy to do anything, both wanting to tame her and be tamed by her.

Ivy sat forward, her hands stroking his sides and around to his back, where his muscles were taut with anticipation. She reached up to his shoulders, her neck raised to look in his eyes, and pulled his shirt down his arms. Ivy explored him with her hands and eyes, then flicked his left nipple with her tongue. She looked up at him with those green eyes and then mischievously bit his nipple. Ruben groaned in response, ready to let her torture him with a thousand love bites. There were worse ways to go.

"Stand up. I want to look at you." Ivy's ragged voice was just as much a turn-on as her body. "This might be our only time together before I break your heart."

Ruben bent down and picked her up, standing them facing each other. Ivy could talk about heartbreak all she wanted. After tonight, she wouldn't be able to say no to him ever again.

Ivy put her index finger on the fuzzy trail that led from his flat waist down into his pants. Then she slowly traced her fingers up the midline of his six-pack, through the small valley between his pecs, and over the collarbone that framed his chest. She put her hands on his shoulders and felt the rounded muscles beneath, then caressed his arms down to his palms. Ivy pulled his hands to her mouth and kissed his fingers before releasing him to continue her inspection.

While he stood in place, Ivy walked around, trailing her hands across his back and following the V-shaped outline to his waist. Her fingers dug in just below his belt, teasing him with her plans. Ruben turned around to face Ivy and she pulled her sweater over her head, red hair disappearing for a moment as her lacy blue bra came into view. Ruben's breath caught in his throat.

Her upper chest was sprinkled with pale freckles. He vowed to explore every single one.

Ivy threw her sweater to the floor and put her arms around his neck, their bare skin touching for the first time. They melded together, skin on skin, as their mouths passed secret messages to each other.

"Where is your bed?" Ruben asked, picking her up. "Tell me now or I'll take you on this floor," he whispered.

Ivy wiggled out of his arms, landing like a cat on the floor. "What's wrong with the floor?" She unbuttoned her jeans and slowly shimmied them over her hips and down to the ground. Stepping out of them, she kicked them to the side.

Her ivory skin glowed in the soft light, a beacon calling him home. Ruben unbuckled his belt and unbuttoned his pants, watching her sink to her knees on the floor. He would take her anywhere, everywhere, anytime.

Pants gone, he joined her on the floor, laying her back as his hands explored her silky pale body. Ruben discovered freckles on her shoulders, the tops of her knees, and even a few on the tops of her feet. Her creamy breasts overflowed the barely-there bra, one that could serve no other function than seduction.

Ruben reached behind her to unfasten her bra and gently removed it. He held her exposed breasts with his hands, the fullness overflowing his grasp. His mouth tasted her, hotter than the curry, smoother than the milk.

"Sit on the table," he commanded. Ivy scooted to the edge of the large farmhouse-style coffee table, away from the rapidly cooling dinner plates. Ruben knelt in front of her, reaching for the waistband of her panties and gently tugging them down to the floor. Ivy sat naked in front of him, and he pulled her knees gently apart to appreciate all of her.

Ruben kissed her knees, waiting for her moan of approval before traveling up her inner thigh, kissing and licking his way to her source. Ivy scooted forward, making the journey shorter. As he kissed her center, the core of her being, she grabbed his hair and moaned. Ruben was hooked, and if she chose to break his heart after this, he'd gladly let her. The treasure was worth the price.

# # #

Ivy had never been so glad that she bought this ridiculously huge coffee table for her small flat.

Ruben pushed every button on her body, and he pushed them hard. Ivy's senses overloaded, his hands and tongue and lips all over her body, worshiping her like a goddess. Ivy knew having sex with him would be like glue to their impossible not-quite relationship, a complication in her life she couldn't afford right now. But she couldn't be bothered with the future when the present consumed every thought and sensation.

Ruben's attention to her breasts erased the worries of what might happen tomorrow or next month or next year. From breaking his heart or not being able to follow through with breaking his heart.

"I want you, Ivy. I've wanted you from the moment I first saw you." Ruben's voice was soft, but his hands were not. "I have to have you now." Ivy slowly nodded, locking eyes and ready to join bodies. He pulled a condom from the pocket on his crumpled pants on the floor and stood. Ruben tore the package open with his teeth, looking down at Ivy on the table as he rolled it on. She felt like he was wrapping a gift for her.

He placed her feet onto his shoulders and leaned over her, biceps bulging and eyes sparkling with desire. Her head fell back when he entered her, a cry escaping her mouth as he filled her completely. His hands gripped the edges of the coffee table as he thrust, her blue polished toenails framing his eyes. They moved as one, a rhythm as natural as breathing, pace increasing along with their passion.

Ruben consumed her with every stroke, her hips bending and flexing to accommodate him. He seemed to sense when she couldn't handle more and backed off, a devilish grin on his face when her body urged him to resume.

Intensity burned on his face as he edged closer to his release, his body calling for her to join him. As she followed his body's command, Ivy felt the familiar sensation build, and her body tightened in anticipation. Ruben's eyes grew wide for a moment, feeling her close around him.

"Oh, Ivy," he whispered, the sound of him saying her name bringing her closer to orgasm.

"Ruben, I can't wait anymore," she panted.

Between clenched teeth, he groaned as he leapt into a sea of release. Then the flood overtook her, waves of pleasure rolling out from the center of her being, all the way through her fingers, toes, and scalp. They both rode the sensation until the very last gentle ripples of euphoria lapped at the shore.

Panting, Ruben put his hands on either side of Ivy's head on the coffee table. He leaned down and kissed her gently. "You said you'd break my heart, but I think you broke something else." He nibbled at her ear and neck, soft kisses and gentle bites as their heart rates returned to normal.

"I should have told you my aim isn't very good," Ivy said, laughing when he tickled her side.

"You can go ahead and take it back," Ruben said.

"Take what back?"

"What you said about leaving. Because there is no way you can go after that," Ruben said, kissing her shoulder.

"You might be right, Ruben. You might be right." Ivy reached up to smooth his hair where she'd mussed it. Warmth glowed from her belly, and she was content in a way she hadn't felt for years.

"Of all the ways I imagined being with you, the reality was far better. But next time, I think we should use the bed." Ruben lifted her from the coffee table and turned to sit, a move so smooth they stayed connected. Ivy curled her legs around his waist.

"You know that no one has ever been in that bed but me." Ivy brushed his hair back with her fingers.

"Don't tell me you're partial to coffee table sex because I don't know if I can do that again." Ruben laughed and then kissed her chest in between her breasts, licking the salty beads of perspiration.

"No, I don't invite men here. This is my home, my sanctuary. Until now, I've never wanted anyone else to see it. But you can't blame me for not taking you all the way to my cocoon the first time out." Ivy smiled and then kissed the tip of his nose.

Ruben cradled her hips in his hands and stood, allowing her to drop her legs to the floor as they came unbound from each other. "It's not the first time anymore," he whispered as he bent to kiss her.

"Always negotiating, aren't you?" Ivy asked.

"Only for things I want, Ivy. Only for the very best." Ruben kissed her again, pulling her tight, the sweat cooling on their bodies and making them sticky.

"Why don't we take a bath and reheat our dinner? I think we've worked up an appetite." Ivy caressed his back as she spoke, knowing she'd never be able to forget the hard body he was hiding under those well-tailored clothes.

"I hope you're not hungry because the bath is going to take a while." Ruben raised one eyebrow and Ivy looked down, smiling as she led him to the tub.

"You'd do anything to avoid another bite of curry."

# # #

"Don't get used to this," Ivy said, slicing their bagels on the counter with her back to him. "I'm a yogurt and granola type of woman, usually. But we depleted some vital energy reserves last night." She wore a kimono-style robe cinched tightly at her waist, tangled red hair hanging over her shoulders. Ruben wanted nothing more than to eat her for breakfast.

She put the plates of overcooked scrambled eggs and bagels on the table, failing to look directly at his eyes. The morning after was too raw for her, something to which he could relate. Or was it more than that? Ivy could have easily sent him home last night, or shooed him out the door first thing this morning. He had been on the other side of this equation more times than he cared to count, feigning sleep in hopes his latest conquest would leave, or making excuses about an early work meeting just for the ease of waking up alone.

Ruben pushed the plunger on the coffee press, the aroma of dark roasted beans infusing the air. Ivy cleared her throat as he poured.

"Um, can you put a shirt on? It's a little distracting."

Ruben wore his tight boxer briefs and nothing else. It didn't occur to him to cover up after the night they'd just shared. He wished Ivy had come to breakfast in her underwear. But if she did, they probably wouldn't have gotten around to eating.

"Oh sure. Sorry about that." Ruben walked to the couch and picked up his shirt, buttoning it over his boxers. "Pants, too?" he asked with a grin.

"I wouldn't want to accidentally spill hot coffee on you," Ivy threatened, a smirk on her lips as Ruben's face paled.

"Good point. I forgot what a dangerous woman you are." Ruben slipped on his pants and sat back down at the table, grateful for the break in awkwardness.

"What time is your flight?" Ivy asked.

"Getting rid of me so soon? I was hoping to at least finish my breakfast," Ruben replied, only half telling the truth. Ivy's eggs were terrible. He made a mental note to take her out for breakfast the next time they spent the night together.

"I'm a little rusty with morning-after conversation. I'm used to having breakfast alone, too." Her smile was conciliatory, so Ruben gave her earlier comment a pass. They were both feeling a little exposed this morning, her more than him. He would tread lightly.

"I know you've got work today. I'll head back to my hotel when we're done with breakfast. But I want to see you again. I can stay another night if you're free." Ruben didn't want to sound clingy, but if there was even a remote chance of a repeat of last night's sex, he wanted it.

"Sorry, got to prepare for a big meeting coming up. And arriving late this morning means staying late tonight." She smiled. "Not that I mind." She reached her hand across the table to his, fingers touching in an act he thought was as intimate as anything they'd shared the previous night. Ruben's heart pounded in his chest. Normally he'd feel his fire quenched at this stage, his curiosity sated. But with Ivy Cross, he was just getting started. No way she was moving, not if he could help it.

Play this slow, Ruben. Don't get greedy.

"I can come back to London after your big meeting," Ruben offered, ignoring his own advice in record time. Ivy pulled her hand back and stabbed her eggs with her fork. She took a bite and chewed, the delay in her response speaking volumes. Ruben knew her tactics because he'd done them himself a dozen times before.

"Sure. Let me get past it and then we'll make plans, okay?" Ivy gave that same maddening smile that he knew so well, the one to placate a demand without committing to anything. What else could he do at this point? Pushing her would only make things worse; he knew this from experience. "I do have a question for you, though." She placed her fork on her plate and looked him in the eye. "Why didn't you tell me you and Christof were in competition right now?"

Ruben saw the warning signs in his peripheral vision as he

hurtled toward the cliff at the end of this conversation.

"Why would I talk to you about work when there are so many other things to discuss?" Ruben displayed his best charming smile, wishing for a quick end to the date he'd wanted to last forever just five minutes before.

"I find it strange that you'd warn me away from working with Christof because he's such a bad guy without telling me that he's your direct competitor for a huge contract. You made it sound like he was using me to get even with you, but it looks like you were using me to punish him." Ivy crossed her arms, hands hidden in the long kimono sleeves falling elegantly to the side. Ruben couldn't shake the image of her as a judge and him as the defendant.

"I would have told you about his character even if we weren't in competition. He's bad news, Ivy. But I'll leave it to you to judge for yourself." Ruben thought it wise to keep his answers brief. He knew it wouldn't be long before a smart woman like Ivy saw through Christof. He was only interviewing her to get at Ruben, and once he left town he doubted Christof would follow up anyway. Besides, they'd made a huge step forward last night. Best to let this thing die a slow, natural death and not make it into a fight.

"You can see why it's hard for me to trust you on that. And I don't blame you for keeping your cards close to your chest. I would probably do the same." Ivy's face was stone, impossible to read. If this was her business face, he hoped to never be across the table from her in a negotiation.

"See how compatible we are?" Ruben grinned, hoping to put this conversation behind them. He still had time for one more romp before he had to catch his flight to Madrid.

"That's the problem, Ruben. I think we're too much alike, and that's bad news. I told you I'd break your heart, and you were fine with that. But I'm not okay with you breaking mine." Ivy stood and put her dishes in the sink, leaving the rest of her eggs to grow as cold as the mood in the room. Ruben thought of their salsa lesson, one step forward, one step back. He put on his shoes and left before the situation could get worse.

CHAPTER ELEVEN

Ben was seated in front of Ivy's desk when she walked into her office that morning. Ruben was already on his way to the airport.

"Rifling through my desk for government secrets, Ben?" Ivy took off her coat and hung it on the rack by the door before walking around to sit at her desk.

"I don't think your secrets are government-related, Ivy. What's going on with you? You haven't applied for the promotion yet, even after Jack's personal invitation." Ben stared at her as if trying to peer inside her head.

"How do you find time to do your job, Ben?" Ivy asked.

"It's not my job we're talking about. What gives, Ivy? You have always wanted this job, which means you must have something else in the works." Ben crossed his arms, waiting for her answer.

"Ben, a person with my experience is always going to attract headhunters. It doesn't mean I have to respond to all of them." Ivy kept her tone neutral.

"All of them? Interesting. So you do have another offer on the table. It must be a lot of money because you know you could take the promotion here and turn it into something big in the long run. I hear Sylvia has already set up her own shop. What better way to announce you're available than a very public resignation for no reason?" Ben seemed to be reevaluating his opinion of Sylvia at that moment, and Ivy had to admit she was, too. Good for Sylvia.

"Ben, I'm working on this Berlin conference Sylvia set up. Without her, it is going to take up all my time." Ivy tried to sound exasperated, even though she wasn't. Anything to get him out the door.

"That's why I'm here. Jack sent me to help you prepare, and I'll be going to Berlin, too." Ben's smile showed practically every single one of his teeth. He was giddy about this assignment.

"I don't need your help, Ben. I've got it under control." Ivy frowned, not happy to have a tagalong on this trip.

"You just said it was taking up all your time. Which one is it, Ivy? And why don't you want me to help—afraid I'll suss out your secrets?" Ben smirked, enjoying this entirely too much, in Ivy's opinion.

She wasn't seeing an upside to this, but if Jack sent him over, there wasn't much she could do about it. At this point, what did it matter? If things went well with Christof, she'd be giving her notice soon anyway. And if they didn't, at least she'd have him to be the face of the Embassy while she took care of her personal business.

"Fine, then you can take on coordinating the presentations among the delegates. I don't want any last-minute technical glitches because someone didn't read the instructions." Ivy was glad to have Ben manage this, as the tedium of those details always annoyed her.

"Yes, ma'am! Better get used to calling the shots, boss," Ben said, grinning.

When he left, Ivy leaned back in her chair. *Boss.* She liked the sound of it. Though she didn't know if she'd even have a staff to call her own at Christof's company. Still another question to ask. Ivy typed it into her phone, keeping a running tab of the issues and demands she'd clarify when the offer came through. The conference in Berlin was perfect timing, and she was glad Sylvia was gone to free her up from oversight. Her plan was to get away one evening and meet Christof at his office to discuss her contract. Ivy hated negotiating over the phone. Reading someone in person was much better, especially when asking tough questions.

Like the one she'd asked Ruben over breakfast. She was still pissed he didn't tell her about the ConStead deal, even though she probably would have done the same thing in his position. He had no good reason, other than reiterating that Christof was a jerk and she should stay away from him. What could she do with such vague information? Especially in the face of such an excellent offer and no evidence to support his claim.

She sighed in frustration. It had been a mistake to sleep with him, no doubt. Even worse because it was the best sex she'd ever had in her life. Ivy could never tell Rose about that, worried the news would make it to Mateo and then back to Ruben. She could not fan the flames of this connection. It was already white-hot, and she needed a bucket of cold water to put out the fire. After one more time.

Images from last night flashed in her mind, vignettes of physical connection, lusty laughs, and mind-blowing pleasure. Her favorite mental snapshots were of Ruben's shoulders and back, a perfect V-shape. His body was a lean muscular type that reminded her of a mountain lion ready to pounce. And the memory of the way he used his mouth on every part of her body sent a shiver down her spine.

This morning's questioning was a necessary break in the connection from last night, a way to keep her from falling for Ruben. He held back vital information in advising her not to pursue a job with Christof. And then there was the logistical difference of him living in Madrid and her in Berlin. At least in London he had ongoing business. But Berlin? There was no reason for him to go there except to see her. And Ivy had a feeling she'd have very little time for any relationship if she began the job in Berlin.

She picked up her favorite mug and walked to the breakroom to make coffee. People were gathered in small groups in the hallway, as usual. What wasn't usual was having them stop talking when she passed. Ivy wondered if Ben had been talking about her, or if he'd picked up on the gossip from someone else. What were people saying?

Ivy walked into the breakroom and made her coffee, the aroma of the roasted beans clearing her head. What did she care if people talked about her? She wasn't going to be here long. On the way back to her desk, she made it a point to say hello to everyone she passed, even walking up to a group near her office and casually asking what was going on. People looked down and scattered like the wind as fast as they could.

Hmmm. Why would anyone think she was the shoo-in for this promotion when there were two senior people ahead of her? Unless people knew Jack came to see her. Or unless Ben was spreading this rumor. The good news was if they thought she was leaving, they would be asking questions, curious about her next move. If they weren't asking, it meant her secret was still safe.

Back at her desk, she had an email from Jack.

Still waiting for your official application for the position, Ivy. This is the government, remember? We can't go ahead with just our conversation. I'll need your official application by the end of next week. ~ Jack

Christof had offered her a job and new life in Berlin after a lunch date at a swanky restaurant. He'd sent her a handwritten invitation on personal stationery, and he hadn't even seen her résumé. Jack knew her and treated her like some stranger on an anonymous job site. Ivy knew Jack had to do it this way, but she couldn't help but compare the two scenarios. Christof made her feel wanted, important. Jack made her feel like another cog in the wheel, a box to be checked. No wonder the job held no appeal to her anymore.

Ivy composed a reply to Jack, wondering if she could hold him off long enough to sign a contract with Christof.

Working on the Berlin conference details now. Thanks for sending Ben to help. Will send my formal reply by the deadline. ~ Ivy

Short and sweet and vague. Hopefully he would read it the way he wanted to.

CHAPTER TWELVE

On the flight back to Madrid, Ruben tried to refocus on his business. He had seven days to work a miracle on the ConStead deal, and after being with Ivy last night, feeling the power of their physical connection, he was invincible. Also, he was starving, no doubt because he'd skipped most of the fiery curry last night in favor of the no-calorie meal of Ivy. The more he had of her, the more he wanted. The sight of her in that lacy blue bra, red hair spilling across her shoulders, inflamed him. After deplaning, he drove straight to his office, all the while trying to remember the last time he'd had sex three times in one night and still craved more. By the time he pulled into the parking garage, he'd confirmed it was a first.

Ruben tried to erase the disastrous breakfast from his mind. Maybe the two of them were a lot alike, but that didn't have to be a bad thing. Neither one of them had a great track record with relationships, but that's only because they'd never wanted them before. Now that they did—or at least he thought they both did—it shouldn't be hard. They were the type of people who could accomplish anything, so why not this?

Not telling her about the competition with ConStead was a misstep, but it didn't change the facts about Christof. He hoped Ivy would see that, but he knew it wouldn't matter if she didn't. Christof couldn't mask his true nature for very long, and then she'd have her proof.

While Ruben worked through the complexities of their relationship, visions of her naked body kept interrupting his thoughts. If he'd thought having sex would cure him of his infatuation, he was wrong. The feel of her body against his, the curve of her ass and the fullness of her breasts, the way her hips moved just so when he was inside of her—Ruben felt himself growing hard at the thought. He would never figure out a solution to ConStead with Ivy on his mind.

He thought of *fútbol* rules for five minutes until he could get out of his car without scandal. Instead of walking into the office, he headed for the street, too amped up to sit behind a desk.

Madrid was his city, and Ruben was glad to be back. Even though it was the third biggest in Europe, the central zone was still very walkable, with a distinct feel in each neighborhood. You could go from party central to genteel elegance to hipster organic in just a few minutes. Or you could get away from it all at the park, forgetting you were in a city at all.

Mind churning, Ruben turned into a coffee shop and ordered his favorite breakfast, a toasted baguette rubbed with tomato, olive oil, and a little bit of salt. A small *cortado*, an espresso cut with steaming milk, was the pick-me-up his brain needed to find a solution for ConStead.

He sat at the counter, picking up a discarded newspaper. At the bottom, in a small box, he saw that two politicians with very different political ideologies were banding together to fight an outsider. Both parties thought it was scandalous at first, like the serfs joining forces with their overlords, but when faced with a common enemy, it made sense. People were starting to come around and see the logic in an unusual partnership. Ruben wondered if the politicians would continue working together after the enemy was gone, who in this case was a deep-pocket developer who wanted to revamp a historic area of Madrid without paying his share of taxes. He doubted it.

"The enemy of my enemy is my friend," Ruben said aloud, his brain forming an idea.

The barista looked up.

Ruben shook his head, unaware he'd spoken the proverb out loud. He'd been so focused on working against Christof he'd forgotten there was another competitor in the mix. Christof's goal would be to take as much as he could from everyone involved. Take more money from the client, take Ruben's reputation and almost-girlfriend. What would he take from bidder number three, and could Ruben use that to his advantage?

Ruben couldn't deny the desire to best Christof, to walk away with the business and keep Ivy in London. He wanted to win, and in this situation he couldn't do it on his own.

The plan had a few holes to patch still, but for the first time he saw the light at the end of the tunnel, a way to walk away with everything. He just hoped the light wasn't an oncoming train.

CHAPTER THIRTEEN

"Ivy, I'm so glad I caught you." Mrs. Bingham waved from her front door as Ivy walked up. Before Ivy could respond, Mrs. B continued. "A package came while you were gone, and Mr. Baker left it with me." Mr. Baker was their postman, a quiet man who'd been delivering mail on this route for probably thirty years. "With the rain coming down, I shared one of your chocolates with him for his trouble." Mrs. Bingham beamed, and Ivy wondered if she didn't have a thing for their postman. She imagined the two of them together, a chubby and talkative Mrs. B with the slight and quiet Mr. Baker. A perfect pair. Ivy could even still call her Mrs. B.

"Thanks, Mrs. B. I'm glad you both enjoyed the chocolate." Ivy reached for the package, hoping to cut the conversation short. All she wanted to do was go inside and make some lists: what to ask for in her contract negotiation; pros and cons of selling versus renting out her flat; what kind of clothes she needed to add to her wardrobe; where she should live in Berlin.

What to do about Ruben. Or what not to do about Ruben.

Now that he was back in Madrid, this crazy attraction would probably die a natural death. She could move on to her new life. She and Ruben would be friendly at Rose and Mateo's wedding, former lovers with too short of a history to have any drama. The scenario played out in her head perfectly, convincing her that it could happen the same way in real life.

Once inside, Ivy put the package and her purse on the table and hung her coat on the fake red antler rack in her entry hall. She made a note to take the rack with her if she moved. Ivy liked seeing the bold style statement the minute she walked in her door, a reminder of her hardheaded nature. The rack was a gift ten years ago from her friend Lily and was one of her favorite possessions.

Ivy kicked off her shoes, stood at her kitchen counter and pulled back the cardboard flap. Inside was a large envelope with her name on it plus a small box.

She opened the envelope and pulled out the formal offer letter from Christof, outlining her job duties in analyzing and pitching government clients for his company's data storage solution as well as her compensation package. Ivy put her hand out on the counter to steady herself. During lunch, no money was discussed. Nor job duties. It was a meeting of the minds, deciding whether to become a team or go their separate ways. Ivy knew the money would be more than she made working for the US government, but she had no idea it would be four times as much, and with a bonus for every client she signed.

Ivy's head was swimming. She was not one to base her

success on money, but she did base her success on how much money someone was willing to pay her for her smarts. And this was a definite sign of success. The only sticking point she could see was the requirement to move to Berlin immediately. She would live there and work at his office at The Werks and travel throughout Europe convincing the powers that be in every country that they should be working with Christof. And her. If Ivy did this, she would be part of Christof's team.

She read to the bottom of the letter, mouth dropping open.

P.S. I'm attaching the keys to your car. You seem like a woman who belongs behind the wheel of something sleek and powerful.

The black box sat in the package. She reached in and pulled it out, setting it on the counter. Ivy crossed her hands over her chest and stared at the box. She leaned down, elbows on the counter, and gently opened the hinged lid. Inside was another box labeled *Original BMW™ Accessories.*

Ivy took the box out, sliding the cover off to reveal a key fob with the tiny blue-and-white logo. The key fob alone probably cost more than her first car. Ivy didn't know a lot about automobiles, not having owned one since moving to London all those years ago, but she did know expensive.

She put the key on the bar and stepped back, examining it.

The life she was contemplating—correction, leaning heavily toward—included an expensive car, a salary four times more than her current one, plus more independence and control over her projects. Not a bad setup for a woman in her early forties looking to make some serious bank to fund a cushy early retirement.

Ivy shook her head. A few days ago she was wondering what to do next, and now she had more options than she ever thought possible. On the one hand, there was a personal request to apply for the promotion at the US Embassy, a prestigious job that she could use to secure an even better job in just a few years. On the other, she could have a brand-new life in Berlin right now with four times as much money as she currently made, not including bonuses. And a hot car to drive. Plus the most fabulous sex with the most irritating and compelling man she'd met in years.

Three distinct possibilities, none of which worked well with any of the others. The economist in her couldn't help but map out probable outcomes based on her choice.

Plan Christof: Money now and possible prestige later.

Plan Embassy: Prestige now with possible money later.

Plan Ruben: Hmm.

No matter how hard she tried, she couldn't pin down the outcome with Ruben. Would it fizzle in just a few short weeks or months, just like her other relationships? He lived in Madrid, and the best she could hope for was seeing him a couple of times a month when he came to London on business—if she was still even in London.

She picked up a pen and started doodling on the pad she kept on her counter. She sketched Ruben as she thought of him, the outline of his lean muscles on his taut body. He was a modern-day Vitruvian man, her sketch not nearly as good as Leonardo's original. But Leo probably had more time than she did. Ivy had to make a decision soon, and the only option without a clear pro-and-con list was Ruben. He was the biggest complication in her decision-making process, and it was just too soon to tell if it would work out.

The only guarantee she had was using her smarts to land a good job. Finding a good man, the perfect man, the most irritatingly perfect man, was the long shot. It also came at a heavier price if things went wrong. Ivy sat down at the kitchen table and started composing a message to her friends. This time of day, everyone would be awake, and Ivy hoped they were near their phones. Oh, who was she kidding? Of course they were.

Send to Group: Late_Bloomers

Ivy_Cross: Time for a vote! A: Stay in London and go for a promotion. B: Take new job offer with 4X salary and move to Berlin. C: Explore crazy chemistry with Ruben (who also drives me crazy). Can't combine any of them. Voting lines are open for one hour.

RoseGarden: Ruben. You are a smart cookie. You can always find work. Love is rare.

Daisy_Eats: Berlin! You've exhausted London. Time for a fresh start. Berlin is hot HOT right now.

VioletStackDesign: Prestige vs. Money vs. Love. What about the one that will make you happy?

Ivy_Cross: Can I get some consensus, please? Not making this easy for me.

LilyL: No help here. I don't think you get love + money + happiness all at once. Pick the one you want most right now, worry about the others later.

Ivy gritted her teeth. They were supposed to be helping her out, and instead they were clouding the issue even more. But that's what she got for sending a poll via text message. Rose was still on a love high, living in Australia with Mateo and starting a brand-new life together. Of course she'd pick love. Daisy was always looking for something new to discover. As a food writer, she traveled to some great cities in the world, and if she said Berlin was hot, it was true. But did that mean it was right for Ivy? She'd practically lived on curry since moving to London, so food variety wasn't a huge motivator for her. Violet was the introspective one, the designer who could always see many ways of doing a thing, but only one way to see it through once picked. Her friends weren't helping at all.

The phone rang, and Ivy picked up.

"I'm in Africa right now, the birthplace of humanity. Where we all started. Where I just treated the medicine man for intestinal parasites. Where I should be able to give you all the answers," Lily said by way of greeting.

"So give it to me, Lil. What's my best choice?" Ivy respected Lily's opinion, knowing she was the second most logical of all of them, a doctor to her economist, someone trained to evaluate facts to make decisions.

"You got me, girl. I have the most expensive education money can buy, share an apartment in New York with three other doctors, and I spent half the year living in a hut treating diseases in forgotten places around the world. I'm divorced. I don't have money, prestige, or love! Tell me again why we're friends, Ms. Fancy London Diplomat?" Lily laughed.

"How many times do I have to tell you, I'm not a diplomat!" Ivy's exasperated voice was Lily's goal all along.

"No doubt, my friend. I don't think anyone would ever accuse you of being diplomatic. So tell me the story. What's going on with you? And this call is costing me a fortune, so make it quick." Of all her friends, Lily knew how to manage Ivy best when she got wound up.

When they were kids, Lily was one of the few Asian children in their small town. Her mother was Chinese, and her father was a small white man. Lily never had a chance to be anything but short and slight, and different and tiny meant a lot of bullying, at least until Ivy stepped in. No one messed with Lily once they knew she was under Ivy's protection. Every kid for blocks was scared of the wrath of the tall, redheaded girl who rode her bicycle around the neighborhood like a Hell's Angel with purple streamers on her handlebars.

Lily was still a small woman, but a hard one. Her straight black hair was glossy and simple, a fitting frame for her almond-shaped eyes and high cheekbones. She trained in martial arts and gymnastics, honing her body to work for her. Lily could take care of herself these days, but it was the head start with Ivy's protection that helped her get there, and Lily would never forget it. She paid her back with logic, a more factual view of the world than the others—more evidence, less woo-woo.

"A few days ago I wanted my life to change. Today, I've got three options and no clear winner," Ivy said.

"Even for you, that's fast, Ivy. Tell me why you sought three different options in the first place," Lily said.

"That's just it. I didn't. My goal was to find a new job, so I made a list and started making contacts. But then Ruben came to town, and I just can't get over this chemistry. He riles me up like no one else, and he challenges me like no man I've ever met. I really like him, except when I hate him. The sex is blistering hot. But I met a guy in the hotel lobby who ended up calling me for a job interview. A guy that Ruben hates, by the way. And then my boss left the Embassy and her boss personally asked me to apply for the job. That about sums it up," Ivy rambled.

"You met a guy in a hotel and he offered you a job? That seems like a downward career move," Lily said. They laughed like the old friends they were, comfortable in calling each other out over questionable ideas.

"I was waiting on Ruben, and this guy Christof walked up with his dog and we started talking. He's apparently a competitor of Ruben's, and they're both in town for some big conference. He said he wanted to get more government contracts, and he thought I'd be the right person to help him do that. And I probably would be. But it's a little crazy. He is willing to pay me four times what I make now, and he sent over a key fob for a BMW in the offer letter. Can you believe it?" Ivy shook her head, even though Lily couldn't see it.

"Ivy, you met this guy in a hotel lobby, he's Ruben's competitor, he knows you're with Ruben, and he offers you an unbelievable job the next day? Sounds suspicious to me." Lily said what Ivy had been thinking in the back of her mind but didn't want to admit.

"I'm smart enough to do this, Lily. He wouldn't offer that kind of money just to get one over on Ruben." Ivy was in a huff.

"Of course you are. But I'm not sure you're the queen in this game of chess. What did Ruben say?" Lily asked.

"Of course he doesn't like it. But that's because the job is in Berlin with his rival," Ivy said. "If I take this job, it cancels out the option to see where this thing goes with Ruben."

"Tell me why you don't want the promotion in London," Lily said.

"I'm ready for a change, Lil. I've been doing the same thing forever, dating the same type of guys, going to the same places. I'm not meant to live in this kind of routine, and it's driving me crazy. I am Ivy Cross, dammit!" There was silence after Ivy spoke, a quiet that went on so long Ivy thought the connection dropped. Then Lily started laughing.

"Well, if Ivy Cross is so screwed up that Ivy Cross is going to start referring to Ivy Cross in the third person, then we'd better figure this out quick. Lily Lang is on it!"

"I know it sounds crazy, Lily. I can't figure out why I'm so torn up. First Rose finds true love by accident, and now she's off to happily ever after on another continent even. I can't even stay in a relationship longer than it takes a carton of milk to spoil. What does that say about me? Maybe I've just waited too long to fall in love and my career is all I've got left. I'm too hard, too suspicious, too wary." Ivy's voice dropped, the real story finally coming to the surface.

"Ivy, you asked for a change and now you have options. No matter which one you choose, you're going to be okay. I know that, and you know that." Lily waited for the message to sink in. "Now let's carry these three experiments a little bit further. Can you delay your answer on the new job until you find out more about this guy and his company?"

"Yes, I think so. I'm going to Berlin for some Embassy work, and we have another meeting. Christof will want my decision by then, though." Ivy's wheels were turning, seeing the brilliance in Lily's suggestion. "And then I'll also put off the promotion at the Embassy for a bit. They won't stop taking applications for the job for another three weeks. That gives me time. You're freaking brilliant, Lil. Thank you." Ivy felt the weight of those decisions fall off her shoulders.

"What about Ruben? Wasn't he an option?" Lily asked.

"I don't know, Lil. I think that ship has sailed. Best to go with a sure bet, one that comes with a legally binding contract, preferably with a fat signing bonus."

"Hey, don't close down your options just yet. You don't even have to sleep with him again. Just keep the door open. It won't be long until you have to make your choice." Lily was right.

The three options were experiments in a lab, options for the Economy of Ivy that she needed to analyze. She was going to take each one as far as she could to predict the best outcome for her. Then she'd make her decision. It was the logical thing to do, and if anything, Ivy considered herself a rational person.

"Thank you, Lil. You are right. No need to lock it down until the last possible moment. I'm so glad you called. I could have done something foolish," Ivy admitted.

"Hey, I know you pretty well, and I predict you will still do something dumb, but like a cat you'll scrape through to live another day. And tell another wild story."

"Touché!" Ivy laughed.

"Now that you've burned through my minutes, I'm going to dinner. Tonight we're celebrating a local wedding, the medicine man's son. He's curious about Western medicine though we can't talk about it when his dad is around. Love you!" Lily was off the phone before Ivy could even return her affections.

CHAPTER FOURTEEN

The chaos of Alejandro's house used to bug Ruben. Children's toys, a blaring television, and the smell of cooking food or coffee, no matter what time of day he arrived. Alejandro and his wife, Pilar, were on the small back terrace of their apartment in the transitional neighborhood of Lavapiés. The place they owned would be worth twice as much in other parts of Madrid, and in ten years or so their investment would pay off big. Alejandro had the patience of a saint, taking the long view on everything from love to real estate to family. It wasn't even logical that a man like him would be friends with the fast-acting and impatient Ruben, but they'd been like brothers since childhood.

Two small children came racing past, screaming with delight. Ruben would make sure to say hello to his godchildren later, once they'd calmed down a bit.

"Did you ever think when we were kids that we'd be like this in our forties?" Ruben asked as Alejandro ushered him inside the house.

"Every day, *mi amigo*. This is the life I've always wanted."

Alejandro stopped in the living room and picked up a few children's books from the floor. On the table was a vase of fresh flowers, something Ruben knew Alejandro bought for Pilar every week since they first started dating after university. Ruben used to tease him about it, that he was wrapped around her little finger. Still, he couldn't dispute the fact that Pilar and Alejandro were one of the happiest couples he knew. "Let's sit outside. The weather is warm today."

"My life is the one I thought I always wanted, too," Ruben said.

"*Thought*? Past tense?" The lawyer in Alejandro caught the details, the slips that would make his cross-examination sharp and brutal.

"Everything was great until I met Ivy."

Pilar walked out at that moment, her black hair gleaming in the sunshine. She had the kindest face of anyone Ruben knew, and she was a real catch for Alejandro—smart, funny, and as crazy about kids as he was.

"You are way too old to be having your first heartache, Ruben. What kind of emotionally stunted playboy life have you been living?" Pilar put the small white cup of coffee on the table and embraced Ruben when he stood. She looked closely at him when they parted and put her hands on his cheeks, examining his face like he was a sick child. "You poor baby. You really are sad! I'm sorry I made light of it. Sit, let's figure this out."

Pilar walked around the table, her arm trailing over Alejandro's shoulders as she did. He reached up to touch her hand as she reached the end and sat down.

"What happened?" Alejandro asked.

"I met her in London with Mateo, and the chemistry has been hot from day one. The main problem is that she lives in London, and I live here. But we can work that out!" Ruben stopped to take a sip of his coffee. "Mmm, good stuff, Pilar. Thanks." He set the coffee back on the saucer. "Then she got a job offer from a guy I hate in Berlin, and even though I told her he was a jerk she is still considering it."

"A woman with a mind of her own. Who knew they were out there, Ruben?" Pilar winked at him. "Back up for a minute. Tell me about Ivy. What makes her so special to you?"

"She's so sharp, Pilar. No matter how much crap I put out there—and I admit it can be a lot—she will call me on it. Ivy likes my cocky attitude, but she doesn't tolerate it. I can't explain it. She's the only one who can manage my energy, make me feel calm. And now that I've had that connection, I can't live without it."

"By connection, you mean sex," Alejandro clarified.

"Don't even get me started, man. I cannot divulge details of my sexual skill in front of your wife or she'd leave you," Ruben said with an evil grin. Alejandro punched him in the shoulder in reply. "But it's more than the sex. I want her brain, her sense of humor, even her mean streak. I like who I am when I'm with her, who we are together when we finally open up."

"I don't understand why she would consider a job from someone you hate if she respects your opinion." Pilar shook her head, trying to understand the situation.

Ruben toyed with his coffee cup. "She said she wanted a big change in her life, that she was shaking things up. I thought seeing Rose and Mateo made her think more about a relationship"—Ruben paused before his admission—"and I might have complicated things. I forgot to tell her that I was in competition with Christof for some business and she found out. She thinks I told her to stay away for my own reasons and that I'm a jerk."

Alejandro laughed. "She got that right!"

Pilar clucked her tongue at Alejandro. She turned to Ruben. "Don't pretend you forgot to tell her, either. I've known you too long. You can't have it both ways, Ruben. You can't ask her to trust you if you hold back."

"Not to burst this personal growth moment here, but what about the obvious complication? She lives in London. Or maybe Berlin. And you live in Madrid." Alejandro got serious. "I know you, Ruben. Long-distance is not going to work, no matter how much you like her now."

"For any other woman and any other relationship I would agree with you. I would run the other way. But this is different. I can't explain it," Ruben said. "If she'd just stay in London I can make it work. I have clients there."

Pilar rolled her eyes. "Nice that you can fit her into your schedule like that. Hope she doesn't make any changes to her life without consulting your assistant first." Pilar reached over to pat his hand. "Ruben, I think you are a jerk, but you're our jerk, and we're going to help you figure this out. Want to stay for dinner? I made *buñuelos rellenos* for dessert." She flashed a toothy smile, knowing Ruben couldn't resist her stuffed fritters.

"You knew I was coming over?" Ruben asked.

"No, I make these every week for Alejandro. It's why he's getting soft in the middle." She poked at Alejandro's love handle and leaned over to kiss him.

"Soft in the head, more like," Ruben said. "Maybe I'm better off without a woman. It will keep me sharp and good looking," he teased.

Ruben was happy to be in their cozy family setting. Usually when he came for anything but a party, he didn't stay long, always restless to get to the next thing. But now he could see the allure of hearth and home, a longstanding relationship where each person did nice things for the other.

Still, there was no way he could imagine Ivy cooking sweets for him every week. Or anything, for that matter. If she couldn't cook eggs, she probably couldn't cook anything.

"So you think I was wrong to expect her to stay in London to see where this goes? When she said she wanted something different in her life, I thought she was hinting about me," Ruben said. "I thought we could try London for a while, and if that works out she could move to Madrid."

"If this Ivy is anything like you've said, it doesn't sound like she knows how to hint," Alejandro pointed out.

"She wanted a change before she met you, and you think because you show up in her life at the same time she's going to throw her entire career out the window to move to Madrid with you? *Qué locura*, Ruben. She sounds too smart for you!" Pilar laughed as she stood to go back inside and finish dinner. "Seriously, Ruben. Find out how you can meet her halfway, make it a decision that shows you're in it together, and she'll come around."

"And if she doesn't, Pilar's ready to fix you up with Joaquina from her yoga class." Alejandro created an hourglass shape with his hands and raised his eyebrows when he thought his wife wasn't looking, nodding his head and smiling.

She stopped in the doorway, back to both of them. "Alejandro, you know I have eyes in the back of my head. No dessert for you!" She turned her head back to a sheepish Alejandro and winked as she walked back inside.

Alejandro groaned at getting caught. "Women. You can't live with them, but there's no way in hell I'd want to live without that one."

For the first time, Ruben knew exactly what he meant.

# # #

"Do you send car keys to everyone you interview?" Ivy asked, cradling her cell phone against her shoulder.

"I want you to know what you're getting into," Christof replied, voice as smooth as silk. Ivy kept battling with herself over Christof. Was he this smooth and confident, the George Clooney of the technology world? Or was he hiding a ruthless personality like Ruben said? Ivy had no doubt Ruben believed it, but she didn't know if it was real. Would Ruben still be against Christof if he were unattractive? From a middle-class family? Ivy tried to quash her doubts.

"That's exactly what I want, too. I'm coming to Berlin on Embassy business next week, and I'd like to tour your office, meet some of the people I'd be working with, and then make my decision. I hope it's okay that I come by in the early evening; I'll be at work all day." Ivy tried to sound confident, like she belonged in this world and could command people to stay late to meet her.

Christof's laugh told her she didn't fit in yet. "This is the tech world, Ivy. Most of these guys don't even get here until noon. Why don't you meet us downtown? We're celebrating the completion of a big project, and it will be more relaxed than at the office. You like to dance, right?" Christof added that last sentence without a pause, making it sound like the most natural thing in the world. Ivy flashed back to her night of salsa dancing with Ruben. Dancing wasn't working out so well for her these days.

It felt strange to schedule a business meeting at a club, and she wouldn't be able to see his office. Ivy couldn't tamp down the unsettled feeling in her gut. From Ruben's warning to the overly generous salary to the vague details on the actual job, Ivy's internal alarm system was beeping.

Christof continued. "Maybe you can drive us to the restaurant in your new BMW. I should have told you we have Mercedes as a lease option if you'd rather. Just say the word."

"Why is it we've talked more about the car than we have the actual job and my qualifications?" Ivy asked.

Christof's tone made her feel like a little kid getting scolded by a parent. "Ivy, you know more about this position than I do. I want you to create this job yourself. I don't know how to sell to large governments, what they need and how they share information. You do. So I'm counting on you to design the job. Were you not clear on the project?"

She winced, glad they were on the phone instead of in person. She promised herself not to disappoint him again.

The job was even bigger than she imagined, which both thrilled and terrified her. Ivy hadn't worked in the private sector for over a decade, and never in Europe. A lot of international commerce was conducted in English, but knowing the language and knowing the business culture were two different things. Some of this would be as foreign to her as speaking German.

"Then I guess I should negotiate for more money before we finalize this," Ivy responded, only half joking.

"I don't joke about money or business, Ivy. Something else you should know—I take confidentiality seriously. I can't tell you who to date, but I can tell you that almost everything we do here will be off-limits for conversation with Ruben. You need to decide which relationship will be best for your future, because there's not enough room for both."

Ivy's mouth fell open. Christof made clear what she'd only suspected, that she couldn't have both. But she never thought it would be up to him to decide.

"I appreciate your candor," was all she could say.

"Speed is important to me, and I want your answer before you leave Berlin." His tone changed with that last sentence, and Ivy glimpsed what it would be like to work for him. No excuses, no delays, no problems.

And if she said yes, no Ruben.

CHAPTER FIFTEEN

Ivy stood in her bedroom, staring at the closet. The dress code at the Embassy was conventional, and she wore suits and heels every single day, even when she didn't have meetings. It was expected.

But Christof was part of the startup world, breaking rules and redefining normal on a daily basis. This was not a guy who wore a tie without a very good reason. Ivy didn't want to make a wrong first impression, to have his employees think she was old-fashioned or too set in her ways to fit in. But she didn't want to look ridiculous, either. No way was Ivy showing up in jeans with torn knees or lugging a ratty backpack. That wasn't her style, and it never would be.

Ivy sat on her bed and crossed her arms, looking into the closet. A new job, a new industry, and a new life were good reasons to reevaluate everything. Should she keep her suits? Invest in a pair of hipster jeans and bold eyeglasses? Pierce her nose? Ivy laughed at the thought. What would her friends think? She picked up her phone and sent a group message.

Ivy_Cross: Diff job, diff wardrobe. What do you think?

RoseGarden: Stay in London and save the money.

She should have known that was coming. Ivy would have to tread carefully with Rose until everything was finalized in Berlin. God, what if Ruben already told Mateo they had sex? Before she had time to worry about it, the phone buzzed again.

VioletStackDesign: "Beware of all enterprises that require new clothes" ~ Thoreau

VioletStackDesign: "Do whatever the hell you want." ~ Vi

VioletStackDesign: Choose the one that feels right.

Ivy_Cross: Your artist logic baffles me, as usual. But I love you anyway, Vi.

Her jewelry designer friend always dressed as if she were going to a garden party. Ivy existed in the real world, where appearance did matter in business deals every single day, and she worked her appearance to her advantage. Look like you know what you're doing and people will think you do. Even if you don't have a clue.

Daisy_Eats: What does your new boss wear?

Ivy_Cross: Aloof sexiness and intimidating power.

Daisy_Eats: You already have that outfit! You'll fit right in.

Ivy_Cross: I do look good in that, don't I?

LilyL: Three options in play, don't commit yet.

Ivy promised Lily that she'd carry forward on all the options for her future, so no drastic decisions yet. Once she saw the office, met the others, and saw Christof in his own element, she'd be able to make a decision on her job, her personal life, and her wardrobe. For now, business as usual.

Ivy tossed the phone on her bed and zipped her bag. Her flight to Berlin was tomorrow, and her future started sometime shortly after. She just had to come to terms with the fact that Ruben probably wouldn't be in it much longer. But she hoped they'd have a vigorous and exhausting goodbye.

# # #

"Ben, the flight is only two hours." Ivy looked over the contents of Ben's work bag, stuffed with snacks, magazines, a Kindle, and a backup drive full of movies, no doubt illegally downloaded.

"I always come prepared, though I'm expecting to get most of my entertainment from you, Ivy." Ben popped a chip into his mouth, crunching loudly. "Besides, this is my first business trip. I think you might be grooming me to take over for you when you get Sylvia's old job. Or take this mysterious offer." Ben grinned, baiting her.

"It will be a lot more boring than you think. And it will do absolutely nothing for your career, I can guarantee it." Ivy returned the grin, then sat back in her seat and closed her eyes.

"I thought bigwigs were always working. Don't tell me you sleep on the plane." Ben was starting to get on her nerves.

"You are going to be on your feet for at least twelve hours a day over the next few days. You'll drink too much booze at night, and you'll have to get up far earlier than you want. And you have to be on all the time. You take your rest where you can, Ben." Ivy never even opened her eyes.

"See, this is the kind of mentoring I was expecting when you brought me on this trip. The kind of stuff they don't teach in school." Ben was giddy, and Ivy was irritated. She put her hand over his on the armrest, still with her eyes closed.

"Ben, if you say another word before we land, I'll throw you out the window. Promise." Ivy felt his hand tense and knew he wanted to say something. She patted his hand three times and then said, "We'll talk again after we land." Then Ivy went to sleep.

She turned her phone on when they landed, a buzz indicating her messages. The first was from Lily, who was coming back from assignment in Africa on her way to New York.

LilyL: How long are you in Berlin?

Ivy_Cross: Three days.

LilyL: Excellent. Coming to disrupt your life for a day.

Ivy_Cross: In Berlin?

LilyL: Yes, flight to London overbooked. Chance to change for no fee now. Okay with you?

Ivy_Cross: YES.

Ivy smiled to herself, thinking of how great it would be to see Lily, even for just twenty-four hours.

"What are you smiling at?" Ben peered over, trying to read her messages. Ivy turned her phone away from him and frowned.

"Do that again and I'll throw you out the window," Ivy said.

"But we've landed. At most I'd skin my knee." Ben's smart mouth was going to get him in trouble.

"You've underestimated my strength." Ivy stood and pulled out her carryon from the overhead, revitalized from her short nap and the message from Lily. This situation was going to be a lot easier to navigate with a trusted friend beside her. Most of the time she kept her guard up, and sometimes that meant not seeing everything as it truly was. Lily would be her gauge, a way to not screw up the amazing opportunity in front of her.

# # #

Ben turned out to be a good helper, leaving Ivy free to imagine the different variations of her future as attendees from all the European Union countries mingled together at the opening night cocktail party. Ivy was well practiced at having conversations at these events with only half her attention, and without the worry of the logistics of the conference, she found the whole thing almost relaxing. Maybe she should have brought someone like Ben with her long before now.

Ben, on the other hand, was already exhausted. "Don't

sprint the marathon," Ivy warned. Ben was zooming around the room, using considerable energy to check details and answer attendee questions. She watched him, remembering her first conference and how hard she worked to make a good impression on her bosses. If she went to Christof's company, she'd be starting over in a sense, not quite as far down the ladder as Ben, but still with a steep learning curve. Was she ready to do that again? Ivy must have frowned because the woman she was talking to asked her what was wrong.

"My apologies, Madame Branchard. I just remembered something I have to do before tomorrow. Would you excuse me?"

Ivy slipped out the door and into the stairwell, climbing a few flights rather than risking running into someone on the elevator. As a tall American with red hair in a mostly male-dominated field in Europe, it was hard for Ivy to go incognito. Today she'd done her best by wearing neutral colors, pulling her hair back in a tight bun, and staying on the periphery of the room all day. She even modulated her laugh, the one thing guaranteed to get her noticed in any room. Not being herself was hard, but it was a small price to pay for the ability to slip out the door to meet Christof undetected.

Ivy went upstairs and slipped into her room, kicking off her shoes and walking into the bathroom for a quick change.

She shook her hair loose, feeling the constraints of the day leave instantly. She touched up her makeup, adding a more dramatic line to her eyes and shading with smoky gray. Her lips were neutral and glossy, a perfect look for a night out.

Ivy took off her suit and changed into a gold silk tank top and black silky pants. A few bracelets on her arms and strappy heels on her feet completed the look. Sexy, but not slutty.

The vision in the mirror was the opposite of the quiet, professional woman she'd been just a few minutes before. This woman was ready to change her life, to shake things up, and to take some risks.

A knock on the door gave her a smile. Showtime! She flung open the door and was shocked to see Ben standing there, holding a stack of papers.

"Wow, Ivy. You look hot. I mean, if I can say that." Ben's eyes were wide, and Ivy froze, for once not sure what to say.

"Uh, Ben. Hi. What can I do for you?" The last person she wanted to see her like this was Ben. Why hadn't she used her peephole? Mainly because she thought Lily would be too short to register.

"I just talked to the keynote speaker for tomorrow. He says his talk is twenty minutes longer than we allotted. Do we allow that, or do I tell him we'll cut him off like a drunk actor at an awards show?"

"Let him talk. It won't matter. Anything else?" Ivy wanted Ben to leave before Lily arrived.

"When I couldn't find you downstairs, I just took a chance

on finding you here. You know, working, or something," Ben said as he took in her outfit.

Ivy heard the elevator ding in the hallway, and out walked Lily, black hair in a messy bun on her head, wearing an orange crocheted cape over blue jeans and flip-flops, boho chic all the way. Lily saw Ivy standing at her door and waved as she started down the hall with her bag. Ben looked at Lily, then at Ivy, and then back at Lily.

"I thought I was never going to get here. And you look like all the stars in the sky, Ivy." Lily reached up to hug her. "It is so good to see you!" She looked over at Ben. "Hi, I'm Lily. Who are you?"

"He's just leaving, that's who he is. I'll see you tomorrow, Ben." Ivy's dismissive tone would have sent most people away.

"Hi, I'm Ben. Ivy and I work together." Ben held out his hand.

"Nice to meet you, Ben. Got to hit the shower if I want to catch up with America's Top Model over here." Lily pointed at Ivy before rolling her bag into the room.

"Good night, Ben." Ivy started to close the door, but Ben stuck his foot in.

"You know I am an excellent wingman. And I speak German." Ben leaned against the doorframe. "You'll have more fun with me, I promise." He lowered his voice. "And I won't tell a soul."

"Ben, you don't know what you're talking about. I'm catching up with a friend who's passing through. That's all." Her fingernails tapped against the doorframe, impatient to be done with him.

"That's not what she said, America's Top Model. I had no idea you were juggling two careers." Ben crossed his arms over his chest and left his foot jammed in the door.

"Fine. We leave in one hour. Get the meeting room set up, confirm with the keynote speaker, and meet us by the back elevator. If you're late, we'll leave without you. And if you talk about this," Ivy started.

"I know, I know, you'll throw me out the window. You're such a violent person, Ivy."

CHAPTER SIXTEEN

Ruben hung up the phone, a smile spreading across his face. The plan was going to work. In twenty-four hours, he would watch Christof's aristocratic face melt in front of him, his pride taking a near-fatal hit. Ruben liked to consider himself a modern man, above the macho fray, but he enjoyed payback as much as the next guy. Maybe even a little more than the next guy. And it was even better to deliver revenge personally and publicly.

The ConStead deal was his—well, mostly his. Alegre Data could now afford some expansion and still keep a little safety net in the bank. Ruben was an ambitious businessman, but he was not foolish. Ruben only took big chances when he knew he could handle the failure. He lived by three basic rules:

Protect yourself and the things most important to you.

Take risks only when those things are safe.

Then take as big a risk as you can handle.

These three rules worked well for Ruben in business, and

now he applied them to winning Ivy. Once he won the ConStead deal, he would take as big a risk as he could to win her. He couldn't let her go to work for Christof. The guy was bad news, and even if Ruben couldn't have Ivy in his life, he didn't want her to get hurt. And she would definitely get hurt—professionally and personally—if she trusted Christof.

Ruben called his right-hand man, Tomas. "It's settled. Come to my office and we'll finalize the paperwork before I head to the airport."

"You know this is going to start a war with Christof, right?" Tomas couldn't mask the nervousness in his voice. Things were about to get very interesting at Alegre Data.

"You know the story of David and Goliath?" A slow smile spread across Ruben's face. "Christof is too cocky to anticipate all the rocks I've got to throw at him." Ruben was on the verge of righting a wrong, evening the scales of justice, and in the process he was doing something good for his company. He would do almost anything to keep it, still smarting from the memory of how Christof ruined the company where he used to work. The scent of revenge made him hungry for it, his appetite still strong after all these years.

Ruben was a vice president back then, a trusted member of the team and like a son to the owner. He knew he was being groomed to take over, and he saw his life play out as head of the company. The contract was straightforward, supplying an electric company with data storage for millions of transactions for hundreds of thousands of customers in a region of France. It was a profitable deal, but also a fair one. Then Christof came through, taking their customer out to lunch, spreading rumors about vulnerabilities in their system. Over the course of six months, he planted a seed of doubt in the customer's mind. Ruben could tell by their attitude, the way they questioned even good news.

And then the problems started. Little glitches here and there, problems they couldn't easily identify. It wasn't until later they realized Christof hired a hacker to apply for a job, paying him a double salary to sabotage their system from the inside. When contract renewal came through, the hacker dealt the deathblow to their system.

Then Christof swooped in just in time to offer an emergency recovery with the help of their hacker ex-employee, taking the entire business from them. Word spread and they lost three more accounts in one week. Then four more that same month. Within three months, they were struggling to make payroll.

In the end, Christof got what he wanted, his plan one of diabolical genius. While he distracted Ruben with the electric company and obvious rumor mongering, his hacker was quietly at work destroying their infrastructure. The entire plan had been to break the company, to make it struggle so much that Christof could swoop in and buy it for a song. And that's what he did, restoring the technology the minute the contracts were signed.

Within two weeks of signing the deal, Christof folded the

entire company into his own, only retaining two employees. He laid everyone else off and the company was no more. The owner left Madrid after that, retiring to his little farmhouse in the south. Ruben still had a hard time imagining him as a gentleman farmer, spending his days drinking coffee with the other old men at the cafe or tending a small garden behind the house. That would never be Ruben, banished by a lesser foe. Never.

Where his old boss felt resigned and beaten, Ruben was angry and vengeful, and the years hadn't softened him. Ruben wanted to make Christof pay. On his last day at the company, cleaning out his desk and imagining elaborate plots of murder, Christof appeared in his doorway.

"Don't be too hard on yourself. You were beaten by the better man." Christof gave him a fatherly smile, even though they were about the same age. "But I see a spark in you, Ruben. I can train you to be the better man in every situation. Stick with me and you'll be rich beyond your wildest dreams."

"I think you have the wrong definition of a better man," Ruben said, continuing to clean out his desk. "The better man in this case was the one whose work you destroyed." Ruben piled the last of his belongings together in the box and stood.

"If it was that easy for me to take, then he didn't deserve to keep it." Christof's lips formed a smile, but the grin never reached his eyes. "You're mad now, but when the passion fades you'll see what a smart move it was. And I can teach you to think that way, too." Christof continued to use his twisted logic to justify his actions.

Ruben saw a successful future in front of him, one where he'd hold on to everything he built and protect it from vultures like Christof. Where he'd use his power to cut enemies like him off at the knees. He wanted to be a benevolent dictator, but still a dictator over what was his.

"Fuck off, Christof. You've got nothing I want." Ruben then walked out of the company he thought he would one day own.

When Ruben received his final check, there was a note from Christof inside on his rich-boy stationery.

If you change your mind you still have a place here, but you'll have to start at the bottom.

~ The Better Man

Ruben kept that note on the wall next to his computer every day for the next few years as he built his own company, a reminder to protect what he built and destroy anything that came close to threatening it. Strike first, ask questions later.

Ruben thought his revenge would be success and living well. But now on the table before him was a chance to get even with Christof, to win the ConStead deal with his own brain instead of a hired gun. Ivy might lose her opportunity to work for Christof in the process, but Ruben wouldn't lose any sleep over that. He'd consider it a bonus to save her from the misery of a professional association with Christof. There was no better way to show Ivy and the world the true nature of Christof Brandt than to put him to the test.

This time Ruben would be the teacher.

CHAPTER SEVENTEEN

Ivy and Lily stood in line at the club while Ben went to sweet-talk their way in. Ivy could have told him his German was no good when she and Lily were dressed like that, but it was nice to not have him hovering for a change. Ivy squeezed Lily's shoulders. "It's so good to see your face, Lily. I've missed you. I've missed you all."

"Weird how you can even make it through the days without my constant presence and advice. Maybe I should come visit more often, keep you on track." Lily poked Ivy in the belly button with her finger, a habit that had irritated Ivy since childhood.

"On second thought, maybe we should start heading for the airport now. Don't want you to miss your flight, you know." Ivy elbowed her and then looked at the line behind them, stringing around the block. She wasn't a club-goer, at least not much in the last ten years, and she'd forgotten how uncomfortable it was to stand in heels on the pavement. Maybe this was a bad idea. What if they never got in?

Ivy looked ahead for Ben, still nowhere in sight. The little jerk probably started flirting with someone in line and forgot all about them.

"Ivy Cross. Your chariot has arrived." Christof stood next to her on the sidewalk, holding his hand out so she could step over the velvet rope. He wore a dark brown jacket with flaps and zippers all over, a worn, buttery leather look that was either vintage or an incredibly expensive reproduction. Ivy didn't picture him haunting the secondhand shops, so it was probably the latter.

"Just in time. These shoes are made for dancing, not standing." Ivy took his hand and stepped onto the sidewalk. "This is my friend Lily. She stopped in Berlin for the night on the way to New York." Ivy noticed Christof taking in Lily's appearance, her truly vintage outfit a perfect match to his own. She wore a white, fake-fur capelet over a black bodysuit and stiletto boots. Peeking out from the capelet were strands and strands of gold necklaces. Her hair was pulled back in a sleek ponytail, and her almond-shaped eyes were lined with kohl. She looked like she stepped out of a sleek Cadillac in a 1970s disco movie. Ivy loved Lily's style and knew she spent hours scouring the second-hand shops around the world for her finds. It was her one guilty pleasure, a way to make up for spending half her life in scrubs and clogs.

"Welcome to Berlin, Lily." Christof was smooth, and Ivy wondered if she saw a spark there. "Shall we go in, ladies?" Christof held out his arms on both sides so they could accompany him, pimp-style, into the club. Lily laughed and linked her arm through his, up for the adventure, and all Ivy kept thinking about was the power play. Why was he doing this? It wasn't a date. Did she want such a casual relationship with her powerful boss?

At the front of the line, they saw Ben begging the doorman in German to let them in. Ivy turned to Christof and said, "He works with me."

"*Guten abend*, Marius," Christof said, not stopping for a response from the doorman.

"Mr. Brandt. Enjoy your evening." Marius unhooked the rope to allow them in. Ivy grabbed Ben and dragged him inside behind her, deviously enjoying his red face.

"Your German was a huge help out there, Ben. Thanks so much for coming along. Not sure how we would have gotten in without you," Ivy said, mock seriousness on her face.

"Did you just pick up this guy in line, or what?" Ben whisper-shouted in Ivy's ear, trying to process what just happened. Ivy remained quiet, walking ahead with a faint smile on her face. "You're gonna make me work for this, aren't you?"

"That's the problem with today's youth, Ben. You want everything handed to you on a silver platter. Back in my day, we walked twelve miles uphill in the snow just to get a good piece of gossip. You embarrass me with your lack of initiative, young man." Ivy turned her back to him, enjoying the taunting a little bit too much. It was risky having him here, but at this point she was eighty percent sure she was going to take the job, so it would only be a matter of days before it was public knowledge. Ben was a good guy. No harm in letting him suss out the news a few days early. He'd be the most popular guy in the office for a week after she resigned.

Christof angled them toward the VIP area, nodding at the attendant at the top of the stairs as they passed. The rounded red banquettes surrounded low black tables with votive candles, the light reflecting on the mirrored ceiling, which was covered with mismatched crystal chandeliers. The effect was funky and intimate. In front of them, designer metal screens gave glimpses of the dance floor below but shielded their activity from the rest of the club.

They'd barely sat down when a waitress in the skimpiest dress Ivy had ever seen brought two bottles of champagne and fluted glasses. She leaned over to put them on the table, her dress showcasing just about everything for Christof. He smiled in appreciation and gave her a hundred Euro note, acting like a gratuitous flash of breast was an everyday thing for him. Maybe it was.

"You must come here a lot," Ivy said, trying to make sense of the businessman with the little dog she met in London before and the well-known playboy clubber in front of her.

"Not as much as I should, probably. I own this place." Christof leaned in to pour their champagne.

"So that's how you got in so easily! How can I compete with that?" Ben's goofy grin like a happy Labrador, thrilled that his owner found the chew toy that was lost behind the couch.

"*Zum Wohl!*" Christof clinked glasses with each person in turn, toasting their good health. "Ivy, I hope you find Berlin to your liking," he added before taking his drink. Ben's eyes grew wide at the comment, but Ivy wouldn't look at him.

"How long have you owned this club?" Lily asked, body already moving to the music.

"I opened it about three years ago, which is a lifetime in this business. But Berlin is hot right now, and people keep flooding the door, so I'll enjoy it while it lasts." Christof stood and walked over to the screen to look down on the dancers. "I bought it for half the market rate, can you believe it? Find a guy who is hurting, and you can ease his pain and line your pockets at the same time. I'd call it a win-win, but I don't like to share the glory."

Ivy wondered if everything he touched turned to gold. Had this guy ever had a failure before? For some reason, that worried her. Setbacks were an important lesson in business, a way to check growth and prevent a towering collapse. Ivy thought of the mortgage crisis in the US, the hubris of bankers and how devastating their fall was on everyone around them. His father was an investment banker, so maybe he hadn't felt the sting of failure before.

"Let's dance, Ben." Lily grabbed his hand and headed for the stairs, not waiting for an answer.

"Your friend is a decisive one." Christof walked back to the couch and sat down, arm across the back like he owned the place. Which he did.

"She's all business when she's working for Doctors Without Borders, but outside of that she is all about having fun. Her job is a lot harder than ours." Ivy checked herself. "Well, harder than mine. I shouldn't say that about yours because I don't know. Are you a full-time playboy club owner and professional dog walker, or do you have an office job, too?" Ivy felt her natural bullish personality work through, despite her efforts at staying quietly professional. The urge was too great to discover more about the mysterious man who might soon be her boss.

"See, this is the problem with being rich. People think I have it easy, that I don't have to work as hard as everyone else. That's true in a way; I don't. But because I choose to work, I have to do more than the average person to be taken seriously. So yes, in addition to being the German Hugh Hefner and Fritz's human slave, I do have a day job that consumes most of my time. You aren't going to be working for a hobby business owner, if that's your worry," Christof said.

"I thought you said some of your employees were coming out tonight. I'd like to meet them," Ivy said.

"They are coming, but probably not for a couple of hours. One thing to know about a team of young single men in a technology company is that their day starts after lunch and ends just before dawn. You don't have to adapt to it, but you should know the lifestyle going in," Christof said.

"Tell me what you like most about living in Berlin," Ivy asked. She tried to picture herself living there, though sadly she'd not seen much of the city yet beyond the hotel and this club.

"Vibrancy. You'll feel it everywhere, from the art to the music to the startup community to even the graffiti on the walls. This city is humming with the future." Christof's passion was clear. "In contrast, Berlin also honors the past. You'll see remnants of the Wall, an outline in the street of where it used to sit to separate us from our East German neighbors. Berlin is very much about the future, but we also accept our imperfect past and how we changed it."

"A good motto for life, isn't it? Look forward, but learn from the past." Ivy wondered how he could learn from the past if he never lost or made a mistake.

Ivy walked over to the edge of the platform to look for Lily and Ben in the crowded dance floor below. Lily's white fake fur stood out in the darkness, made easier by the fact that she was dancing in a clearing with a man who was clearly not Ben. This guy was twice her size, with shiny black hair tied back at the nape of his neck. He looked Native American from this distance, a modern-day warrior with a broad, stoic face and beardless skin. The two of them together, fully in command of their bodies and seemingly unaware of every other person in the room, were mesmerizing. Christof stood beside her, watching.

"Your friend Lily likes Berlin," Christof said.

"I don't think his name is Berlin," Ivy replied.

They watched Lily and her new friend bend and sway to the music, lost in the moment but completely in tune with each other. Less than four hours in town, and Lily was already at home. Maybe it was her job, always adapting to new environments and people from all over the world. Ivy wondered why it was so much harder for her to give in to the moment. She was too bossy for that, too much of a leader to ever follow or allow fate or something else to decide her future. Maybe that was her problem. Maybe she should let go like Lily, indulge completely in the moment, and go with the flow.

Except for the slight problem of not knowing the first thing about how to surrender.

"What do you think of Berlin?" Christof asked. He reached over and touched her shoulder, turning her to face him. "Better yet, what do you think about working for me?" Christof pulled her closer, the thumping of the music beating in time to her heart. She was inches away from her new boss's face. His breath smelled like champagne, and she detected a faint hint of musk. His green eyes looked down at her, and she noticed his eyelashes had a hint of red in them, just like his hair. What a striking redheaded child the two of them would make.

Ivy's eyes went wide at the thought. *Where did that come from?* She pushed the thought out of her head, replacing it with an image of the two of them making that redheaded child. Now Ivy was really in trouble, because the thought of Christof naked and below her was not unpleasant. Or on top of her. Or beside.

No, it was not unpleasant at all. Ivy pegged Christof as the submissive type, a guy who bossed everyone around by day but liked to be bossed himself at night. Ivy could do that. Ivy definitely could do that. Her eyes closed halfway at the thought, and then she remembered that he was actually in front of her, waiting for an answer to his question. And that he was still her future boss.

"I think both Berlin and you are full of surprises," Ivy stammered, taking a small step back.

"You have no idea, Ivy," Christof said with a sly smile.

Ivy wished Lily would come back, or even Ben at this point. She was getting into hot water, and she did not want to turn up the heat. She looked out over the dance floor and Lily was still dancing. Her only hope was Ben, or having to cool things herself.

"Do you always mix business with pleasure?" Ivy asked.

"Business is my pleasure, and I take pleasure in business. There is no need for them to be separate." Christof took another step forward and put his hand on Ivy's waist. "Would you like to dance, Ivy? We can stay up here."

"Let's go downstairs. It's more fun in a group," Ivy said. She hoped her nervousness didn't show through.

"Oh, now you're surprising me, Ivy Cross. I like it in a group, too." Christof winked and laughed, and Ivy didn't know whether he was joking or not. This was not the Christof she knew.

They took the stairs down to the dance floor and melded into the crowd, dancing as one giant body with everyone else. Ivy moved farther away from Christof toward Lily. She touched Lily's shoulder and mouthed *help*. One nod of her head and Lily moved over to Christof, taking Ivy's place. Ivy was left staring at Lily's stranger, a giant of a man who accepted the change without missing a beat.

Away from Christof, Ivy felt her guard drop. This was like salsa dancing with Ruben, though there was no pressure to impress. She could just feel the music and dance, the closest Ivy ever came to letting anything take control of her. She danced until her feet hurt, only stopping when Lily touched her on the shoulder and pointed upstairs. Ivy leaned in to her dance partner and thanked him. He bowed his head in thanks and then melted back into the crowd. Lily's magnificent stranger never said a word.

Ivy followed Lily up the stairs to the VIP area, collapsing on the couch. Christof spoke with the waitress, who arrived a few minutes later with more bottles of champagne and some much-needed water.

"Christof, you have been very generous. But I still have to work tomorrow." Ivy looked at her phone, shocked that it was already three a.m. "Scratch that, I have to work in four hours."

"One more and then I'll have Marius call you a cab." Christof was a man who didn't take no for an answer, a problem Ivy was starting to realize. He poured their drinks.

"Lily, you seem to be liking Berlin more than Ivy." His point landed. Ivy felt like she was failing a test, and she did not like being tested.

"That guy was incredible!" Lily gushed.

"Kan. He calls himself a warrior artist, whatever that means." Christof took another sip, his back slightly turned away from Ivy. She could feel the chill coming off him and wondered exactly where she made her misstep. Was it backing away from his advance? Changing dance partners? Or did he just not think she fit into this world as well as he thought? Ivy would find out more tomorrow at their meeting, but for now she wasn't going to play this stupid game. If he wanted to spend all his time talking to Lily, so be it. They were leaving after this drink anyway.

"You know him?" Lily asked.

"Everyone knows Kan. A guy like that tends to stand out. He says he goes where his creative battles take him, which is a fancy way of saying he's a drifter with money. He shows up here a few times a year." Christof paused. "Did he talk to you?"

"No, we just sort of found our way to each other on the dance floor." Lily talked like she was in a dream state.

"Don't take it personally. He never talks to anyone." Christof turned farther away from Ivy, her penance still not over. She wasn't fond of this immature side of Christof, and she was past ready to go back to the hotel.

"We should go. Lily has a flight to catch, and I have to be at the opening speech of the conference at nine." Ivy was leaving, even if it cost her the job. "Thanks for a fun night, Christof. I'll see you later today at your office." Ivy picked up her purse and she and Lily began walking toward the stairs. Christof didn't say a word. *What was his deal?*

On the way to the door, club still packed with people, they found Ben. Ben! Ivy had forgotten about Ben and would have left him behind if she hadn't seen him. That would not have gone over well at the conference.

He was at a small table talking to a guy with pink hair and at least a dozen piercings. Pink Hair wore a leather jacket and army boots with a cartoon-embellished T-shirt. They appeared to be deep in discussion, though what they had in common Ivy couldn't imagine. Ivy tapped him on the shoulder.

"Benny Boy, time to go," she said.

"Is that your mom?" Pink Hair asked.

Ivy's eyes narrowed at Pink Hair, who shrank back in his chair.

"Don't say that. She'll throw you out the window." Ben smirked. He stood up and shook Pink Hair's hand. "Thanks for the info." Ben threw a twenty Euro bill on the table. "Next round is on me." He squeezed the guy's shoulder like they were old friends or new lovers and turned to walk out with Ivy and Lily.

"You like the dangerous ones, don't you?" Pink Hair called out to Ben.

"There's no fun in playing it safe." Ben laughed.

CHAPTER EIGHTEEN

Ivy poured coffee down her throat in an attempt to wake up. She was not cut out for the party-girl life. Lily was still sound asleep in bed, hand over her face just like when they were kids. Ivy made a mental note to come wake Lily by ten o'clock to make sure she caught her flight to New York.

The bathroom mirror was not kind to Ivy. Evidence of her late night was written all over her face, from the smeared mascara to the dehydrated skin. She wiped off her makeup with a washcloth, slathered her skin with moisturizer, and then piled the makeup back on again, her armor for a day of glad-handing and networking. She'd also have to deal with Ben today, who would be more obnoxious than usual after last night's adventure.

Ivy dressed in a smart purple dress with nude peek-a-boo heels. Her legs looked a mile long in this dress, and the color contrasted nicely with her red hair. She looked professional and polished, the exact opposite of how she felt.

Ben was waiting for her near the meeting room, hot coffee

in hand.

"Black, just like you like it." He gave her the cup, relishing the look of gratitude on her face.

"You are a lifesaver, Ben. Thanks." Ivy closed her eyes and took a sip, waiting for the caffeine jolt to hit.

"Oh, I definitely am." Ben crossed his arms over his chest.

"Do I even want to hear this?" Ivy asked. "If the problem is already resolved, I don't need to know. My brain can't handle it this morning."

"My new friend from last night gave me the scoop on Christof. He's not a nice guy, Ivy. I don't think you want to get friendly with him."

"This is not the time or place to talk about this, Ben." Ivy couldn't deal with his drama today.

"We should talk about it soon, because I have some intel." Ivy rolled her eyes as Ben spun on his heels and walked toward the morning's keynote speaker, a distinguished man from Germany who generally kept his talks humorous and interesting. Ivy booked him specifically because of this, knowing that even among economists these kinds of conferences could get boring fast.

How could Ben be so lively after such a long night? Ivy wondered if there was some magical cutoff at forty that made sleep more appealing than dancing the night away.

The morning schedule was packed, which kept Ivy awake and alert. Ben was an asset, no doubt. He kept everything going, and all Ivy had to do was interact with the attendees. This made it easy for her to sneak back to her room at ten o'clock to wake Lily.

"Hey, sleepyhead." Ivy sat on the edge of the bed and rubbed Lily's head. She was rewarded with a big yawn and stretch as Lily slowly came back to life. "Time for you to get out of here if you want to catch your flight." Ivy stood and walked to the mirror to retouch her lipstick.

"Do I have to leave?" Lily rolled over in the bed.

"You can sleep on the plane, Lil. Get your lazy ass up." Ivy sat on the chair and kicked off her shoes, giving her toes a quick massage.

"I don't want to sleep. I want to find Kan." A slow smile spread across her face. "My god, he was hot."

"Well, I'm glad one of us had a good time last night." Ivy walked over to her bed and flung off the blankets.

"I should kill you for that." Lily rose from the bed, pajama pants dragging on the floor as she shuffled to the bathroom like a zombie. She emerged five minutes later looking like a completely different human being, her hair pulled back in a neat ponytail and face scrubbed clean. After a quick change back into yesterday's jeans and poncho, she zipped up her suitcase to leave.

"She's alive!" Ivy linked her arm through Lily's, moving toward the door. "Let's get you some coffee and a taxi, dancing queen. I can't believe you're going already."

"It was basically a layover, so I think we made the most of it." Lily stopped walking and hugged Ivy tightly. "Though next time we meet, let's just curl up on the couch with some wine and talk, okay? I miss your sassy face."

"Deal. Then you can tell me why you packed an outfit like the one you wore last night for a work assignment in rural Africa," Ivy said with a smile.

As they walked past the front desk, they heard a messenger ask the clerk for Lily Lang. "I've been instructed by the sender that she is definitely here. Can you check again?" he asked.

Lily walked over. "I'm Lily Lang. Are you looking for me?"

"Yes, a package for you. Can you sign here?" He held out an electronic signature pad, which Lily scribbled on like the doctor she was. He handed her a large envelope and then left without saying another word.

Ivy and Lily looked at each other.

"What the hell, Lily? Open it!" Ivy was curious, wondering if Christof sent something. Who else could it be? The room was in Ivy's name, and no one else but Ben and Christof knew she was even there.

Inside the package was a pencil sketch of Lily dancing, arms flung wide and a look of ecstasy on her face. Her hair was loose, flying out behind her. The image was sensual, as if the artist captured a private dance with no one else around.

The two of them looked at each other, unsure what to make of such an intimate gift.

"You look incredible, Lil. I didn't even know he looked at you long enough to draw something like that. Or that he could draw at all." Ivy tried to reconcile the Christof she knew with the man who drew this picture. It just didn't compute.

"I don't know what to say. This is strange." Lily's forehead was scrunched, her head tilted as she studied the drawing.

"I'll ask him today at our meeting why he's being a creepy weirdo. You've got to catch a plane, missy," Ivy said.

Lily placed the drawing back in the envelope. "You know, I would have expected this more from Kan. This is how I felt when I was dancing with him. How weird that Christof picked up on it and captured it so well." Lily frowned. "None of my business, Ivy, but this guy Christof puts out a strange vibe. I didn't get him before, and with this picture, I'm even more confused. Just watch your step and do all your research before you sign on to work with him, okay?" Lily reached over to hug Ivy goodbye.

"I'm following your advice, Lil. Three options, and I'm tracing them through until the end. We'll see which works out." Ivy frowned a little, already missing her friend. "When do we see each other next?"

"I guess that all depends on where you end up living and where my next job assignment is, huh? No worries, we'll figure something out. Love you, babes." One last squeeze on the arm and Lily was out the door, on her way back to New York and a three-month break until her next assignment.

Lily stopped and called out to Ivy. "You do know that you're allowed to make other friends, right? You don't have to wait for the occasional visit from one of us to share your secrets." She blew her a kiss and got in the cab.

With a heavy sigh, Ivy looked at her watch and hurried to the lunch banquet. She'd kill for a thirty-minute nap right now.

Ivy's phone buzzed.

RubenAlegre: You're thinking about me, aren't you?

Ivy_Cross: You text me just so I have to. Otherwise, no. Should I be?

RubenAlegre: Is it working?

Ivy_Cross: Get back to work.

RubenAlegre: Found a curry place in Madrid.

Cheeky monkey. Ivy couldn't help but smile, followed by an intense wave of guilt over the evening with Christof at the club. She never told Ruben she was coming to Berlin. Ivy frowned. Even on the minuscule chance she went ahead with Plan Ruben, it wouldn't work in Madrid. Ivy had no contacts there, no way to build on her career. It would be a step back, and at this stage of her life, she couldn't take that risk.

Ivy_Cross: Careful. Curry makes you take off your clothes.

RubenAlegre: I'll wait to try it with you.

Ivy_Cross: Could be too spicy for you.

RubenAlegre: Then I should build up my tolerance.

Ivy_Cross: Repeated exposure?

RubenAlegre: Like a lab rat.

Ivy_Cross: When are you coming back to my lab, little rat?

RubenAlegre: Two weeks? Traveling now.

Ivy_Cross: See you then.

A brief flash of Ruben naked appeared in her mind. How

could she have known that he was so hard underneath all his stylish clothes? So, so hard.

If Plan Ruben didn't work out—and let's face it, all along this was the long shot of the three options—she was going to be disappointed. Ivy had known a lot of men in her life, some she even liked a lot, but she had never known a man like Ruben. And if it took her until she was forty-two to find him, what were the odds of being struck by lightning twice in one life? Not choosing Ruben meant probably never having that feeling again.

Ivy put her phone in her pocket and walked into the banquet room. She was used to decisions clarifying as she worked through them, not getting muddier. This decision was as muddy as it got. It reminded her of that crazy Spartan race she ran with Rose, Daisy, Lily, and Vi last time she was in Arizona.

They had started clean at the start line, hair tied back in bandanas and wearing matching T-shirts for their Spartan team. By the end of the day, after crawling through mud, rappelling up ropes over pits of water, and scaling fences, they arrived at the finish line a hot, sweaty mess. In between, they pushed each other, sometimes literally, to get through the race. The five of them stuck together, chanting silly songs when they were working the hardest, and never leaving a woman behind. It was a team effort, and Ivy felt the love. The photo from the end showed women covered head to toe in mud, their white smiles the only clue they weren't evil swamp monsters. Would Ivy be muddied but smiling at the end of all this? Or would she trudge through all the obstacles and mud and lose her way to the finish line?

Unfortunately, she couldn't rely on her friends this time. It was her decision, and even though she knew they'd back her no matter what, it was hard to know which way to go. If she only had a map or a flow chart to tell her what would happen with each decision.

Before all this started, Ivy's life was neat and tidy, if not a little boring and unchallenging. Now it felt like it was only a challenge. Ivy smiled to herself, enjoying the thrill of it all. She might be scared out of her mind, but she was definitely not bored anymore.

# # #

"How goes the conference, Ivy?" Jack's voice was deep and powerful, a man used to being in charge.

"Great, Jack. Germany took the lead as usual, and we had some interesting exchanges about Greece. I'll give you the full details in my report," Ivy said in a rush, wondering why Jack would be calling her at the conference for any other reason than the promotion. She couldn't think of one. God, she didn't want to do this over the phone.

"Glad to hear it," Jack said.

"Ben's been a huge help. Thanks for sending him." Ivy decided to throw Ben a bone, give him a bit of praise in front of the big boss before she left. She was starting to ramble to fill the empty air and caught herself. "What can I do for you, Jack?"

"You can get your application in for the promotion. You know we have to do this by the book, Ivy. I can't just give it to you." Jack's voice was even, but the fact that he'd called meant he was getting impatient.

Was Plan Embassy at the end of its trial? Doing a gut check, Ivy thought so. Less salary, less freedom, and very little change in her life. Exactly what she was not looking for. Ivy's heart beat a little faster as she realized she was closing down one of her three options. Even if Plan Christof didn't work out, she didn't want to stay at the Embassy.

So why not tell him no now? Without giving it much more thought, Ivy dove in.

"Jack, I appreciate your confidence in me. That's a huge compliment. But I've decided not to apply for the promotion. It's not the right move for me now, and you have two other great candidates to choose from. The department will be in good hands." Ivy bit her lip, angry that she started smoothing this over, explaining away her decision to make it okay. Why did it matter how many candidates he had to choose from? If she wanted to be a player in the big leagues, she had to stop acting like a peon. This kind of talk would not work in Christof's world.

"I am disappointed to hear this, Ivy." Jack sounded like a parent, waiting for her to apologize for breaking the living room window. Ivy held her ground, zipping her lip and waiting for his next move. When she didn't speak, he continued, "I'll expect your report on my desk Monday morning. Have a good flight back." The phone went silent.

Ivy's heart pounded in her chest, the realization of what she'd done hitting her full force. Jack wouldn't consider her for anything now, and if the job with Christof didn't come through she'd have to find something else soon. She'd just killed her career at the US Embassy. Even though she was ready to move on, the goal was always to do it on her own terms, to not burn any bridges. This one was definitely smoldering, unsafe to cross again. Why didn't she think it through before talking? *Because that's not my M.O.*, she thought, with no small amount of regret.

Ben appeared at her side with a coffee in hand.

"Thought you could use a little pick-me-up." Ben's smile was kind, and Ivy needed a friend in the moment. "What's up, buttercup? You look like your dog just died, and I know for a fact you aren't nice enough to have one."

Normally after a big decision Ivy felt an overwhelming calm, a rightness of being. Oh sure, she usually said the wrong things, in a way that was slightly offensive to other people, but generally she came out of a tough situation feeling right. Ivy did not feel that now, and it unsettled her. Had she just made a huge mistake? Jack wasn't the type of guy to hold grudges, but he wouldn't be helping her out in any way, shape, or form, either. She'd just lost a very powerful name on her contact list, and she didn't know if he would spread the news.

"I just turned down Sylvia's old job." Ivy let the words hang out in the air, feeling the weight of them.

"So what if you missed the deadline. If Jack wants you for the job, you know it's yours. Tell HR to take a hike." Ben sat in the chair in the lobby and patted the seat next to him. "Did you know the official from Croatia is also a mixed martial arts champion? You economists are a weird bunch, Ivy. Totally unpredictable inside those boring suits."

"I just told Jack I didn't want the promotion. He was handing it to me on a silver platter, and I said no." Ivy spoke in a monotone as she sat, staring straight ahead.

"Whoa. You turned down the man? On the phone?" Ben stared at her, shocked.

"He called me, Ben. I didn't plan to do it that way!" Ivy shook herself from the stupor and looked at Ben. "I might have rejected this a little too soon. Nothing else is in place, and I just torpedoed my career at the Embassy."

"So what else do you have going? C'mon, Ivy. What does it matter now? Your secrets are safe with me." Ben touched her arm, willing her to trust him.

Ivy sighed, realizing after this confession and last night's escapade that Ben was in this whether she wanted him to be or not.

"Christof wants me to go to work at his tech firm. I'm not sure if I should. He's wildly successful, but I don't know if I trust him." Ivy stopped for a moment, considering whether to go all in or not. *Oh, what the hell.* "My almost-boyfriend Ruben hates Christof more than anything in the world because of a bad business deal a few years ago. And I can't figure out if Christof wants me for my skill, for my government connections, or just as a big 'screw you' to Ruben."

Saying it out loud for the first time gave Ivy pause. She was worried Christof was using her, and Ivy despised being used. And hurting Ruben was not something she wanted to do, but she couldn't live her life worried about everyone else. Ivy had to take care of Ivy. There was no one else to look out for her.

Not true. What about the Late Bloomers? What about Ruben? Hell, what about Ben? Ivy had plenty of people on her side, she just wasn't asking for their help, letting them in. She was doing it all on her own like she normally did, taking charge whether she knew the direction or not. Ivy pushed those thoughts out of her head, resisting the personal growth opportunity as if it were a germ.

"Christof seems like the kind of guy you don't want to owe. I was worried for you when I thought you were flirting, but even more if you're planning to move to Berlin to work with him." Ben's words were calculated, even. His usual flippant manner was gone.

"I'm forty-two years old, heading toward the peak of my

career, and if I don't make the right choice now it will affect everything else I do for the next twenty-five years," Ivy said.

"A little dramatic, don't you think?" Ben asked with a raised brow.

"You aren't even thirty yet, Ben. You don't get it." Ivy dismissed his comment with a wave of her hand.

"Grade me, O Wise One. You've hooked up with Christof for a job that makes you squirmy but pays big bucks. You just kicked your gravy train to the curb at the Embassy, even though a few years in Sylvia's job would have set you up for a good consulting gig of your own. Basically, you took the quick money instead of the sure money, and you're hoping it pays off because you don't have enough years left to do it all over again." Ben examined his fingernails. "How am I doing?" Without waiting for her to answer, he said, "Oh yeah, and you forgot to consider your lady bits in your master plan. And I hear the winters in Berlin are really cold."

Ivy elbowed him in the side. "My lady bits, as you so elegantly call them, are none of your business, Ben."

"I love you for your brain, Ivy. You know that. Besides, I'm meeting Herr Pinkie for drinks tonight—if I can stay awake, that is." Ben took Ivy's untouched coffee and drank. "So what's the next move?"

"Well, I guess I'm wading into my destiny. Tonight I meet Christof at his office and give him my final decision." The weight of the choice was heavy on Ivy's shoulders. Was it just a week ago that she wanted something different? Now she wished she could go back for just another couple of weeks to sort through this a little bit better. Things were moving too fast, even for Ivy. And her three options were quickly narrowing down to one, the one she now felt the least comfortable with.

Was it fear of something new or a genuine warning bell from her brain? Ivy didn't know, but now she'd have to go with it. She hadn't left herself any other options. And she hated being out of options.

CHAPTER NINETEEN

The Werks loomed in the distance. Ivy was surprised to see an actual factory, not just a clever name for some upscale building like she first imagined. The ugly building had been coaxed into a communal office space, a workspace for creative and technological types.

Outside was a small garden and barbecue space, and the large recycling bin lid was tipped open, showing a mountain of beer bottles. Ivy wondered if she was going to work at a frat house. There were still so many things she didn't like or understand about the tech world, but she'd have to make a place for herself here if she wanted to be successful.

To Ivy's left was what she guessed was the reception area. There was a long wooden counter with an elaborate Lego robot on top. The couches and chairs surrounding it were an eclectic mix of casual but well-made furniture in shades of gray and tan, the kind of furniture you'd see in a magazine about loft living.

Ivy looked around, wondering where to go next. This was unlike any kind of office building she'd ever been in. For one thing, there was a pool table in the lobby and two men playing a game. One wore torn jeans and a hoodie, and the other wore a black kilt with heavy boots. Neither one of those guys would have gotten past security at the Embassy. Here, they were probably executives. They ignored her completely.

Another deep breath and she walked toward the lift, an old-fashioned freight elevator with a gate. Despite the ancient appearance, everything electronic must have been new because it didn't make a sound as it rose to the fifth floor. She unlocked the gate and walked down the hallway, peeking into the open doors as she went. Every person she saw in this building was under forty, and Ivy wondered if there was a ceiling on innovation. *Or maybe people my age don't want to risk everything to start over.*

The end of the hall opened into a big office suite, a reception desk, waiting room, and multiple offices inside. Like below, there was no one at the desk.

"Hello?" Ivy called out, unsure whether she should just walk in or not.

Christof appeared in the doorway of the corner office, arms bracing the doorframe. His sweater stretched tightly against his chest, showcasing his pecs. This man spent some time in the gym. A tiny bit of flat, tanned waist showed between his raised sweater and the front of his cargo pants.

"Good to see you again, Ivy. My assistant is out walking Fritz. Come in." Christof walked back into his office, expecting her to follow. It was a little thing, but it set Ivy on edge. Did everyone in the world follow his instructions without fail?

She shook her head to clear the irritation. *Not a big deal, Ivy. Get over yourself.* Christof sat behind his desk looking like a king on a throne. Ivy couldn't be sure, but she thought his chair was on a platform to make him seem even taller to whoever was in the seat across from him. A mind game, a power play. Even though she figured it out pretty quickly, she couldn't deny the effect it had on her. She did feel smaller, less powerful. Her irritation grew. Ivy reminded herself that she found flaws with most people, including every boss she'd ever had, so why should Christof be different?

"I've given you generous contract terms, and there will be no negotiation. It's a firm offer, a good one, and I'll be surprised if you don't accept. And I'm rarely surprised," Christof said.

Ivy's mouth twitched. His cocky attitude pushed her buttons, and she wanted nothing more than to tell him to get over himself. Well, almost nothing more. Ivy wanted this job, this chance to do something completely different and test herself in the big leagues. And to do that, she'd have to put up with a little more testosterone and macho posturing than usual. She could see why Ruben didn't like him, though being cocky didn't necessarily mean he was a bad person. She'd worked with cocky men all her career.

She pasted a grin on her face. "The contract meets my needs. I'm ready to come work with you, Christof."

"You mean for me," Christof corrected.

Touché. He was right on that one, so she wouldn't push.

"When can you start?" Christof asked.

"Two weeks to start working from home in London, and however long it takes to rent out my house in London to move to Berlin. Shouldn't be longer than eight weeks, though. It's a good market." Ivy couldn't believe she was having this conversation. One week ago she wanted to shake up her life, and today she was getting a new job, a new country to live in, and becoming a landlord because of one decision.

One thing she wasn't getting—Ruben. Ivy knew saying yes to Christof was a nonverbal way to say no to any kind of future with Ruben. She had a huge opportunity in front of her, a way to dramatically change her future. Ruben could go back to dating twenty-something women who weren't savvy enough to see through his moves yet, and she could go back to men in suits who valued career over love, just like Ivy said she did. Ruben and Ivy would probably both be happier in the long run this way.

As usual, Ivy was able to convince herself she was doing the best for herself and everyone else involved, despite the nagging feeling in the pit of her stomach. *Just nerves.*

"Too long. I'll give you two weeks to leave the Embassy and sort out what you need for your house, and then I need you here. We'll get you a furnished apartment to live in while you look for something more permanent." Christof tapped his pen on the desk three times. "You need to start thinking of the highest and best use of your time, Ivy. If you can make more money working for me, then you need to outsource everything else. I can't have you splitting your time to find a renter for a little flat in London when you could be bringing in multimillion-dollar government contracts. Understood?"

Christof stood and offered his hand. "Welcome to the team, Ivy." She looked at it for a moment, knowing the minute their hands touched it was a done deal. The other options were gone. She took a deep breath, plastered a smile on her face, and shook his hand.

The decision was made.

# # #

Stepping off the plane in Berlin, Ruben felt the crispness of autumn. The season was barely starting in Madrid, but from the plane window he saw the leaves were already turning in Berlin. He buttoned his jacket and wheeled his bag down the jet bridge and toward the taxis. The excitement swelled in his chest, only a couple of hours from the meeting with ConStead and righting a wrong Christof made long ago. Ruben had a box of cigars wrapped and ready to mail to his old boss the moment the deal finalized.

He smiled to himself when he thought of the plan. Genius,

it was. And out of nowhere. Everybody wins except Christof. Ruben could taste the victory on his tongue.

What he wouldn't give to see Ivy tonight. His energy was already pegging out the charts, and a night with Ivy would bring him back to center. Ruben still wasn't sure how she'd take the news of him besting Christof, but at this point it didn't really matter. As far as he knew, there hadn't even been a formal offer yet. Christof was just playing her to get back at him, and he'd toss her aside when she was no longer of use to him.

The drive to the hotel was faster than expected, and Ruben took a quick shower to prep himself for the meeting. Beating Christof was a special occasion, and he wanted to look his best.

He checked the time on his heirloom Patek Philippe, a gift from his grandfather when he graduated from University. As he rode the elevator down to the lobby, he thought about his grandfather. Ruben loved that man, his old-fashioned manners charming every man, woman, and child he met. No wonder he was such a successful salesman. He'd opened a store in Madrid that sold dry goods, and when Ruben was a boy he'd loved looking at the old pictures of his *abuelo* behind the counter of his shop, a white apron tied over his dapper suit. Over the years, his grandpa grew his business to include ten stores, which Ruben's father and uncles eventually sold to a huge chain after he died. The business may no longer be in the family, but Ruben knew he had his *abuelo's* instincts for business—and style.

In the lobby he spotted Lars, wearing a suit that made him look even more like a mortician than usual.

"Lars. Ready to win?" Ruben grinned.

"Always. But even more ready to try that new steakhouse afterward. My wife has me on a low-cholesterol diet, and I only get red meat once a month. Can you believe that? Who wants to live forever if you have to eat turkey breast for every meal?" Lars frowned.

"Tonight we dine like kings." Ruben patted Lars on the back and guided him toward the door. The taxi waited to take them to the final bid meeting at ConStead.

When they arrived, the two of them were immediately shown into a sleek conference room. A decanter of water and a selection of cookies and fruit were on the long, dark table. Five notepads and pens were positioned around the end of the table. Ruben guessed that meant the three bidders and two ConStead reps. He regretted the audience wouldn't be bigger.

Christof walked into the room, nodding at the two of them. "Gentlemen." He poured himself a glass of water and sat at the right-hand position to the end, ceding ownership of the head chair to the client. Ruben remained standing, too wound up to sit down.

Gregor and Henrika walked in, closing the door behind them. Christof stood, walking over to them like a long-lost brother, shaking hands and backslapping. Ruben and Lars stayed back, waiting for the pageantry to finish before professionally greeting their new client. Henrika sat at the head of the table, and Ruben and Lars sat on the two chairs to her immediate left. Gregor remained standing.

Christof realized too late his error in taking Gregor's seat to the right of Henrika, and Ruben watched him squirm in recognition of the mistake. With Gregor remaining standing, his irritation obvious, the power balance in the room was thrown off and it was not in Christof's favor. It was a rare misstep for a master player.

Still, everyone in the room knew the decision was already made. Today's meeting was a formality, and nothing anyone did at this point short of murder would alter the course of events. Henrika and Gregor had reviewed all the proposals, including the optional addenda from last week, and awarded the contract. Today was simply the notification.

"Thank you all for coming. We at ConStead are excited about moving forward with this project. As you know, it is the most ambitious growth strategy our company has ever taken, and having the right supporting partners is key to our success." Henrika nodded at each of them in turn. "You three are the final candidates, and as we told you at our last meeting, there was something missing in each proposal, some small or large bit of support that wouldn't derail our project, but it would make it slightly less than perfect. We wanted things to be perfect, and after last week's addendum submission I think we have succeeded." Henrika beamed, taking credit for pushing the bidders to go further than they wanted in service to her employer. She'd likely get a bonus or a promotion for that.

Ruben looked over at Christof, who was at full attention. No doubt he wondered what the addendum submission included. Ruben knew from his contact at ConStead that Christof didn't send one, confident he would win with his original proposal. He would have, too, if Ruben hadn't exercised his talent as the better man.

Gregor picked up where Henrika left off, walking around the room as he did. Ruben watched Christof's head turn as he tried to catch Gregor's attention. Everyone in the room knew something Christof didn't, and the knowledge was dawning on him. Ruben tried not to laugh.

"Creative thinking is what we look for in our business partners. We want to be number one in our industry, and we won't get there by doing business the way everyone else does." Gregor stood behind Christof's chair, staring directly across the table at Lars and Ruben. His smile was genuine and warm. "What we want are partners who will lead the charge with us, supporting our services with creative solutions that allow us to meet our objectives even if they don't fit into a preordained list of services." Gregor nodded at Henrika, giving her the floor for the final announcement.

"We're awarding the seventy-five-million-Euro contract to Betterman Industries." Henrika smiled as if she had just announced the winner of the lottery. In a way, she did.

"Bitterman? Who is that? They weren't on the list of bidders." Christof's brow furrowed, his hands flat on the table as he leaned forward and looked at Lars and Ruben. He expected them to protest as well. When they didn't, his eyes narrowed. "What's going on here?"

"The name is Betterman, Christof." Ruben's voice was steady and strong. "As in, I'm a Betterman than you." The rush he felt in saying those words was as good as anything he'd ever felt before. Well, anything that didn't include Ivy.

Lars used his long hands as he spoke, almost like a conductor of a symphony. "Betterman is a partnership between Alegre Data and HDS. By combining forces and buying a small technology company that fills the gap in our individual bids, we are able to completely satisfy the requirements for ConStead. It is an elegant solution, and one that benefits us all."

"Well, all but you, I guess," Ruben smirked.

Henrika regained control of the meeting. "Thank you all for your contributions, and especially to Ruben and Lars for thinking outside the box to make this a perfect solution for us." She turned to Christof. "Thank you for your proposal, Christof. It was a strong one, and I hope we have the opportunity to do business together in the future." She extended her hand, and Christof just looked at her. Then he turned his head toward Lars and finally Ruben. "Well, maybe not, then," Henrika said with a shrug, drawing Christof's attention back to her.

"ConStead is my deal. This has to be some kind of joke, one I do not find particularly funny." He crossed his hands over his chest like a petulant little boy.

"I can assure we do not joke about business deals at any level, but especially one of this size. It is an exciting time for our company, and we're happy to move forward with Betterman." Henrika stood, and Ruben and Lars stood, too. She rounded the table to shake their hands. "I'll send you an email next week to schedule the kickoff meeting for this project. I'm looking forward to working with you both." She looked back toward Christof. "Gregor will show you all out." With a nod of her head, she was out the door.

The room was silent for about ten seconds, testosterone choking the oxygen out of the room. The four men looked at each other, Christof wild with anger, Ruben and Lars smug to have won the bid, and Gregor monitoring the cockfight about to erupt in his yard.

Ruben wasn't the type to beat someone when they were down. If Christof stayed quiet, Ruben would, too. But he secretly hoped for a verbal showdown, and it didn't take Christof long to reward him.

"Betterman, huh? You've been waiting a long time to use that one on me." Christof's fingers tapped on the table.

"You aren't the last thing I think of every night before I go to sleep, if that's what you were hoping," Ruben responded.

Christof snorted. He turned to Gregor. "Did you know she was doing this?"

"Uh, not sure I'm following you," Gregor answered.

"She made this decision on her own, didn't she? These guys played some kind of sympathy card with her. No way a man would make that decision." Misogyny was a new side to Christof, but one that didn't surprise Ruben.

"That's an old-fashioned view of how business works, don't you think?" Gregor was clearly offended at Christof's remark, and his candor snapped Christof back behind his mask.

"Of course, Gregor. Excuse me. I let myself get carried away for a minute. I'll be catching up with your CEO over dinner this weekend and will discuss it more then." Christof's rich-boy dismissal didn't go over well, as anyone but Christof would have expected.

"Be sure and tell him what you think of how Henrika handled this deal. He hand-picked her to run this project, so he'd probably be thrilled to hear about how she, ah, made a decision like a woman." Gregor opened the door to the room. "Gentlemen?"

#

"You think you won this round, don't you?" Christof snarled as they walked out of the building, no longer chastened by the client.

"I don't have to think it. The proof is in the contract."

Ruben kept his gloating to a minimum, knowing that acting like it was no big deal was an even bigger insult to Christof's ego.

Ruben held up his hand to flag down a cab.

"You aren't going to make as much money with a partner, you know. The deal you won is one I wouldn't have taken anyway." Christof grasped at straws trying to get in the last word.

"You would have never come up with the arrangement because you don't play well with others," Ruben said.

Christof's eyes gleamed. "It depends on what that partner looks like, I guess. Your new partner Lars is not nearly as attractive as Ivy."

He got the reaction he wanted. Ruben dropped his hand and turned to Christof. "You can leave Ivy out of this."

"Oh, but she's very much a part of it. You see, Ivy agreed to come work for me just last night. She's now your competition. Bet that won't help you get in her bed, Ruben." Christof laughed and walked over to the car waiting for him. "I hope her confidentiality agreement with me doesn't intimidate you. We'll be sharing lots of secrets together." His driver stood holding the door open, but Christof turned to look at Ruben one last time. "You should have seen our negotiations, Ruben. That Ivy, she's very thorough." Christof sneered at him one last time before sinking into the backseat of the Mercedes.

Ruben felt the rage building inside like a ticking bomb. Ivy took the job. And not that she had to get his permission, but wouldn't she at least have told him about it? All his careful planning to take down Christof, and he never dreamed she'd accept the job without telling him first. Truthfully, he never thought Christof would take it this far.

Maybe he really did want her to work for him. And maybe she really wanted to.

CHAPTER TWENTY

RubenAlegre: I can be in London tonight.

Let her try to weasel out of that one.

Ivy_Cross: But I'm not there. Traveling on business.

RubenAlegre: Where are you?

Ivy_Cross: Berlin. Conference. Back in two days.

RubenAlegre: I'm in Berlin, too. Are you following me?

Ruben waited for her response, hoping Christof had lied and Ivy was not throwing her career and their fledgling relationship out the window.

Ivy_Cross: Let's meet for dinner before I leave.

That was a surprise, a good one.

RubenAlegre: No schnitzel. Except for mine.

Ivy_Cross: Texting you the address to a restaurant I think you'll like. See you at seven.

RubenAlegre: See you then, American Woman.

# # #

The restaurant was like stepping back into Spain. Ruben sat at the bar drinking a glass of Rioja wine and snacking on a small plate of olives and Manchego cheese as he waited on Ivy. What was he doing with her anyway? She'd never live in Madrid, and he wasn't going to leave. Spain had everything for him— friends, family, work, food, wine, music. Well, almost everything.

The bartender walked over and asked him in Spanish what he was doing in Berlin. Work was an easier answer than love, so that's the one he gave. Out of curiosity, Ruben asked the bartender why he moved to Berlin. Why would anyone choose to leave Spain? The bartender smiled and said that he was actually German, born to Spanish parents who came there during the time of Franco, the dictator who held sway over Spain until just after Ruben's birth. In the post-war years, Germany needed rebuilding, and his father saw a way to escape Franco and start a new life. The bartender had only been to Spain once, on a vacation to Mallorca. He only worked in this restaurant because he was fluent in Spanish and got paid more because of it. His final words stuck with Ruben: "You don't miss what you don't know."

That was Ruben's problem. He did know what it was like to be with Ivy. And now that he'd had her, no amount of logic in his brain would allow him to walk away, no matter what she'd done.

The door to the restaurant opened and Ivy walked in, her red hair falling over the collar of her raincoat and her scarf. The hostess took her coat and Ivy walked up to Ruben at the bar. She was wearing a blue dress that skimmed her curves—professional yet sexy as hell. How did she do that? Her lips were paler than usual, but her eyes were smoky and bold. He couldn't help but stare into them.

"Fancy meeting you here. We should make all our dates at Spanish restaurants," Ivy said. "Oh wait, I think we have."

"Or you could just move to Madrid, where every restaurant is technically a Spanish restaurant," Ruben quipped. He motioned to the bartender to bring Ivy a glass of wine. She perched herself on the stool next to him, her bare knees touching the side of his leg. Ruben felt a jolt of electricity run the short distance from his leg to his groin. This was going to be a very hard night.

"Are you asking me to move in with you and play house, Ruben? Because you should know upfront that I don't cook." Ivy's hand rested lightly on his knee for just a moment, one precious moment, before she turned to accept the glass of wine from the bartender.

"What if I did offer that to you. Would you come?" Ruben asked.

Ivy looked startled, as he knew she would be. She took a sip of her wine to delay her response. "Where is this coming from, Ruben?"

"Answering a question with a question. Amateur move, Ivy. Don't the spies at your embassy teach you any better than that?" Ruben toyed with her, waiting to see how long it would take for her to tell him about the job with Christof.

"Officially, there are no spies at the US Embassy. And even unofficially, if there were, they wouldn't train a bull like me. With bright hair and a loud mouth like this, I'm hardly inconspicuous." Ivy motioned around her face, demonstrating her point.

"But you are good at dodging a question, so I'll ask it again. What if I did ask you to move to Madrid with me?"

Ruben pressed.

"Well you haven't asked me, so you don't get an answer. That's a chicken's way of doing it, if you ask me. If I say no, you turn it into a joke like you weren't going to ask me anyway. And if I say yes it smooths the path for you to ask without any risk. C'mon, Ruben, you're better than that." Ivy turned toward the bar, removing her knees from his leg.

"Will you move to Madrid with me, Ivy?" Ruben laid his cards on the table, knowing her answer already. But she didn't know he knew. Ivy frowned, tracing the rim of her glass with her finger, looking inside the Rioja for an easy out. There wasn't one, and they both knew it.

"There is no work for me in Madrid, Ruben. I can't move there." Ivy didn't look at him when she spoke. "Are we eating at the bar tonight, or should we get a table?"

"We should probably finish this conversation before we ask for a table." Ruben's voice was steady, a contrast to what was going on inside his head. He could feel the breakup coming on, the lurch in his stomach and rapid beat of his heart. It felt almost like catching the flu, the first inkling that he'd be weak and miserable for weeks, the only recovery to let the illness run its course. Poison Ivy. That's what this was.

"Sounds serious." Ivy still looked into her wine glass, avoiding his gaze. The bartender came over and placed a dish of sautéed almonds and cured ham and cheese in front of them. Ivy picked up an almond and nibbled on it.

"What's the real reason you can't come to Madrid, Ivy? Is it because you took a job with Christof here in Berlin?" Ruben's voice dropped to almost a whisper, but in the silence between them he could have just as well shouted it.

Ivy looked up at him, eyes wide. He held firm, waiting for her to speak.

"Looks like you're the one who should be a spy. It hasn't even been twenty-four hours since I accepted the job and you already know about it," Ivy said.

"I didn't have to go looking for the information. Your new boss was happy to share it with me," Ruben said.

Ivy's eyebrows shot up in surprise.

"Why would you be talking to Christof? I thought you hated him."

"Today I won the ConStead deal. As he was licking his wounds, he shared the good news of your partnership." Ruben frowned, then picked up his wine. He looked her in the eye. "Now that you work for him, I guess we're competitors." Ruben drained the rest of his wine, set the glass down on the bar and stood.

"You're leaving?" Ivy asked.

"This is what you call sleeping with the enemy. I'm not giving you a chance to tattle to Christof or use me to further your career. Because that's what you've chosen, Ivy. You picked work over us."

"What the hell do you want me to do, Ruben? I told you I was interviewing with him. I told you I wanted a change in my career and life. You act like this is some kind of big surprise!" Ivy's fury was instant, a far cry from the easygoing woman who walked in tonight. "There is no 'us!'"

"You can fight it all you want, but I can see it in your face, hear it in your voice, and feel it in your touch. Talk your way out of it all you want, but I don't understand the language you're using."

"Ruben, you're asking me to give up everything secure for a future with someone I hardly know, someone who has no track record with relationships, and someone who lives in another country. What Christof offered me is job, a secure future, a fucking contract!" Ivy's chest was heaving with anger.

"I told you what kind of man he was. And then you and I were together, Ivy. Really together, in a way you cannot deny. And still you chose to go with him. I don't care that you're moving to Berlin or taking another job. What I care about is that you aligned yourself in secret with someone I warned you about. Let me ask you this, if you'd gotten a job with any other person on the planet, in any other location in the world, wouldn't you have at least called me to tell me you were taking the job? Or right after? Examine yourself, Ivy. You are ashamed of what you're doing, and that's why you haven't told me." Ruben felt like a lecturing father, but he was secure in his moral high ground.

"You want to lecture me, Ruben? Why wouldn't you tell me you were in competition with Christof on this deal? Or that you were in competition with him often? You conveniently left that out, only telling me your sob story about how he bought the business from your old boss. You know what, Ruben? That's how business works. People buy and sell companies all the time. Why do you get to judge him? You won today, and do you think he's going to be whining about it for years to come?" Ivy picked up her purse and stood. "I chose work because it is straightforward. Clean. Logical. And I know Christof wants me because there's a contract waiting for me to sign that says so. With you, it's always guessing. You want me, but how much? How much are you willing to offer? Nothing. You want me to stay in London to be your convenient booty call. Or better yet, move to Madrid to be near you. Me to change jobs. Me to find new friends and a new life. What about what you're offering me? Think about that the next time you judge my decisions, you sanctimonious prick." Ivy turned in a huff and walked toward the door, snatching her coat and scarf from the rack.

Ruben stood, pulling out his wallet to throw some Euros on the bar.

"It's on the house, *amigo*. Go after her." The bartender stood behind the bar, a look of sympathy on his face. "You don't find a fiery woman like that every day." Ruben nodded his head in thanks and rushed out the door. He looked right and then left. Where was she? Down the street he saw her, coat flapping behind as she raced away in those heels. People parted in front of her, allowing her a wide berth.

Ruben ran down the street and turned in front of her, arms out to grab her shoulders.

"If you want to keep those hands, you'd better get them off me," she growled through clenched teeth.

"Dammit, Ivy. Why are you so difficult?" Ruben yelled. He dropped his hands to his sides, heeding her warning.

"If you want easy, then you're on the wrong path. Now get out of my way." Ivy's eyes narrowed, and she stood with her hands on her hips.

"Don't walk away, Ivy. We've both made mistakes, and we can work this out. If you haven't signed the contract yet, don't. We'll find something else. And I'll show you how much I want you." Ruben grabbed her by the shoulders again and pulled her into a kiss, a hard, possessive one. She resisted him, unwilling to be claimed.

"If that's your form of an apology, it is seriously lacking. Now get out of my way. I'm going to my hotel, alone, and I don't care what you do. I made the right choice, and tonight is proof. Goodbye, Ruben." Ivy stepped to the side and kept walking, not once turning to look back at him.

He watched his future disappear into the night, knowing the next time he saw her it would likely be as an adversary across the table, an extension of Christof but with the ability to elicit far more pain.

# # #

Send to Group: Late_Bloomers

Ivy_Cross: Fancy visiting me in Berlin?

Daisy_Eats: You took the job?

VioletStackDesign: Time for a visit to the US before you start?

RoseGarden: What about Ruben? I thought it was going somewhere?

Ivy_Cross: Ruben who? And no time for a visit, Vi. Gotta start in two weeks.

Daisy_Eats: Meow!

VioletStackDesign: No drama there, eh?

RoseGarden: What happened?

Ivy_Cross: I took the job, that's what happened.

VioletStackDesign: She's not the enemy, Ivy.

Ivy_Cross: Why can't life be easy for once?

Daisy_Eats: I think that's on you, girl. You are the queen of difficult.

LilyL: She's got you there. We love you, but we also know you, dear.

RoseGarden: Happy for you, Ivy. You are a smart woman, and I know you'll make waves in Berlin and beyond.

Daisy_Eats: Just so I'm clear, Ruben is a no-go now? Or just on pause?

Ivy_Cross: Ruben is the past that didn't work. Berlin is the future that will.

VioletStackDesign: Sad we won't see you before you start, happy you're getting what you want.

LilyL: You are getting what you want, right?

Ivy looked at the screen on her phone, tapping the side of the case as she considered her response. Of course she was getting what she wanted. She went after this job and landed it. She said no to the promotion at the Embassy she no longer wanted. And she didn't let a little thing like love—*wait, not love, why did I say love?*—stand in the way of her plans.

Yes, she wanted this. But why did it feel so hollow? Ivy blamed Ruben for her mix-up of feelings, for tainting what should be excitement over her new job. She'd worked him out of her life, but she didn't know how long it would take to work him out of her head.

Ivy_Cross: Yes, I'm getting what I want.

Daisy_Eats: Took you a long time to respond.

Ivy_Cross: Gotta go now, ladies. Will send details of the move when it is all arranged. Love you!

Ivy turned off her phone, feeling strangely uncomforted after the chat with her friends. They always had her back, but like sisters they also knew her weak points, her hot-button issues. And only they could call her out like that without getting burned—especially Daisy and her innocent way of questioning Ivy's decisions. She hated it because Daisy was so often right. Not that she'd ever tell her that, of course.

Was Ruben a no-go or on pause?

Ivy fell back onto the bed in her hotel room, grabbing the pillow and placing it over her face. If she was so happy, why did she feel like crying?

CHAPTER TWENTY-ONE

The knock propelled Ivy out of bed, for a moment wondering where she was. Berlin. The conference. Ivy looked down to see she was still wearing yesterday's clothes. Ugh. What time was it?

"Coming!" she said.

A glance at the mirror on the way out revealed a disheveled woman with bed hair, mascara smeared over her swollen eyes, and sheet marks on her face. Great. Was it too much to hope for room service with hot coffee, reading her mind?

"You look like death." Ben stood at the door, eyes wide at Ivy's appearance. All Ivy could see was the coffee in Ben's hand.

"I was just dreaming about this," Ivy said, grabbing the cup.

"Me or the coffee? Because this sounds like something I should report to HR." Ben closed the door and walked in. "What in the hell happened to you, Ivy?"

"I need a shower first, Ben. Don't be creepy and go through my things while I'm in there, okay?" Ivy trudged to the bathroom and shut the door.

The water pelted her head, easing the pressure headache she had from crying. What a mess she was—and in front of Ben, too. Ivy didn't like to show her vulnerable side, or even admit she had one. She was a cool customer at all times, at least until the last week. She let the hot water hammer her face until she couldn't breathe, and then turned around to massage her back with the strong spray. Ivy felt herself coming back to life.

When she emerged from the bathroom a few minutes later, hair wet and wrapped in the hotel's white, fluffy robe, she found Ben seated on the chair watching BBC News.

"What's going on in the world?" Ivy asked.

"Nothing as exciting as what's going on with you," Ben responded. "Spill it, sister."

"No harm in telling you now," Ivy said, rubbing moisturizer on her face. "My almost-boyfriend is now my never-boyfriend. He wasn't happy that I took a job with the enemy. Go figure."

"Whoa. Who could have possibly predicted that, Ivy? Oh wait, every single person but you. You know, for an economist you are spectacularly bad at predicting your own life." Ben muted the television with the remote. "Did I tell you Sylvia is getting paid six figures to act as a consultant for one of the big banks in London? And that's just one gig. She's going to end up making millions." Ben shook his head. "Who knew she had all this in the works? It's the quiet ones you have to watch out for."

Ivy screwed the lid back on her moisturizer and turned toward the bathroom, hiding her face from Ben. What the hell? Sylvia was quiet, always efficient and steady. Ivy would have never pegged her as the type to build a new empire under their noses. She was surprised at how Sylvia made the whole situation work for her and a little mad that her own efforts were not quite so smooth. Ivy was mad at herself for dismissing Sylvia so easily. Seemed there was a lot more going on there than she thought.

"Good for Sylvia. Give me a minute to put on my face." Ivy walked into the bathroom and quickly applied her makeup and dried her hair, pulling it back into a French twist. She pulled a gray sheath dress from the closet and changed in the bathroom, adding a silver choker to complete the look.

"Holy transformation, Batman," Ben said. "I would have never thought it possible to go from monster to model in just thirty minutes. Now that you're human again, tell me the deal with your new job."

Ivy sat on the bed, sliding her feet into her gray Louboutins. She crossed her legs and turned to Ben. "I'm moving to Berlin, Ben. The deal with Christof is done. Well, almost done."

"Have you ever been to Berlin in the winter, Ivy? It makes

London look like the tropics. Better invest in a good coat." Ben looked down at her sexy gray heels. "Probably some warmer shoes, too."

"I share my big news and all you can talk about is the Berlin weather? See, this is why I'm getting away from working for the government. Too many people telling me I can't do what I want for a bunch of boring reasons. Every move being questioned to death by people who have no vision," Ivy said with a huff.

Ben rolled his eyes at her. "Diplomacy is not a fast-paced business, Ivy. If it was, it wouldn't be called diplomacy. Besides, details matter. You know that." Ben crossed his ankle over his knee, revealing his yellow socks with orange dots. "Remember the guy with the pink hair from the club?"

"That look is not for you, if that's what you're asking."

"Very funny, Ivy. I told you I had some dirt on your boy Christof, and you never followed up. Do you want to hear it now, or should I keep my mouth shut since you've already made a deal with the devil?" Ben's foot started tapping.

"A deal with the devil? You should be writing soap operas, Ben." Ivy put her earrings on and took one last turn in the mirror before picking up her bag.

"Christof is a spoiled dude. Apparently he tries to buy his way into what he wants, and then when he has it he gets bored and trashes it. 'It' being anything from cars to businesses to people. Pinkie told me he stopped the alcohol suppliers from delivering to the club until the previous owner sold it to him at a loss, then he cut the drink prices in half to become the most popular club in Berlin. Is that the kind of guy you want to work for?"

"There are always going to be rumors about rich people, Ben. They use their money to get what they want because they can. It doesn't mean they are any more or less decent than the rest of us," Ivy said.

"And you call yourself an economist. We're all equal. No variances. Outside factors don't matter. Do you hear yourself, Ivy?" Ben stood and walked toward the door. "Well, don't say I didn't warn you."

As she shut the door behind him, her phone buzzed.

CBrandt: Final paperwork ready for you to sign.

Ivy_Cross: Will come by same time today.

A small thrill went through her body. Once she signed, it would be official. Ivy would make more money than she ever had before, with a chance of ridiculous bonuses. She'd help Christof land countries as clients, not just companies. She would be a valuable asset to him, make a name for herself, and live the glamorous life she'd always wanted, regularly eating at restaurants like the Chiltern Firehouse and driving her fancy new BMW down the Autobahn at top speed. She'd be respected, valued, appreciated.

But still alone.

CHAPTER TWENTY-TWO

"Shall I wait?" The cab driver's English was perfect. Ivy's Spanish was fluent from growing up in Arizona, but she didn't know any German at all. Would that impact her success at her job? She had no idea, but it was just one of a hundred nagging concerns. In a few minutes, Ivy would be asked to sign the agreement with Christof, and she still wasn't completely comfortable.

"No thanks, I think I'll be here a while." Ivy paid the cabbie and stepped out, taking in a deep breath.

Her phone buzzed—Ruben. She couldn't handle talking to him right now. Ivy's nerves were raw, and she felt like she was walking into the biggest decision of her life. Ivy turned off her phone and put it in her bag. *Only one scary situation at a time.*

She walked into The Werks slowly, taking everything in with more detail than her first visit. If she worked here, this is what she would see every single day. It was certainly different from the Embassy, where she had to pass through security, scan her bag, and show her ID. Her heels clicked on the marble floors in London, but here in Berlin the floor was concrete—

polished and stylish concrete. This would be hell on her shoes, though looking around, she probably wouldn't fit in if she kept wearing towering heels and form-fitting suits.

The wall in front of her was exposed brick, and the dropped lights from overhead were an industrial style, but obviously reproductions. The heavy pipe connecting the lights was painted bright red, a touch Ivy appreciated. It reminded her of the fake red deer antlers in her entryway at home.

A man walked out from the elevator with Fritz, Christof's dog.

"Hey, I know that dog," Ivy said.

The man stopped, letting Ivy reach down and ruffle Fritz's ears.

"If you're looking for Christof, he's in his office. But I wouldn't recommend it." The man frowned as Fritz tugged on the leash, ready for his evening walk.

"Why do you say that?" Ivy asked.

"He's mad about something, and you'd better hope it isn't you. Good luck." The man was pulled out the door by the dog's tug on the leash.

Ivy paused, wondering if this was going to be another display of Christof's moodiness. His back and forth between good guy and bad guy troubled her, and the economist in her looked for a pattern. If they were going to work together, she'd have to find a way to predict his behavior and adjust her schedule around it. Ivy was confident she'd figure it out and make the best of it. After all, weren't geniuses supposed to be temperamental? It was the price of learning from the best.

The drawing of Lily was what intrigued her. Normally she'd bet it was the mystery man Kan who drew it, but how could have known Lily's name, much less that she was staying with Ivy at the hotel? It had to be Christof. But how could a guy so intent on being the top dog in business, a guy that Ruben disliked and other people feared, be such a talented artist? And so generous with his work? Any woman would love to be seen the way he saw her that night. Ivy wanted to be seen like that. She focused on his artistic talent and his love of the dog. This man had some good qualities, and she could make a good career working with him. After she figured out the temper tantrum schedule, of course.

"I wondered if you'd show up." Christof's tone was cool, a contrast to the very warm feelings his look inspired.

"Am I late? You said you'd be here all evening."

"No, not late. I'd say your timing was impeccable. Come on in." Christof's words were confusing, but he backed away from the door and she walked through. His office was minimalist, a sleek walnut desk and black executive chair against a wall of windows with some kind of treatment to let the sun in but keep the glare at bay. To the right was a white couch with gray pillows and a large coffee table, as big as the one she had at home, which instantly made her think of Ruben.

If she took the job here, she'd think of him every time she walked into this office. And she'd realize she'd chosen a life without him.

Ivy walked toward the couches, thinking they would have a more informal conversation after their night out together, but Christof walked around to his desk. Ivy sat, waiting for Christof to start the conversation. To the right of the desk was a plaid doggie bed with toys in it, Fritz's work area. Ivy kept remembering his gentle way with the dog, his delicate drawing of Lily, and all the other unknown qualities of this man she was about to tie herself to for the foreseeable future. Because that's what this was, right? If she had no intention of working for him, she wouldn't be here. If she planned on saying no, she wouldn't have told the cab to leave. If she wanted to stay in London, she wouldn't have silenced Ruben's call.

The butterflies in her stomach flapped their wings in a fury. Ivy was glad she hadn't eaten yet.

"How long were you supposed to distract me while Ruben revamped his deal with ConStead?" Christof picked up the black Mont Blanc pen on his desk and tapped it against the wood, waiting for her response.

"Distract you? Why are we talking about Ruben?" Ivy couldn't follow his train of thought and struggled to figure out where he was going with this. Was it a test of some kind?

"I suppose I should have pushed a little harder in our negotiations and at least gotten a good shag out of this. You would have gone that far for him, wouldn't you?" Christof's voice was icy, any warmth she'd seen before gone.

"What did you just say to me? Because it cannot be what I think I just heard." Ivy felt like she'd been slapped in the face, the shock of his words activating her fight reflex. "I'm tired of this yo-yo crap you keep throwing at me, Christof. If you want my brain, you're going to respect all the other body parts that go with it. Is that clear?" Ivy's chest was heaving, her heart beating as fast as a hummingbird's.

She took a deep, cleansing breath while he stared, surprised at her response. He wasn't the only one. But Ivy was done allowing herself to be manipulated by this guy. Still, she was curious enough to wonder what drove this. Did Ruben do something? She had to know what shook a confident guy like Christof. If nothing else, she was going to learn from this experience.

A mask came over his face, an instant smoothing of his anger.

"Forgive me, Ivy. I shouldn't have spoken to you that way. I work with all these men, all this testosterone floating around, and sometimes I turn into a caveman. It won't happen again." Christof motioned toward the couches. "Should we sit somewhere less adversarial?"

The power in the room shifted, and Ivy felt it. She didn't need a chair on a platform to hold court.

"This suits me just fine. What the hell is going on,

Christof?" Ivy asked.

"Today has not been a good day. A huge deal that I expected to win was snatched away from me at the last minute by your friend Ruben." Christof paused before the word friend. "I wondered if you'd been sent to distract me, if Ruben had become a sly fox in the years since we first met. I can admire that kind of strategy, you know."

"You think I'm some kind of pawn for your business?" Ivy's ire was at an all-time high, her blood pressure at a boiling point. "Is that how you planned to use me here?"

"Ivy, business at this level is cutthroat. If you won't do what it takes to win, like your friend Ruben, then you won't last. And yes, I would have used all of your talents to win business, just like I'd use all of mine." Christof sat back, his once gorgeous eyes now looking reptilian.

"Is that why you sent the drawing to Lily?" Ivy asked.

Christof looked genuinely confused. "Lily is of no concern to me." He said it as if he were talking about a piece of furniture or clothing.

"Did you ever have a real job for me, Christof? Or was this all about revenge on Ruben?" Ivy's voice was matter-of-fact now, the anger flooding out. How could her instincts have been so wrong? *Because I didn't want to admit Ruben was right.*

"Of course I have a job for you. You'll be a great asset to me, and I still think we can work together. Now that all the cards are on the table, I think we can work together in many ways." Christof stood and walked around his desk, positioning himself right in front of her. She had to crane her neck to look up at him, a position she thoroughly disliked in a confrontation. Ivy might not be an expert in the casual ways of the tech world, but she had a lot of experience with men around the world and their subtle power plays in the boardroom.

"Is this how you want to play it?" Ivy challenged him, her voice cold as ice. "Because you need to think very carefully about your next move."

"I've been thinking about my next move for a long time, and I think you have, too." Christof leered at her, a gross distortion of his normally handsome face. Ivy felt disgust at herself for ever thinking he was attractive.

"I don't know what happened between you and Ruben today, but if this is how you close a deal, I can see how he beat you. We're done here." Ivy stepped around the chair, picked up her bag and walked toward the door.

Christof crossed the room in two long strides, blocking her exit.

"I like this fiery personality better. You shouldn't hide it from me." Christof pulled her to him and kissed her roughly, tightening his grip when she punched and pushed at his chest. Ivy tried to step on his foot with the heel of her shoe, but he widened his stance so she couldn't reach him.

She felt the air leaving the room. How far was he going to

take this? Was he marking his territory like a dog, or worse? Her mind raced through her options for getting away. She'd dropped her bag, which contained a canister of mace. What else could she do?

His arms were on her shoulders, pinning her against the wall, but her hands were free.

Ivy reached down to his groin, found her target, and gripped his manhood. Then she squeezed harder than she'd ever squeezed in her life. Even when he let go of her shoulders and bent double, she stayed with him, twisting as much as his designer pants would allow. Ivy felt his balls crush between her fingers, like the water balloons she and her friends used to throw at each other as kids.

Christof fell to the floor and Ivy knelt over him, her hair falling like a curtain over their faces. She watched the agony on his face, enjoying it a little bit too much. She squeezed harder, remembering how many times she burst those water balloons with her strong grip even as a child.

Quietly, Ivy said a final message to Christof.

"You lost twice today, Christof. And if you ever touch me again, you'll lose in a way that you'll remember every single day of your miserable life." Ivy wiped her hands on her skirt, picked up her bag, and walked out the door as Christof rolled on the floor.

His assistant walked in with Fritz as she breezed through

the door.

"Do you have an ice machine here?" Ivy asked.

"Um, yeah, down in the kitchen." He motioned out the door.

"Oh, it's not for me. And I'm afraid I just made your day a whole lot worse." Ivy walked out, shutting the door on her new career in the technology sector.

# # #

LilyL: The drawing was from Kan!

LilyL: Are you there?

LilyL: Answer, dammit!

RubenAlegre: Need to talk ASAP.

RubenAlegre: Pick up your damn phone.

RubenAlegre: Where are you?

BennyBoy: Let's make up, boss lady. Want to have a

drink?

BennyBoy: Where are you?

Ivy picked up her phone to find the world looking for her. A check of the time showed she had only been at Christof's for thirty minutes. Thirty minutes to blow up the career move she thought she'd be celebrating tonight. Thirty minutes to make her question her ability to judge character. Thirty minutes to finally use the one trick she remembered from Lily's drunken martial arts training that crazy weekend in Mexico.

Now what?

Ivy found a cab at the curb and got in, her first lucky break of the day. As they drove back toward the hotel, she answered her messages one by one, more to distract herself from what just happened than anything.

Ivy_Cross: Kan? How did he find you?

LilyL: Not sure, but it was def him. Found a note in the envelope.

Ivy_Cross: Where is he?

LilyL: Don't know. But his full name is Howahkan.

Ivy_Cross: Kan Howahkan? A rhyming name?

LilyL: No, just Howahkan. One name, like Sting. Kan for short.

Ivy_Cross: Have you talked to him again?

LilyL: Can't. No number/email. Nothing. Total mystery.

Ivy_Cross: That's kinda hot. But frustrating.

LilyL: Enough about me. Tell me about the job.

Ivy_Cross: Christof is an asshole. Just left his office. Not gonna happen.

LilyL: Hmmm. Not surprised. Two options left, though!

Ivy_Cross: About that...

LilyL: Uh-oh.

Ivy_Cross: Finally got to use your ball crusher move from Mexico, though.

LilyL: Calling now.

Ivy_Cross: Don't. Need some thinking time. I'm okay, promise. Will call later. XOXO

LilyL: Take care, girl.

Ivy wasn't sure how Kan found Lily at the hotel when she wasn't even registered, but it made sense that the picture wasn't from Christof. He wasn't a sensitive artist, and his assistant took care of his dog.

But enough about Kan and Christof. Time to focus on a guy who was neither mysterious nor an asshole. The guy she should have been focusing on all along.

Ivy_Cross: What's up?

RubenAlegre: We need to talk.

Ivy_Cross: Sounds important.

RubenAlegre: You could say that.

Ivy_Cross: Where are you?

RubenAlegre: Waiting for you. As usual.

How could she face him again, knowing all his warnings about Christof were true? She'd chosen his enemy over him. Judging from his reply, this was not going to be a happy reunion. Ivy started wondering if she had closed down her final two options at the same time, leaving her with even less than when she started.

Plan Embassy: Ditched. Was there a hope of getting it back?

Plan Berlin: She'd just squeezed the life out of that one.

Plan Ruben: The answer was coming tonight, whether she was ready for it or not.

Back when she and Lily talked about her options, going after all three plans seemed logical. Why not keep her options open until she had time to figure it out? The one factor she hadn't considered in all three scenarios was the most obvious —the other stakeholders in these situations. She'd banked her entire plans on her own needs and never considered the other people. It was one-sided all the way, like most of her life.

Jack wouldn't wait for her to pursue her other career options before he filled the position at the Embassy.

Christof would never forget her relationship with Ruben and their long rivalry.

And Ruben wouldn't stay with her if he knew he was the last available option.

She'd misread every situation, and she kicked herself over it. Predicting outcomes was what she was trained to do, at least in a professional capacity, and she'd broken every single research rule while applying it to her personal life.

All Ivy wanted was to rev up her life, to live true to her personality and grab what would make her happy. And now she had less than when she started. In economic terms, this situation was called a deadweight loss, when an equilibrium was not achievable.

In personal terms, it was a heartbreak, pure and simple.

CHAPTER TWENTY-THREE

"Look at what the cat dragged in." Ruben sat on the lobby chair, trying to look like he'd only been there a few minutes. A friend casually waiting, not a potential boyfriend frantically pacing. One ankle sat on the opposite knee and he leaned back, trying to appear relaxed when every fiber of his being was wound like a spring.

"Where did you learn that phrase? Do they say that in Madrid?" Ivy put one hand on her cocked hip and looked at him. She had a tired look about her, a little bit haggard even.

"We have cats, you know. And they drag things in. Forgive me for saying so, but you look a little, uh, dragged." Ruben stood, walking toward her but not touching her. He wanted to, to take her in his arms and hold her tight, but if he did, he wouldn't be able to say—and mean—everything he wanted to say tonight.

"That's fair. I'm feeling a little dragged today. Want to come up to my room?" Ivy asked.

Ruben wanted to laugh, thinking of the last time they were

at a hotel and she wouldn't even come up to his room to get a box of chocolates. Now she wanted to seduce him to avoid talking about what happened today. As much as he wanted to feel her body on his again, he had to be the strong one now if there was a chance of this relationship moving forward.

"Let's go to the hotel bar. It looks pretty empty right now." Ruben held out his arm to usher her there, touching her back for just a moment. He remembered that night in her apartment, kissing his way up her spine. Where his hand was right now, there was a tiny mole. Ruben felt the heat rush to his center just thinking of his secret knowledge of Ivy, something no one else in the room knew.

But did Christof?

Focus! Ruben cleared his mind, thinking of the list of terrible food choices he'd have at the bar. With the news from today, he hadn't eaten since breakfast and he was starving. He hated German food. And English food. And French food. Come to think of it, he hated almost everything but Spanish food. For a while, he and his friends had co-owned a restaurant in Italy, and he did learn to love Italian food. But he still thought it was better when paired with Spanish wine.

Ruben was a man of distinct tastes. When he loved something, he loved it all the way and nothing else would do. Anything that didn't fall in the "love it" category went into the purgatory that was "not as good as Spain," or in the case of love, "not as good as Ivy."

But even the food in Spain was sometimes a

disappointment, and Ruben wondered if Ivy would be, too. How could he throw his heart to a woman who let it fall to the ground, and then walked all over it? Ruben was a little ashamed of the way he'd behaved over the years with women, always making them work harder to be in a relationship with him. Now that he knew how it felt, he promised himself never to do it again. Though he hoped he'd never have the chance.

When they were seated, Ruben ordered a sandwich, thinking it the least objectionable of the food on the menu. Ivy ordered flammkuchen like she ate it all the time. Ruben worried that she was settling into Berlin a little bit too easily.

"What is a flame cooch-in?" Ruben asked.

"It's flammkuchen, and it's like a flatbread pizza with onions and apples. In the autumn, this is a specialty along with the late harvest wine. I first tried it one year in Munich at Oktoberfest. I hardly ever come to Germany, so I never get to have it. If you're nice, I'll let you try it," Ivy said with a friendly smile. No snark in any of her comments so far. She must really have felt guilty.

"Tell me about your meeting with Christof." Ruben threw her off balance on purpose, waiting to see her reaction. He wasn't disappointed.

"Don't kick a girl when she's down." Ivy's mouth formed a straight line, as if she wanted to keep her words from spilling out. Ruben saw her eyes water, but the Ivy he knew would never cry in front of him. At least not in a public place. Every part of him wanted to reach across the table and comfort her, but he knew this was likely the most important conversation of their relationship. He couldn't smooth it over just because it was difficult. They were adults; they could handle this. Or so he hoped.

"I screwed up, Ruben. Is that what you want to hear?" She put her elbows on the table and leaned forward, not an ounce of meekness left. This was more what he expected from Ivy, and he was glad to see the mousy girl gone.

"I just want to hear the truth," Ruben said.

"You can't handle the truth!" Ivy held her anger for a second and then laughed, her movie line reference the icebreaker she needed to carry on the conversation in a less combative way. "I needed that. This has been a really crappy day."

"Ivy, you have known how I felt about you from the very first day we met, when I didn't even know you were Rose's friend. From that day I've wanted you, and I've never been less than clear with you. I've made it very easy, probably too easy, for you to be with me. And you've done nothing but make me jump through hoops to be with you. That ends today." Ruben felt the heat of his anger rise, his frustration over what should be so clear and simple turned into a gut-wrenching experience, one that they may not make it through.

Ivy's eyes went wide, but only for a moment. Ruben caught her off guard, but she recovered quickly. He could almost see the wheels turning in her head.

"Don't try to paint yourself like a perfect romance book hero. You were a player, and I was a target. Why else approach a strange woman in a restaurant like that? Because you saw straight through to my heart? To my winning personality? No, you were looking at my tits," Ivy fired back.

Ruben could feel himself growing hard under the table. This woman did not back down. The intensity between them was like nothing he'd ever known, and he couldn't live another day without it. Ruben would not leave this table without knowing they were together.

The waiter arrived with their food and drink, silently placing it on the table and leaving. Ivy cut into her flatbread pizza with gusto, her knife scraping against the plate. What was the word Rose had once used to describe the feeling of anger when she was hungry? Oh yeah, *hangry*. He let her eat in silence for a moment, taking a bite of his sandwich and judging it okay—not a Spanish *bocadillo*, of course, but not bad. The Germans did have delicious dark bread and a good selection of meat and cheese. The spicy mustard was a nice touch, too. Maybe he shouldn't be so harsh toward the food and drink of other countries. Or toward Ivy.

"I will admit that my first reaction to you was physical. But it didn't take long to include all of you, even that hard head of yours," Ruben said.

Ivy put down her fork and dabbed at her mouth with her napkin. Then she took a drink of the sweet wine and sat back in her chair, sated for the moment. The edge was still there, but not quite as razor-sharp as before.

"I wanted the job with Christof. It seemed like my lucky break, a sign of some kind because it came out of the blue the day after I decided to change jobs and shake up my life. A job always seems more reliable to me than a love affair, something more permanent."

Ivy paused, waiting for a reaction. When Ruben didn't give her one, she continued.

"Every warning sign was there, but I thought I knew best. I ignored your opinion, the tiny voice in my head, the message in my gut, and all the clues Christof left for me to discover. I jumped head-first into this, and now I've ruined everything." Ivy stopped to take a drink.

"Don't be so dramatic, Ivy. It was just a job." Ruben couldn't let her get out of hand with this or it would turn into one of his mother's telenovelas, an overwrought soap opera.

"That's just it, Ruben. It wasn't just a job. It was possibly my final chance to make a big career move when I'm nearing the peak of my professional powers. It's different for women. We don't get more responsibility and kudos when we get our first gray hairs like you do. I'm a single woman in my forties, and I have to think about my future, what the second half of my life will look like. And I don't want it to be in the same job at the Embassy, dating the same kinds of guys, and having the same conversation about the weather every day with my neighbor. I want more, and if I keep waiting around I'll never get it. I seized an opportunity, but it turned out to be the wrong one." Ivy finished her rant, picked up a piece of her pizza, considered it, and then threw it back on her plate.

"I don't want you dating the same kind of guys, either. I want you to be with me," Ruben said.

"Ruben, I have royally screwed up every part of my life in less than two weeks. I'm not sure you want to expose yourself to my kind of luck. I'm more like poison ivy these days." Ivy looked him in the eye, challenging Ruben to respond. Wisely, he didn't. "Christof was using me, though you probably know that. And he thinks I was some kind of spy for whatever business ninja move you did to him. Luckily I told my boss at the Embassy I wasn't going to take the promotion just before I found out that Christof was a total ass. So now I'm back where I started."

"Ivy, were you with Christof?" Ruben asked quietly.

"Today? Yes, I just came from his office. Gropey bastard." Ivy took another sip, stopping midway when she finally understood Ruben's meaning.

"*With* with? God, Ruben, of course not. Why would I sleep with someone I'm going to work for? I don't need that kind of complication in my life." Ivy set her glass down on the table, still holding the stem as if to anchor her in place. "You thought I did, didn't you?" Ivy's voice was quiet, disappointed.

"It bothers me that your first reaction wasn't that you didn't sleep with him because you were with me," Ruben said with a sigh.

"Don't be ridiculous, Ruben. I wouldn't have slept with him even if I didn't know you. It was always just business with him, or at least I thought it was, and now it is nothing. Absolutely nothing. It's over, and I never have to see him again." Ivy crossed her arms over her chest.

"That's the thing. It's not over. We haven't seen the last of Christof, trust me." Ruben stood and walked around to Ivy's chair, pulling her up to him in a warm embrace. "But let's not talk about him right now. For the last hour I've held myself back from touching you so we could talk. I thought I could hold out, but the truth is I want to feel you. I need to feel you. And I want to celebrate with you."

"What do we have to celebrate?" Ivy asked.

"For one thing, I won the ConStead deal from Christof. For another thing, you're not moving to Berlin. And for a third thing, there is nothing standing between us now but these clothes. Any one of those things is worthy of a celebration, but all three means it is going to be a very long night." Ruben took her hand and led her to the elevator, then up to her room, where they didn't emerge until the sun came up.

CHAPTER TWENTY-FOUR

"Ivy, where have you been? We're on closing remarks right now. I thought I was going to have to go to the airport without you!" Ben was frantic.

"Relax, Ben. I've been here the whole time." Ivy's voice was dreamy, relaxed, and very un-Ivy-like, especially for the last day of an important conference. Ivy knew she was phoning it in, but given her refusal to take the promotion, her career at the Embassy was toast anyway. She made a mental note to talk Ben up when she got back to at least help him gain some career traction.

Traction. Ivy stopped. The last forty-eight hours seemed like an eternity to her with all the drama, but to the outside world, it was just forty-eight hours. Two days. How much could have happened in that amount of time for everyone else?

"Ben, I know it's a big favor, but can you cover for me just a little bit longer? It's important," Ivy pleaded.

"What you owe me after this trip is more of a check than your ass can cash, Ivy. But yes, I'll cover for you. We leave at five o'clock, so don't be late. And whatever you're going to do, good luck. I want all the details later." Ben squeezed her shoulder and then turned back toward the hotel ballroom.

Ivy took a deep breath and ducked into an unused conference room, shutting the door behind her. She ran down the list of ways she could approach this, knowing that groveling was not a good style for her. Plus, Jack wouldn't respect it. She had to sell it in a way he would listen. At least having this job back on track would put some of her life back to normal and leave room to pursue the relationship with Ruben. Unfortunately, taking the promotion would also mean giving up her job search. It would look too strange at her level to get a promotion and leave right away. Potential employers would think she couldn't hack it, or that some big scandal must have happened as soon as she took over. No, if she went this route, she was locking herself into a career at the Embassy.

After last night with Ruben, that no longer sounded so bad. Sure, they weren't in the same city, but London and Madrid weren't so far apart. And she was good at her job. And she had Ben as a wingman, someone she could trust and mentor.

It all seemed so clear that Ivy wondered why she ever thought of leaving the Embassy. Shoulders back, head clear, priorities in order, Ivy hit the speed dial for Jack.

"Good morning, Jack. Ivy Cross." She was going to be all business, coming from a point of power, treating it like a silly misunderstanding.

"Ivy. I didn't expect to hear from you." Jack left the

comment to hang in the air, and Ivy was unsure if he meant "ever again" or just "today." This was not starting the way she wanted.

"Jack, it's been a crazy few days. But the conference is going really well. I'm excited to get back to London, though." Ivy hated the way she sounded, almost manic. Time to dial it back.

"From what I understand, you haven't been seen enough at the conference to know how it was going." Jack's comment hit her in the gut. This was going to be a lot harder than she thought.

"Ben has been a huge help, and I've given him more visibility since this is his first conference. He's doing a great job, and I'm looking forward to mentoring him more when we get back to London." Ivy wasn't going to defend herself or show weakness. Jack wouldn't respect that.

"No need to bother yourself. Ben's going to be reassigned when he gets back to work for the new director. Something else I can do for you, Ivy?" Jack asked.

"I'm glad you brought that up, Jack. I've been thinking about our previous discussion and realize I might have been too hasty in my decision. It's a big job, and I had to consider how best I could contribute. I'm confident I could do a great job in this role, and I'd like to submit my application for the promotion as soon as we get back to London. I wanted to call you first, though, and thank you for your confidence in me." Ivy smiled as she said it, as if she were standing in front of

Jack's desk trying to make a good impression.

"Interesting," Jack said. "I guess this has nothing to do with the fact that the job you wanted to take didn't work out?"

Ivy felt the air being sucked out of the room. She closed her eyes and put her hand up to her forehead.

"You don't get to be in my position without having contacts all over the world, Ivy. And it just so happens that Christof Brandt and I went to the same boarding school. Small world, isn't it?" Jack let the words hang in the air for a moment before continuing. "I know you tried to get a job with him, and I know you didn't succeed. Christof even told me how you tried to sleep your way into his organization. Tacky, Ivy. Very tacky. And frankly not a trait I'm willing to promote as leadership material at the US Embassy."

"You have known me for almost ten years, Jack. And I have never used sex to get what I want. I don't have to." Ivy's rage pounded through every pore of her body. If there were something in the empty room to throw, she would have done it.

"Ivy, I might have known you for ten, but I've known Christof for twenty-five. He's never lied to me, and he has no reason to lie to me now. What does it matter to him?" Jack asked. Ivy thought his naiveté was astounding. He was going to be a terrible senator if he got elected.

"Exactly, Jack. Why would he bother to tell you unless he had an ulterior motive? He lied to you to get even with me because I wouldn't sleep with him or go to work for him." Ivy felt herself coming to center, the focus of her anger allowing a clarity that pure rage did not. Jack was never going to see her way, despite years of proof of her character. One word from a slime ball like Christof tainted her entire tenure at the Embassy. She was done there, and they both knew it.

Ruben was right; Christof was not going to take his loss lying down.

"Ivy, you're embarrassing yourself. Your personal life seems to be too, ah, exciting for the kind of visibility this job requires. I've already got another candidate for the promotion, so there is no need for you to apply." Jack cleared his throat. "Probably best if you continue looking for a new job. I'll give you plenty of time off to get it done. In fact, why don't you take some vacation leave starting now. If all goes well, you'll find something soon and start over somewhere more, ah, amenable to your charms." Jack disconnected, leaving Ivy with a silent phone in her ear.

"Bastard!" she screamed as she threw her phone against the wall.

Ivy felt the ugly cry coming on, and for once she didn't try to stop it. She let it all out, in the privacy of a sterile meeting room at a hotel in Berlin, and didn't care who might see it.

#

Ivy packed her bag, checked out, and left the hotel without a word to anyone. She caught a cab to the airport. Ruben would be looking for her, but even he couldn't soothe her hurt. She had royally screwed up her life in record time. This was an Ivy adventure of grand proportions. No promotion. No new career. And without a job at the Embassy, no visa to even stay in London, much less a way to pay her mortgage. London was one of the most expensive cities in the world, and she lived in one of the best neighborhoods in the city. For how long, she didn't know.

And Ruben. How could she even think about a relationship now that her entire career was in the toilet? First things first—money to pay for her house and put food on her table. Ivy had always been single, with no one else to support her, and she knew it was up to her to fix this thing before she added the complication of a relationship to it.

She was at zero. Less than zero with huge bills hanging over her head.

Ivy messaged her friends as a group, wanting to share the story only one time.

Ivy_Cross: Screwed everything up royally. No fixing it this time. Need a new job. New location. New life.

LilyL: Witness protection program?

Ivy_Cross: Too soon, Lil. :(

RoseGarden: What about Ruben? Can he help?

Ivy_Cross: Don't complicate things, Rosie.

Daisy_Eats: What do you need?

Ivy_Cross: Poison.

VioletStackDesign: For you or for someone else?

Ivy_Cross: Someone else, obviously. Remember who you're talking to.

VioletStackDesign: Glad to know you're okay then. :)

Ivy_Cross: Will keep you posted. Nice knowing you're out there, ladies.

If all else failed, Ivy could crash on any one of their couches. Australia, Portland, New York City—she had several options for a forced sabbatical if she had to take one. She could even crawl back to her hometown in Arizona and stay in Rose's old house until she sold it.

Or Madrid. Ivy immediately banished the idea from her head. She would not run to a man for rescue. She got herself into this, and she would get herself out. At least she hoped so.

What would this next adventure look like? Ivy counted her assets—a large professional network, twenty years of experience, and an ability to move just about anywhere in the world. She couldn't count on Jack for a reference, but she could always reach out to Sylvia as her former manager for a kind word. Even though they didn't bond like best friends, she knew Sylvia respected her professionally.

When this whole idea of a career change started, Ivy had a list of contacts. She'd just work the list, follow up on her contacts, and find a job the old-fashioned way. It was ridiculous to think she'd find a great career move by meeting a guy in a hotel, unless she was looking for a job as a prostitute. Ivy shivered, thinking again of Christof and his kiss. Ivy always trusted her instincts, and the past few days made her realize just how wrong she'd been. Wasn't she supposed to be getting wiser with age? Because in the moment, she felt as ignorant as ever.

The cab pulled up to the airport departure lane, and Ivy went inside. In just two hours she'd be home, ready to regroup. Socrates told her to stop fighting the old and focus on building the new, so that's exactly what she'd do. Brand-new job. Brand-new location. Brand-new love? No, she couldn't go that far yet. There was still hope with Ruben, even though it was just a thread. At this point, that tiny string was the only thing keeping her sane.

CHAPTER TWENTY-FIVE

"You left Berlin without saying goodbye? I thought that last orgasm was memorable enough that you'd at least send me a text message. Too much to ask?" Ruben was not happy to call and find out Ivy was back in London. "You know this whole thing doesn't work if we both don't show up in the same place occasionally."

"I'm sorry, Ruben. You're right; it was a jerk move. It was a horrible day, and I needed time to think." Ivy stuck her foot out from the bubbles in her tub to examine her pedicure. It was past time for a touchup. At least now she wouldn't have to squeeze the appointment in on her lunch hour. Plenty of time now to do everything, but the pedicure would have to be DIY. Without job security, all the extras would be off the list.

"Our friend Christof is an old buddy of my boss Jack. Apparently he called after I left and told Jack I tried to sleep my way into his organization and sell him a list of government contacts. Jack is so dumb he couldn't tell it was an oversell. A liar only needs one reason. Backing it up with multiple excuses is amateur hour. But that's what I'm dealing with here. I can work for Jack for years with a spotless record, and some jerk spreads a rumor and my career is toast. I hate every man in the world right now except you. And possibly Hugh Jackman."

"Hugh Jackman has never done for you what I've done for you. I don't see why he's still on the list," Ruben said matter-of-factly.

"My life is falling apart and you want to talk about my fantasy list?" Ivy asked.

"Ivy, there is never a time I don't want to talk about your fantasies. But I agree there are other things to discuss now. We can come back to Hugh Jackman later," Ruben offered. "Can you look for a job in Madrid? I mean, you already speak Spanish, so it seems like a good choice."

"Ruben, you don't know me very well if you think I'm the type of woman who chases after a man like he's a lifeline. What am I supposed to do if things don't work out between us? Then I'm stuck in Madrid alone."

"Why are you already planning for it not to work? I want you, Ivy. We are good together, and you know it," Ruben said.

"Said like a guy who has absolutely nothing to lose. Your deal went great, you don't have to move, and your reputation is intact. You'll have a more geographically desirable piece of ass. I'm not seeing a downside for you, Ruben." Ivy knew she was pouting, but she didn't want to throw herself all in on a new relationship and not know that he was making a similar effort. It was too easy for him to get in, which meant it would be too easy for him to leave. She wasn't born yesterday.

"You don't want to make the most logical move possible because it doesn't inconvenience me enough to prove I love you? That's insane, Ivy, and you know it," Ruben blurted. The silence that followed was an eternity.

"Did you just say you loved me?" Ivy asked, her voice almost a whisper.

"First Hugh Jackman and now this. You really know how to derail a conversation, Ivy." Ruben sounded as if he were backpedaling, so Ivy pushed harder.

"You said you loved me. I heard it, and you can't take it back," Ivy said, voice growing stronger.

They sat in silence for a few moments, wondering who would speak next.

"I didn't mean to say that. I mean, I did mean to say that, but not like that. And not over the phone." Ruben sighed. "I'm screwing this whole thing up."

"You had a plan of how to tell me you loved me? Tell me what you were going to do," Ivy said, curious. "Pretend this never happened and we're face to face right now."

"Ivy, stop playing around. This isn't the time. Just forget I said it."

"How do you forget something like that?" Ivy asked.

"Ivy, all I do is give you breaks. Do you think for once you could do it for me? I understand you've had a bad day. You didn't get the promotion and now you go back to being a regular economist. Thanks for playing, try again next time. But you will find another job someday. You won't find another me."

Ivy didn't tell Ruben that she was being pushed out of her job, that her days were numbered. Let him go ahead and think they were back at square one, that everything was going to work out happily ever after. She was done trying to figure out men for the day, to advance her career in this cutthroat world, or to care about anything else. Ivy was disintegrating, and she wanted to do it in private.

"Ruben, I have to go. It's just too much right now. I'll talk to you later." She knew it was abrupt, that she was acting like a bitch, and that she'd regret it. But right now, she just needed to sink into a hot tub and cleanse herself of the mess she'd made.

"Let me know when you have time for me in your complicated life, Ivy. I'll just be waiting around like a dog." Ruben disconnected without another word. She felt the tears well up, and this time she let them flow, turning on the faucet in the bathtub. As much sadness and frustration as she had, this bath would turn into a salty sea before the water got cold.

CHAPTER TWENTY-SIX

"What's going on at the Embassy that you and Sylvia both left at the same time? Sounds like a scandal waiting to erupt." Joanna's tone was casual and breezy, but Ivy knew she was digging for dirt.

"You really are in the loop, aren't you? Sure you don't have access to the security cameras? Maybe you know more than I do." Ivy played it off, hoping she'd drop the search party and focus on Ivy's résumé instead.

"Well, I like to know what I'm getting into long before I actually get into it. Forewarned is forearmed and all that. What's going on to have you both leave? Something external, or something internal to you and Sylvia? Might as well tell me now because you know I'll find out."

Joanna Savage earned her name. She made it her job to know the motivations and goals behind every embassy and government client in the Western world, which is why her services as a consultant were in such high demand. Joanna could unearth the BS in any argument. Ivy had watched her bring senior executives to their knees with a few pointed questions, saving her clients billions of dollars. She never wanted to be on the opposite team from Joanna, and she hoped today's conversation would lead to a job.

"My star has never been hitched to Sylvia's, and it's just a weird coincidence that we're both leaving. Or at least I think it is. I still don't know why Sylvia left, but she has landed pretty well. Word is that she's got a few board positions in addition to her own consulting gig. I don't think she's going to miss the stale donuts from the US Embassy breakroom," Ivy said.

"So you don't know why your boss left, you aren't being promoted to her position, and you think that puts you in a good position to come work for me? I'm an information broker, someone who scoops the stories no one else has so I can shine light on the deals and programs on the table. I advise my clients with the benefit of the uncommon knowledge so they go into these deals with eyes wide open, everything on the table. You come to me now to ask for a job and you can't even tell me the real reason you both left?" Joanna's read of the situation was as aggravating as it was accurate. Ivy sighed.

"I hate to say this, but I think Sylvia played dumb most of the time, and behind the scenes she was feathering her own nest. She left and immediately had these other gigs lined up, which tells me she'd been working this angle for a long time. And no one saw it coming, which was brilliant." Ivy decided to show her hand, to gain Joanna's respect by being brutally honest, even if it hurt. "As for me, I decided to shake up my life and seize a bigger paycheck and more opportunity in the private sector. My first chance came right as Sylvia was leaving, and I seriously pursued it long enough to turn down a promotion at the Embassy to Sylvia's job. By the time I decided not to take the new job, the promotion was no longer being offered to me."

"What job were you up for?" Joanna asked.

Ivy paused, not wanting to bring Christof into it. *Oh well, in for a penny, in for a pound.*

"I was approached by Christof Brandt." Ivy decided to keep it brief and pray Joanna moved on to a different topic. Was there any chance she didn't know of him? Ivy could hope.

"Christof Brandt, huh? I can imagine why that didn't work out. I'm surprised you'd even consider working for someone like him. What was your logic in that?" Joanna asked.

God, she's not letting me off the hook here. "It was a strange circumstance, actually. I met him by chance through a mutual friend, and when he showed interest in my career, I began thinking it was a good strategy to combine my experience in government work with a move to the private sector. In the end, I decided it wasn't the right fit, but it got me on the path that led me to your door today." Ivy motioned to their surroundings, Joanna's tastefully decorated office.

"That can't be true," Joanna said, leaning back in her chair and putting her glasses on top of her head. "Christof Brandt doesn't have any friends, and even if he could scrounge up one or two, I doubt very seriously they would be the type to befriend you, too. I don't know what happened with you and him, but I do know you're not telling me everything." Joanna leaned forward, elbows on her desk, and looked Ivy in the eye. "You know what I'm going to say here, don't you?"

"Before you do, can I ask you to reconsider based on my résumé and not on the decisions of the past couple of weeks? I know I veered off the path a little with Christof, but it is time for me to move on from the Embassy, and my experience and contacts can benefit your company, Joanna." Ivy wasn't letting this job go without a fight.

"Ivy, the job was decided before you came in here. I just wanted to hear what was going on at the Embassy. I'm seeing Jack at a cocktail reception tomorrow night, and it wouldn't do for me to show up and not be at least one step ahead of him." Joanna's smile was cold, a warrior so accustomed to winning that it was almost no longer enjoyable. Almost.

"So glad I could help you stay on top of the industry gossip, Joanna." Ivy frowned, showing her displeasure but biting her tongue from saying more. Joanna was a powerful person, and she didn't want to get on her bad side. "I appreciate your time."

"Don't let it get you down, Ivy. Everyone digs themselves into a hole at least once, and the best of us learn how to climb out and stay away from shovels in the future. You'll get there, just not today and not with me."

"If that was meant to be comforting, it fell short of the mark," Ivy said, forgetting her vow to not make a powerful enemy.

Surprisingly, Joanna laughed. "See, you're going to be just fine, Ivy. If you want to discuss a job again in a few years, give me a call. Right now, I think you have a little more growth ahead of you. I can't wait to tell Jack how stupid he was to let you go." Joanna chuckled to herself as Ivy picked up her bag and stood.

"Come back in a few years with more experience? That's a line I never thought I'd hear at the age of forty-two," Ivy said as they shook hands.

"Think on it and you'll see that I'm right. Joanna Savage is always right."

Hey, that's my line. Now I see why everyone thinks I'm a bitch when I say it.

CHAPTER TWENTY-SEVEN

Ruben rubbed his eyes and pinched the bridge of his nose. Not again.

He spoke slowly into the phone, mainly to lower his own blood pressure. "Lars, this is the third time this week you've called me with bad news. We partnered together on this ConStead deal under very specific circumstances. If you can't supply me what I need, the whole deal goes under. We both look bad, and we both lose money. Is that what you want?" Ruben explained it as if Lars was at his first day on the job, not a seasoned company executive.

"Ruben, I get that you're mad. I do. But we're struggling to make money, and if I get a buyer who wants to pay premium pricing for rush delivery, I've got to take it. My cash flow is not what it used to be," Lars explained.

"You're taking a short-term solution to a long-term problem. When you piss off ConStead, we lose the entire contract, and you don't make payroll again." Ruben's joy at besting Christof to win this deal was rapidly turning to regret. This morning, he'd stepped on his favorite pair of sunglasses, and yesterday the check engine light came on in his car. Nothing in his perfectly ordered life was going right anymore.

"That's where you're wrong. My new customer put in a standing order for the entire length of the ConStead contract. Even if it goes away, I'm still making money. And if you give me just another six weeks I can replenish enough to sell to you, too. See? Everybody wins," Lars said.

Ruben swung his chair around to look out the office window. The skies were gray, a normal morning look for Madrid, where the sun normally didn't get out of bed until eleven. The light was coming, he knew it. And there would be a solution to this problem, too. But right now, it looked pretty gray.

Ruben's mind tugged at him. There was something important he was missing.

"Your new client put in an order that is exactly the length of the ConStead contract?" he asked.

"Yeah, weird, huh? Maybe they're on the same bid schedule. Either way, it's going to be a comfy three years for my company, and it couldn't have come at a better time." The relief in Lars' voice was in direct proportion to the alarm growing in Ruben's brain.

"I don't believe in coincidences, Lars. And if you were smart, you wouldn't, either. Who's your new client?" Ruben asked.

"No need to insult me, Ruben. You thought I was smart enough to partner together on this ConStead deal, remember?" Lars's feelings were hurt, and Ruben's stomach sank. Was this guy really going to get emotional about his own failure to live up to their agreement? This wasn't child's play, and Ruben regretted choosing him for a partner. As if he had a lot of options in the moment. But he wanted to beat Christof so bad that he blinded himself to Lars's lesser qualities, like not thinking long-term and taking the easy way out.

"You're already shorting me on the order, which may cause us to lose the deal altogether if I can't smooth this over. The least you can do is tell me who your new client is," Ruben bargained.

"Fine. The client is FritzFolio. It's not Brandt, if that's what you're worried about," Lars said.

Ruben flipped his chair around and starting searching on his laptop. It took him five seconds to discover FritzFolio was a holding company for Brandt Industries. He was looking at Christof's smug face on the "About Us" page. He 'd named the company after his dog.

"Did you even do a background check on your new client, Lars?" Ruben couldn't keep the irritation out of his voice.

"I did a credit check, which is all I care about. What they do with the servers after they get them is none of my concern." Lars sounded smug, and the only thing Ruben was going to enjoy about this entire conversation was bursting his bubble.

"FritzFolio is one of Brandt's companies. You agreed to sell to him, and if you don't he'll sue. But when you fail at delivering on the ConStead deal and lose it, he'll cancel his order. He knows you don't have the money to sue him or wait it out. He does." Ruben shook his head. "You've been played, Lars. And now we're both screwed."

"Are you sure you're looking at the right company?" The alarm was growing in Lars's voice, which was a small consolation to Ruben. He couldn't really blame him for not doing due diligence on his new client. Ruben was guilty of the same thing with Lars, using him to further his own plans instead of making a solid business decision.

His blood boiled when he thought of all the damage Christof had brought to his life.

"Ruben, are you still there?" Lars asked.

"I'm here," Ruben replied.

"What are we going to do now?" Lars asked, his team spirit back in play now that he needed help.

"You mean what am I going to do now that you've thrown us under the bus? Give me a day to think about it and I'll call you back. Don't worry; I won't make a move without you, *partner*." Ruben disconnected and stood, walking around his office. The glass wall to the outer space showed a busy office, livelier since the acquisition of the ConStead deal. He felt the pressure of his old boss, the sinking knowledge that Christof could tank his company, too. But he wasn't going down without a fight.

CHAPTER TWENTY-EIGHT

Joanna Savage's dismissal was the worst, but it certainly wasn't the last. Everywhere Ivy looked for a job, doors were closed.

"We've just filled that position."

"You're overqualified."

"We need someone with more experience in whatever-it-is-you-don't-currently-have-on-your-résumé."

Ivy began wondering if she was being blackballed. Could Christof have poisoned the well of every single company in Europe? Jack wouldn't make that kind of effort; he was too interested in his own career and upcoming election to play any kind of revenge game on someone beneath him. No, it didn't make any sense.

Ivy sat cross-legged on a pillow on the floor, her laptop on the low wooden coffee table in front of her. The last person to sit here was Ruben, when he had her perched on the corner in her birthday suit. What a night that was! And now it was all just a hot, sexy memory. It was a dumb idea to think she could have it all—a great new career, a hot love life, and plenty of money in the bank. At this point, she had none of those things. And if she couldn't find a new job, she'd have to sell the stupid coffee table anyway.

Someone knocked on her door. Ivy wasn't expecting anyone, and the deliveryman usually dropped her packages next door at Mrs. B's by default. He didn't get the memo that she was home now, and because she left the blinds closed, no one else would think she was home, either. Ivy uncoiled herself from the floor and slid her way to the door in her socks. Maybe she'd answer, and maybe she wouldn't.

Ivy looked through the peephole. Ben stood on the front porch, and he held a bag of curry from Indira's place in front of him for her to see. Ivy opened the door and grabbed at the bag.

"Not so fast, babe," he said, holding tight to the bag. "Curry for cocktail, that's the trade." Ben smiled sweetly and held his ground. Ivy stepped aside and waved him in.

Ben put the bag on the counter and sank down into the red couch, a plush zone of comfort that was hard for most people to leave. Ivy dug into the bag and took out the containers, lining them up on the bar and then taking down a bowl. She looked over at Ben and then took down another one.

"When I traded curry for a cocktail, I didn't mean I was actually going to make it for you. I might not be your boss anymore, but I'm certainly not working for you. Gin is on the bar cart and tonic and lemons are in the fridge," Ivy commanded as she plated their dinners. "I like mine strong."

"Yes, Your Highness. How could I have thought that delivering your favorite Indian curry and offering my shoulder to cry on should merit you mixing me a cocktail?" Ben rolled his eyes and pulled himself from the couch to make their drinks. "So how goes the job search?"

"Don't ask. I seem to have caught some kind of unemployable virus, and I can't find the cure. Jack can't outright fire me, but he can make my life pretty miserable until I go. I'm trying to avoid that scenario." Ivy brought their plates over to the table and curled up on the couch, waiting for Ben to arrive with drinks. "What's the word at the office?"

"You don't want to know. Half the people think something happened at the conference, and the other half think it is related to Sylvia leaving, as if you two are going into business together. Can you imagine?" Ben shook his head and carried their drinks over. He kicked off his shoes and curled up on the couch as if he'd been to Ivy's house dozens of times.

"Here's to unexpected friendships." Her sudden warmth stunned them both, and they covered up the resulting awkwardness by drinking.

"You know, we underestimated Sylvia. I feel kinda bad about that," Ben said.

"I think Sylvia was smart enough to work at being underestimated. She never wanted more at the Embassy, so why try? We should have been more like her." Ivy tasted some of the curry. "Nice job cooking dinner, Ben. This is perfect."

"Did you hear that Sylvia is getting married next month?" Ben said it slowly, as if unsure what her reaction would be.

In response, Ivy choked on her rice. "Are you kidding me? Sylvia not only pulled a hot new career out of thin air, she also found time to fall in love? My god, I've done everything wrong." Ivy put her plate on the table and sunk back onto the couch, clutching a pillow to her chest.

"Want to be my plus-one at the wedding?" Ben asked. Ivy kicked him in the leg with her bare foot. "Free booze and a chance to wear fancy clothes. You can't turn that down, Ivy."

Ivy imagined showing up at the venue, running into every person from her office, including Jack, and watching Sylvia live out the life she wanted. And then she felt like a jerk for not being happy for Sylvia when she'd clearly created a great life for herself. When did she turn into such a jealous bitch?

"You know what, Ben? I'd love to come. No more sitting around feeling sorry for myself. If I want something new, I need to create it. Stop beating myself up over my mistakes and being jealous of everyone else," Ivy said.

"Well, I was a little hasty in asking you." Ben pulled an invitation out of his pocket. "You got an invitation, too. She must have mailed these before knowing you were out. Or maybe she doesn't even know. I can't imagine she keeps up with office gossip anymore." Ben handed over the cream-colored envelope with her name in calligraphy on the outside.

Sylvia Pusey and Colin Ferguson invite you to join
them as they commit their lives to each other on
Saturday, October 25, at The Music Room in London.

"I wonder if she hated growing up with the name Pusey as much as I hated Ivy," she contemplated out loud.

"You hate your name?" Ben asked.

"No, not now. But back in school, when everyone else was Jennifer, I hated being different. You can imagine what the kids probably did to Sylvia with a last name like Pusey." Ivy warmed to Sylvia, starting to see some of their commonalities instead of how they were different. As she'd realized over the past few weeks, her read on people was seriously off these days.

"Don't tell me you're going to be best friends now," Ben moaned.

"No, I just want to start giving credit where credit is due. Sylvia set up her own career, found her own man, and is hosting her own wedding. She did it all without fanfare, which is totally opposite from the way I live my life. I could learn a lot from her example," Ivy said. "After I finish another few days of pity eating and watching Bond movies on television, that is. You can't rush personal growth."

"You have a favorite Bond?" Ben asked.

"Like you have to ask. I'm a modern woman, Ben. Of course I'd pick Daniel Craig." She picked up the remote. "I have him on pay-per-view if you're interested."

"Daniel Craig is my favorite, too. I'm in," Ben said. As Ivy clicked through the menu screens to bring up the movie, Ben said, "You know, I never would have imagined sitting on your couch with a takeout and watching movies together. Ever. But I'm glad we're doing it."

"Yeah, me too, Ben. Me, too." Ivy started the movie, but all she could think about was Sylvia and her path to happily ever after. What could Ivy take from that? How could she fix her career and her life? For so long she'd tried the bull approach. Maybe now it was time to be a little quieter, like a lamb.

Or sly like a fox.

CHAPTER TWENTY-NINE

Ivy sat across from Sylvia at the cafe, stirring her coffee while her former boss steeped her tea.

"It feels a little weird being with you in a social situation," Ivy said, addressing the discomfort right away. She wasn't going to make the same mistake with Sylvia that she did with Joanna Savage. Clear communication all the way.

"I never thought you cared for me much, to be honest," Sylvia said.

"Then why invite me to your wedding?" Ivy asked.

Sylvia laughed. "Is it totally unromantic for a bride to do business at her wedding?"

"You know I'm leaving the Embassy, right? I don't know what I could do for you anyway. But I respect a woman who seizes opportunity where she can." Ivy smiled and raised her coffee cup in an informal salute.

"I knew that. It's not a bad thing, you know. Too easy to get stuck in a rut, and at our age you've got to keep moving or you'll close off all your opportunities."

"Like a shark?" Ivy asked.

"Well, maybe not that extreme, but you know what I mean. If you don't create your own opportunities now, you'll slowly get locked in place and overlooked while younger people move ahead," Sylvia said. "Speaking of being overlooked, I'm going to give some attention to those cupcakes in the case. Do you want one?"

"Sure, I'll take the one with the coconut sprinkles on top," Ivy responded.

Sylvia arched an eyebrow. "Already checked them out, did you?"

"Hey, I might be totally oblivious to my career these days, but I do not ignore my taste buds," Ivy replied.

Ivy watched Sylvia walk up to the counter and survey the options before settling on a strawberry cupcake. She chatted with the server for a moment and then pointed to the coconut one. Sylvia seemed so carefree, even with a wedding on the horizon and a new business. Ivy ached for that kind of security and confidence again.

Sylvia set the plates on the table and began unwrapping her cupcake. "Where were we?"

"You did pretty well at creating your own opportunity. No

one saw that coming, you leaving the Embassy so suddenly. At least no one at my level. How did you do that?" Ivy asked, genuinely curious. This was why she'd asked Sylvia to coffee in the first place, to figure out a plan of attack for her own career and life. And to get a reference for a new job.

"I saw the writing on the wall a couple of years ago. Jack surrounds himself with yes-men, and if you're not one of those, then you get pushed to the side. He's testing everyone before he brings them along for his big Senate campaign." She puckered her lips in mock awe. "When I saw it happening, I started making alternate plans, strengthening contacts and creating new relationships that would help me on the outside. It's how I met Colin, actually." Sylvia smiled, a dreamy look in her eyes. She bit into her cupcake, a small bit of pink icing sticking to her lip. She swiped her tongue around her mouth to catch it.

"You say 'on the outside' as if we were both in a prison, Sylvia. It wasn't that bad, was it?" Ivy asked.

"You tell me, Ivy. You've been wanting a new job for months, dying to get out. If I noticed it when I was only half paying attention, then other people did, too," Sylvia said. "My god, these are good. Did I tell you I ordered these for my wedding? Cupcakes instead of a cake."

Ivy blinked, surprised at being read so easily by Sylvia and wondering if they were going to start talking weddings now. "Um, is that a thing now?"

"What, cupcakes or you being so transparent?" Sylvia

smirked. "Yes, the cupcakes are a thing. And no, you haven't always been so obvious. But lately? Yeah. And if I noticed, so did everyone else."

"I'm just feeling antsy, ready for something different. Did you know Jack offered me your old job?" Ivy asked.

"Doesn't surprise me. Jack likes to think he's shaking things up by breaking little rules, but he won't break any big ones." Sylvia's nonchalance threw Ivy. She thought Sylvia would be more upset, but she simply stirred her tea. "What are you looking for, Ivy?"

"I want to move to the private sector, have a little more variety in my work, and make more money. But I'm stuck. My visa is tied to my job, and if I don't find another company to sponsor me, I'll have to go back to the US. All my experience is in Europe, so it makes sense to stay here."

"It's too bad you didn't start planning this before Jack offered you the job. Now he's going to push you out. You don't have a lot of time before life gets miserable," Sylvia said, completely unaware that Ivy's life was already miserable. She licked the icing off her fingers and grinned. "I'm glad you looked me up, Ivy. I think we could have been friends if we'd ever opened up like this before." A look of regret passed over her face.

"Yeah, I think my life would have been a lot different if I'd opened up more. No use crying over spilled milk, though."

"Or cupcake crumbs," Sylvia added as she picked up her

purse to leave.

"Wait, Sylvia. You said you invited me to your wedding to do business. Do you want to talk about it now? I feel like we got sidetracked with the cupcakes," Ivy said.

"No worries, Ivy. I got what I came for," Sylvia said. "I'll be in touch."

Ivy watched her go, wondering if she'd softened her opinion of Sylvia in a moment of weakness. She still had moments when she was frustratingly foggy. Did she only want Ivy's opinion on the cupcakes? Office gossip?

And Ivy had forgotten to ask her for a letter of reference, the main reason for the meeting.

CHAPTER THIRTY

Ruben stood at Ivy's front door, flowers in hand. He knocked and waited. No answer. Was she inside avoiding him, or was she not at home? She wasn't talking to him, so he had no way of knowing. He turned to survey the neighborhood, a tidy street of buildings that looked alike, right down to the potted shrubs flanking each black door with a gold door knocker.

An older woman emerged from next door carrying a wheeled shopping bag.

"Ivy's not at home, but if you want me to take those flowers for you, I'd be happy to put them in some water," she said.

"Uh, thank you, but I need to deliver these in person. Do you know when she'll be back?" Ruben asked.

The woman smiled, touching the scarf that held her brown curls in place.

"How romantic! I can tell by your accent that you're Spanish. You must be the, ah, friend who gave her those delicious chocolates. I hope you don't mind that she shared them with me." The woman blushed as if she were flirting with Ruben. Then he realized she was, in her own way.

"My name is Ruben." He walked over to her and held out his hand. "I'm glad you enjoyed the chocolates." His smile was warm, thinking of his aunts and their preoccupation with telenovelas and matchmaking back in Spain. This woman could have been one of them.

"I'm Mrs. Bingham, but you can call me Mary," she tittered. "I saw Ivy this morning before she went running. She said she had a job interview today. Poor thing. I hope she finds something soon. She's such a hard worker."

"You mean she's not working now?" Ruben asked.

"My, my, my. Maybe you're not as good a friend as you thought," Mary said, putting her hand up to her neck. She eyed him suspiciously. "When was the last time you talked to Ivy?"

Ruben shuffled his feet, wondering why this chubby little grandma of a woman had him so off-kilter. Then he remembered his own fierce grandma and knew. "Uh, we had a sort of falling out recently and I was hoping to mend things," he said.

"High time you did that, then. Ivy's been through a lot lately with her job troubles. She needs all the friends she can get." Mary tilted her shopping bag handle behind her, ready to be on her way. "If I see Ivy I'll tell her you came by."

Ruben stood on the street with flowers in his hand and a sinking feeling in his chest. All this time he thought Ivy simply went back to work at the Embassy while she looked for a new job. He didn't know she was out of work.

Was the taint of Christof ever going to be washed off?

Ruben spotted a trash can on the corner and walked toward it to dump the flowers. Just as he dropped the flowers in, he saw Ivy turning the corner. Their eyes locked and she stopped in her tracks, just for a second, before pulling her shoulders back and continuing.

"Freshening up the trash bins? How considerate," she said by way of greeting.

"Just one of the many services I provide for my good friends," he replied.

"Are we friends, then?" Ivy asked.

"Yes, we are friends. Even when we don't act like it." Ruben took a step forward and touched her shoulder. "I'm sorry, Ivy. Sorry for this whole mess. I don't want to fight with you. Well, at least not the way we've been fighting."

Ivy's shoulders sagged, her armor falling away. "I don't want to fight with you, either, Ruben. But it doesn't even really matter anymore. If I don't find a job soon I'm going to be shipped back to the US. Then this London-Madrid thing is going to look ridiculous in hindsight."

"Did you lose your job at the Embassy?" Ruben asked, pulling her into a hug.

"Might as well have," she said into his ear. She crumpled into him, his hardy Ivy turning into a quivering leaf. Ruben held her close, smelling the shampoo in her hair, her body warm against his. He wanted to make everything right, but he knew that even if he could, she likely wouldn't let him.

"Can we go inside and talk?" Ruben asked.

As an answer, Ivy pulled away from him and started walking. "C'mon in. I'll make us some coffee."

Once inside, she made a pot of coffee and shared what she'd been doing during their radio silence, including the disastrous interview with Joanna Savage and the news about Christof.

"Why is Christof so vindictive? I just don't get it," Ivy said.

"He's a psychopath, that's why," Ruben said. "Is this where I say I told you so?"

"Not if you want to stay in my good graces, *friend*," Ivy replied. She glanced down at the coffee table between them, the sturdy farmhouse table that held their weight for a night of unbelievable sex. Ruben wondered if she was thinking what he was thinking. Sipping coffee and having a conversation in the cold light of day with the memories of that night swirling in his head felt strange. He wondered if he'd ever see her naked again.

Ivy rubbed her shoulder, then slowly trailed her hand across her upper chest and tapped her heart with her fingers. Ruben watched, mesmerized. If he thought for one minute that he could live without her, these few moments together shattered that illusion. No matter how hard this was, how much they had to work it out to be together, he was going to do what it took. Pilar was right; he hadn't given his fair share before, but now he would.

"You know he expects this to break us up," Ruben said.

"He was right about that, wasn't he?" Ivy said. "There aren't a lot of options."

"Aren't you tired of him winning all the time? I know I am." Ruben sat his coffee on the table and scooted closer to Ivy on the couch. He squeezed her knee. "If we put our heads together, I think we can beat him and solve our problems at the same time."

Ivy's eyes sparkled as she put her hand over his. "You might be just a little too optimistic about happily ever after for us, but I'm all for kicking Christof's ass." Ivy grinned.

"You can take the woman out of America," he began.

"But you can't take the America out of the woman," Ivy finished.

"Thank god for that." Ruben leaned in and kissed her, the taste of her like water to a man lost in the desert. When they broke apart, he smiled, eyes crinkling at the corners. He turned to the coffee table and knocked on it three times. "Think we can use your bed this time?"

#

With sunlight streaming in through the windows, Ivy sat Ruben on her bed. He watched as she unbuttoned the first button on her blouse. She smiled when he followed suit, unbuttoning his own top button. They mimicked each other all the way down, a mirrored striptease.

Ivy dropped her shirt on the floor and then reached back to unzip her skirt, slowly edging it down her hips. Ruben watched it fall to the floor, then gazed back up at her standing in her lacy purple bra and matching thong. Against her red hair and pale skin, the vision was striking, and Ivy knew it. She waited for Ruben to catch up with her. He stood up to unbuckle his belt, ripped it through the loops and held it in his hand, one eyebrow raised. They both laughed, breaking the tension for a moment.

"If anyone's using that, it will be me," Ivy said. Ruben's eyes went wide for a moment, and he dropped the belt to the floor.

Ruben stepped forward and cradled Ivy's face in his hands before giving her the deepest kiss of her life. She grabbed his waist, the hard flesh like a pillar of marble in front of her. Ivy's hands journeyed up his back, feeling the indention of his spine and the muscles extending from his shoulder blades. Her fingers traced down Ruben's sides, a perfect V-shape down to his waist. Once there, she pulled him hard into her, the skin from their torsos hot against each other.

Ruben reached behind her to unhook her bra, then cradled her breasts in his hands as the straps fell down. He removed the bra as if he were unearthing a treasure, then leaned down to kiss the freckles on her chest as the bra dropped to the floor.

"Every freckle is like licking the sun," he said between kisses, and they both laughed.

"Come here, you deviant sun worshiper, you," Ivy said as she led him to her bed.

They fell into Ivy's bed, covered with exotic pillows from her travels. Thankfully there was no time to remove all those pillows, because Ivy felt like a queen of some Bedouin tribe in the desert lying on top of them with her servant Ruben doing everything he could to make his mistress happy. The fantasy fueled her desire.

The two of them fit together perfectly, a yin and yang of complementary bodies and moves to delight each other. The light from the windows dimmed, as if the sun went behind a cloud, and Ivy saw Ruben's face and body with a bit of shadow —definition around his muscles, the square of his jaw, and the depth of his eyes. He was gorgeous, like a Greek statue with a substantially better package under the fig leaf than what

Michelangelo gave David.

"Are you ready for me?" Ruben asked, rolling on the condom as she nodded. He stopped and caressed her cheek. "Are you ready for us?"

"I've been ready for you all my life, Ruben," Ivy responded with a sigh. Her eyes watered, but she didn't cry. "I just didn't trust myself before now."

Ruben slowly entered her, a sensation of fullness spreading through her body as they fully connected into one being. She wanted to forever feel this way.

Their lovemaking was different this time, less urgent and more purposeful. The light of day exposed every move, each look, and the lightest caress. Nothing was hidden by the dark, and they were fully open to each other for the first time. It was passionate, and it was uncomfortable. Ivy could no longer pretend to be the dominatrix type, not in her sunny bedroom, opening her heart to Ruben at the neediest point of her life.

"This is too much, Ruben," Ivy whispered, fear darkening her eyes. "I don't think I can do this again."

"My darling, we aren't even done with this one and you're already worrying about the next?" Ruben teased softly. "It is intense, no? This feeling we have for each other. I won't lie; it could burn us up, and it scares me, too." He stopped and just lay quietly with her, their hearts beating in time. "It will always be too much, Ivy. That's why we have to stretch it out over the years, nibble on the feast for decades to come, always knowing where to go when we get hungry."

"Such a poet," she replied, grateful for his patience. Ivy felt the fire building, the hunger for him overtake her fear of such an intimate connection. "I think I'm ready for another nibble," she whispered, and Ruben obliged.

Ivy knew she would never tire of looking at his face above hers, looking down at her with such devotion, skin glistening with sweat. He was the sexiest man she'd ever known, and he was here, in her bed, focused on pleasuring her until she cried for mercy. How could she have ever thought to live without him?

Her anger at the stupidity of the last weeks fueled her desire, the realization that she'd almost lost this man, this connection, and this intimacy. She grew bolder, more forceful. Ivy pulled Ruben down to her, kissing him deeply before wrapping her legs around his waist and forcing them to the side, and then rolling one more time so that she was on top.

"Did you used to work at a circus?" Ruben teased. "Because I'd be happy to install a trapeze in here."

"If I reveal all my talents now, you won't have any surprises left," Ivy replied.

"I don't think in an entire lifetime you could stop surprising me, Ivy Cross."

Ivy placed her hands flat on his chest and guided their rhythm, speeding and slowing as she led them both to the top of the mountain. The expression on his face told her the pacing was excruciatingly good. She sped up, building to a peak of desire that surprised them both when it broke through, waves of pleasure and release flowing to every nerve ending in their bodies.

Ivy cried out, arching her back and throwing her head back, red hair clinging to the beads of perspiration on her back. Now that she'd committed, she finally felt free.

CHAPTER THIRTY-ONE

"Shouldn't you be at work?" Ivy asked, standing in the doorway in a fluffy white robe holding a coffee cup. Her red hair was a wild mess.

"Shouldn't you?" Ben replied. "Nice outfit, by the way. You look like you've been up all night." Ivy's sly smile stopped him in his tracks. "Oh my god. You've been sexing it up all night! Is he still here? Should I go?" Ben peeked around her and into the flat.

"Relax, spymaster. He's gone. Come in." Ivy shuffled to the kitchen to pour Ben a coffee. "Why aren't you at work, seriously?"

"I called in sick." Ben sat down on the couch, placing his bag at his feet. "While you've been getting your freak on, I've been working on your career." Ben took the cup of hot coffee offered. "You're welcome, by the way." He took a sip and then looked down at the couch he was sitting on. "You guys didn't do anything here, did you?" His face scrunched up as if he'd just smelled sour milk.

"Grow up, Ben," Ivy said, smiling into her cup as she took a sip. She tried not to laugh, but she couldn't help herself.

He hit the side of his head with his palm. "Out, out, out. I'll probably need therapy for the mental images now seared into my brain."

"Can we talk about something else, please?" Ivy enjoyed torturing Ben, watching his face turn red.

"Yes, definitely." He set his cup down on the table and removed his laptop from the brown leather messenger bag at his feet. "I have a proposal for you."

"The answer is no. I don't think we have a future together, Ben. You probably snore, anyway," Ivy quipped.

"Very funny. And we do have a future together, at least one where we keep our clothes on." He looked skyward and mouthed, "Thank God."

"I'm listening," Ivy prodded.

"So I'm thinking between us we can land you a plum job somewhere in Europe. I will mine all the resources I still have at the Embassy and do all the legwork and research for you to ace the interview. I can also sweet-talk Jack into writing a good recommendation for you," Ben said.

Ivy cocked her head at Ben.

"What can I say? He likes me," Ben replied, shrugging his shoulders. "He actually likes me more than I like him." Ben scrunched his nose at the thought.

Ivy couldn't hide the surprise on her face. "I'll be damned."

"Anyway," Ben said, dragging out the word to get her attention, "one way or another we can find you a new job soon. All I ask in return is that you take me with you as your assistant." He took a deep breath after his spiel, waiting for her reply.

Ivy set her coffee cup down on the table and leaned back into her chair. She examined Ben's hopeful face, wondering why he'd do this for her. Then she hated herself for being suspicious of this man who'd shown her nothing but loyalty.

"Why do you want to work with me, Ben?" Ivy asked.

"Because you have good instincts—usually. And because you're a straight shooter. I can learn from you, and I can help protect you, too. I see things you don't, and I can get information you can't. Think of it like Batman and Robin. Or something like that." Ben laid his case out like he was in an interview, which Ivy supposed he was. She just didn't know she was hiring.

"How do you see this partnership working?" Ivy asked. Being on this side of the table after her disastrous interview with Joanna Savage was enlightening.

"I'm your right hand. We don't keep secrets from each other. I help you get what you need to excel, and you teach me how to lead and manage complex projects. I'm thinking two to three years together in this arrangement, and then redefining our relationship as I gain more experience." Ben's earnestness was appealing, and his plan was not without merit. Ivy was on board with all of it, but she didn't think Ben could pull off that crucial first step—finding Ivy a job. And without that, there was nothing. She decided to humor him, but only if it wouldn't cost him his job at the Embassy. No need to wreak more havoc than she'd already done.

"I like the idea, Ben, but I honestly don't know how you're going to find me a job better than I can find me a job." Ivy stood up and walked to the kitchen. "I'm making some scrambled eggs. Want some?"

"How can you be thinking of food at a time like this, Ivy? We have work to do!" Ben urged.

"And we can't do it on an empty stomach. I'm scrambling two eggs. Speak up if you want me to add some for you." Ivy pulled the small skillet down from the cabinet, the perfect size for two scrambled eggs. She thought about Ruben, eating breakfast together every morning, and wondered if she'd have to invest in a bigger pan. Or actually learn to cook. The thought made her grin.

"No eggs for me. You cook, and I'll tell you what I've got lined up for you already," Ben said.

Ivy turned from the stove to look at him. "You already have things lined up for me? Wow. You have been busy." Ivy cracked the eggs into a bowl and whisked them with a fork, adding a generous pour of milk and a heavy shake of pepper.

With a thick slice of bread in the toaster, she had the makings of a queen's breakfast. And she needed the nourishment after last night.

"Your first meeting is with Sylvia," Ben said.

"Sylvia?" Ivy turned from the stove, spatula in hand as her eggs burned. "I just had a cupcake with her yesterday. Why would she want to meet with me again?"

"You passed the first stage. Next time is an actual interview." Ben smiled, enjoying her surprise.

"Interview, huh? You set up the invitation to her wedding," Ivy said, realization dawning. "You're orchestrating this whole situation?"

"Let's just say Sylvia is at the top of a select list of companies I've researched for you," Ben said. "She's got a much bigger reach than you think, and there are several opportunities for you to discuss. I'm emailing them to you now so you can do a little homework before your meeting tomorrow." Ben clicked a few keys on his laptop, busily working while Ivy just stared.

"You're a standup guy, Ben. I underestimated you," Ivy said.

"You underestimate a lot of people. But I won't let you do that anymore."

#

RubenAlegre: Ain't no sunshine when she's gone.

Ivy_Cross: Clouds in Madrid?

RubenAlegre: In my heart, woman. I need you.

Ivy_Cross: We're going to break each other.

RubenAlegre: I hope so.

Ivy stretched in her bed, satisfied for the moment to have the virtual version of Ruben in bed with her via text. Why had she thought they couldn't make it work from two different cities? Of course they could.

A nagging voice in the back of her head reminded her that she wasn't working, which is what gave her the time to luxuriate in bed with sexy messages. Once she got a job, that would change. *No sense thinking about that now. We'll deal with that when it comes,* she thought, liking her new attitude.

Build the new. Socrates was right. Ivy wouldn't focus on fixing the old anymore. It was all about the new. The past was passed, and it couldn't be changed.

She rolled out of bed and walked to her closet, the gray pantsuit and lavender button-down shirt for today's meeting hanging for her inspection.

Yesterday Ivy and Ben crammed all day on her options for working with Sylvia and a few other companies. Ivy had to admit, Ben had done his homework. She felt as ready for this interview as she had anything, a far cry from her confidence going into the meeting with Joanna Savage.

Confidence was the key. Ivy was a woman with experience, leadership skills, and a pretty good network. *Not a good enough network to get a job on my own, but no one has to know that.* Ben was definitely her best career asset at this point, her secret weapon.

When Ivy walked out the door an hour later, she was the image of a woman on her way up. And once she fixed this career problem, she'd find a way to fix her relationship problems, too.

BennyBoy: Back straight, tits up, no jokes.

Ivy_Cross: Yes, Dad.

BennyBoy: I'm serious. You think you're funny, but you're not.

Ivy_Cross: I am funny!

BennyBoy: No, you really aren't. Be smart, be sharp, but don't joke or you will undo all my hard work.

BennyBoy: This is tough love, babe.

Ivy_Cross: Okay, no jokes. Will msg when done.

Ivy_Cross: And if I haven't said it, thank you.

BennyBoy: You haven't. And you're welcome. Feel free to practice saying it more.

Ivy_Cross: Don't push your luck.

The Tube station was packed. Ivy had forgotten what it was like to be in the mosh pit of commuters. For the last several years she'd walked to work, buying her flat mainly because of the close proximity to the office. She refilled her Oyster card at the machine, adding enough money to fund several trips on the Tube for the upcoming interviews Ben had scheduled.

The stream of passengers moved in a mostly orderly fashion through the station, down the escalators and onto the platforms. She stood waiting for her train, the sign indicating it would arrive in two minutes. If she took the job, this would be her commute every day. Ivy tried that idea on for size, liking it because it meant she could stay in her flat. *Not so fast, Ivy. Gotta be offered the job first, she reminded herself.*

Walking into the sunshine from underground ten minutes later, Ivy walked the short distance to Sylvia's office building. She'd chosen well, a nice but not opulent space with a directory on the wall. Sylvia was on the fourth floor, the professional sign and logo already in place. It had only been a couple of weeks since she left the Embassy. Sylvia must have had this all arranged for months. Again, Ivy wondered how many times she'd underestimated the people around her.

At the fourth floor, Ivy followed the signs to Sylvia's office. The assistant manning the front desk gave her coffee and seated her in the small reception area. This was a much bigger operation than she imagined, and for the hundredth time since yesterday she appreciated Ben's level of research. She'd have never thought this of Sylvia, would never have taken the time to find out.

In a moment, Sylvia walked in, color high on her cheeks and hand extended for a firm shake. "So good to see you again, Ivy. You didn't happen to bring cupcakes in that bag, did you?" she joked.

"Too risky. I was afraid I'd eat them on the way over. You can trust me with a lot of things, but cupcakes are not one of them," Ivy replied with a smile as they walked into her office.

"Good to know what your weaknesses are up front," Sylvia said as she took her seat behind the desk. "Now let's talk about your strengths. Tell me why you should work for me."

Warm-up must be over.

"The first reason is that I've worked for you before, and you know I can deliver when it comes to sharing complex economic issues with non-economic people. If I can convince politicians who change their minds every five seconds to appease voters of every type, then I can certainly work with CEOs who only answer to a single group of shareholders." Ivy was strong, concise, and to the point, just like she'd rehearsed with Ben the day before.

He'd made her do it on video so she could see herself afterward and notice any weird habits or tics. After laughing at the fact she was wearing a white fluffy robe while extolling her virtues as a key employee, Ivy noticed she nodded her head a lot. She looked like a yes-woman when she was nervous, so in today's meeting her neck was ramrod straight, her gaze powerful and direct. Ivy had no idea where Ben learned all this body language stuff, but she was grateful for his help, especially the help she didn't even know she needed. He would be a good assistant if she ever landed a job.

"The second reason is that I have a security clearance from the US government, should that be needed for any government-specific contracts. Even when it is not required, I've found clients appreciate knowing that their advisor is trusted by a major international government." Boom. Ivy was delivering on all her key points like a pro. Ben would be so proud.

"And the last is that I need very little supervision. You can point me in the right direction and I'll take care of the situation, which frees you up to recruit business, manage your other projects, or even enjoy an extended honeymoon." Ivy smiled when delivering that last line, an acknowledgement of Sylvia's refocus on her personal life.

"Why did you turn down the promotion at the Embassy?"

Sylvia asked. Ivy braced herself, having known this question was coming but still not liking it.

"I wanted something different, just like you, something with a little less restriction and more opportunity. I couldn't get that at the Embassy. My original plan didn't calculate you leaving, which is why it got a little messy with Jack. Had I known you were also leaving, I would have gone about it differently so as not to burn any bridges." Ivy felt relief at having said it correctly, knowing she'd stumbled during her practice session a few times yesterday.

"See, that's where I have a problem. Had you been more aware of office politics and the people at the level above you, you would have been able to predict my moves. But you were too lost in your own world, too narrowly focused to see the big picture. And that's my biggest concern in hiring you, Ivy." Sylvia pulled no punches, and Ivy felt like the wind had been knocked out of her. Her independent nature was killing both her personal life and her career. Great. The thing she liked the most about herself was keeping her from getting what she wanted. Ivy steeled herself for another letdown like the one with Joanna Savage. Why did she even bother to put on heels for this?

Socrates popped up in her head again. "Build the new. Build the new. Build the new." God, he could be such a pain in the ass. But he was right. Ivy couldn't change what happened, but she could focus on the new. She opened her mouth to speak but Sylvia interrupted her.

"There's also the question of judgment. You wanted to work with Christof Brandt. I know you came to your senses, but a decision like that after a stellar career at the Embassy makes me wonder about other snap decisions you might make. You're not working out the consequences of your actions, which I find surprising in an economist," Sylvia said. Ivy was floored. That was a low blow, but she couldn't fault her for bringing it up. Thankfully she and Ben practiced this question, too, though she didn't expect to have to use it.

"You're absolutely right. The past few weeks have taught me some valuable lessons about teamwork, partnership, and vulnerability. Have you ever heard the phrase, 'when the student is ready the teacher will appear'? Well, that's what happened to me. I'm taking a crash course in getting my head on straight in every area of my life right now. And if you hire me, you get the benefit of this new awareness coupled with my knowledge and experience." Ivy took a sip of her now-tepid coffee and placed it on Sylvia's desk. She waited to be shown the door, knowing there was nothing left to discuss. This was the heart of the matter, and if Sylvia couldn't see past this, there was no sense talking about the job.

"I appreciate your candor, Ivy. Let me do some thinking and I'll call you in a few days." Sylvia stood, an indication the meeting was over. Ivy fought the urge to look at her watch, pissed that she'd prepped hours for a fifteen-minute chat that would likely go nowhere. She was mad that Ben got her hopes up at all, that she thought there was a way out of this mess. Even in this meeting, Ivy felt like a yo-yo, back and forth on whether she could really turn her career around and make room in her life for Ruben.

As it was, she'd likely be moving back to Arizona to be a barista. Still, no more burning of bridges on her watch. It was time to shake hands and walk confidently out of the door and away from yet another opportunity.

"Thanks for your consideration, Sylvia. I know we'll work well together." Ivy ended the conversation on a confident note she didn't feel inside. And she was wishing she did have some cupcakes stored in her bag. Maybe she would stop off at the bakery on the way home and indulge a little. Better yet, she could go home, put on her running clothes and sweat out her frustration so she could order a double helping of garlic naan from Indira's place tonight.

Ivy's phone buzzed as she walked out of the building.

BennyBoy: When do we start?

Ivy_Cross: No-go.

BennyBoy: You didn't tell a joke, did you?

Ivy_Cross: Haha. I'm too self-centered. Exercise bad judgment. Apparently.

BennyBoy: Tell me something I don't know.

Ivy_Cross: Are you here to help me or what?

BennyBoy: Exhibit A.

Ivy_Cross: Smartass. Sylvia is thinking about it. Not sure what that means.

BennyBoy: Probably that she's thinking about it.

Ivy_Cross: Why do I keep you around?

BennyBoy: Because I'm the only one who can handle you. Talk soon.

Well, not the only one. Ivy remembered the delightful way she'd been handled by Ruben a couple of nights ago. Now that she'd made the decision to go forward with this whatever kind of relationship they had, she worried she couldn't hold up her end of the bargain. Where would she work? How much money would she have for flights to Madrid? How much time would she have to see him? It was all up in the air, and she felt a significant loss of control. If this was vulnerability, she didn't like it at all.

CHAPTER THIRTY-TWO

"This is how Christof must feel when he's about to take someone down. I've got to admit, it's not a bad feeling," Ruben said.

"Christof deserves to be taken down. We don't," Lars said. Ruben frowned at his business partner, the sour taste of betrayal still on his tongue. He'd stick with Lars through the end of this deal as promised—he was still a man of his word—but he'd never work with him again. Lars was too untrustworthy, and in the greedy way to boot. It was much better to have a vicious opponent like Christof than a gluttonous one like Lars.

"Remember that I'm the one in this deal who kept his word. And for that, I'm changing our partnership agreement to reflect the additional work I've had to do to save us from your mistake." Ruben knew if he didn't cause Lars some pain in this situation, he'd be likely to trip himself up again. Money was a powerful motivator to color within the lines. "My share just went up twenty percent on the net profit, and you're not going to hit me with false margins on your stock, either."

Lars nodded his head, knowing this was a better option than losing the entire deal. Ruben knew he felt bad, but feeling bad and not making the same mistake again were two different things. He couldn't allow this to happen again if he wanted to keep the ConStead deal and his company afloat. And now that he had Ivy back in his life, he definitely wanted less time dealing with problems and more time enjoying the rewards of his hard work.

Ruben's idea was brilliant, and he knew it. Lars shared the purchase order from FritzFolio with Ruben and he spotted a way out. The order was for the previous model of server, not the current one that Lars was supplying for the ConStead deal. Lars planned to fill the order with the new one before talking with Ruben. This little snafu meant Lars could contact FritzFolio and let them know this product was outdated and no longer available through his company. By the time they responded with an updated purchase order with the new specs, he could rightly tell them he was out of stock—all of it going to ConStead, of course.

This way Lars would be in the clear, the ConStead stock would be preserved, and Christof would have no way of retaliating, at least not legally. That was the biggest worry they had, that Christof would tie them up in courts for years to come.

Ruben decided not to tell Ivy about Christof's intervention. She had enough to worry about while finding a new job. But Christof? He definitely wanted to tell him. It was worth the same-day round-trip flight from Madrid to do this in person.

When Ruben left Lars's office in Berlin, he headed straight for The Werks. Every logical part of his mind told him this was a bad move, but the testosterone drowned out the noise. He wanted to see Christof sweat, to make sure he knew Ruben had beaten him again. And he wanted revenge for Ivy.

What an ostentatious jerk. Christof was a billionaire, and he worked out of a factory—a factory with an organic juice bar and a weekend DJ, no less. Did anyone who worked here feel the same sort of repugnance Ruben felt in walking through the door on polished concrete floors and being checked in at a reception desk made of exotic wood made to look like loading pallets? This expensive version of poor seemed like a mockery to Ruben, a slap in the face to all the entrepreneurs out there who really were struggling to make it big, foregoing the fancy offices and sleeping on couches to make it to the big time.

Ruben wondered if Christof did this on purpose as some twisted kind of flaunting of his wealth or if he was truly that unaware. *Probably the latter.*

When Ruben left the elevator he ran into a young man with a leash chasing after a dog. It was the same dog he remembered from the hotel lobby just a few weeks before. Christof's dog, one he apparently didn't even walk himself.

"Fritz! Down boy." The man with the glasses was trying to corral the dog long enough to attach the leash, but the excited pup was too fast for him.

"Looks like you waited too long to take that guy out,"

Ruben said.

"He's always this way. Loves the outdoors and hates being cooped up. Are you here to see Mr. Brandt?" he asked.

"Yes, he's expecting me. No need to show me in." Ruben walked toward the office door while the assistant walked out with the dog.

"I like the look of upscale poverty you've done here. Is this so you can feel like a regular person?" Ruben said by way of greeting.

"Ruben, you've finally come to beg me for a job. You surprised me by holding out this long." Christof stood and then walked to the corner of his desk and leaned against it, arms crossed.

"I'd rather dig latrines than work for you, Christof. Though now that I think about it, the work is probably the same." Ruben was vibrating on every level. He was going to need an intense workout after this.

"Then why the visit? Surely you aren't having problems with the ConStead deal already? I would hate to hear that. Really." Christof's eyes crinkled at the corners, a genuine smile at what he thought he was going to hear.

"Why would you say that?" Ruben asked innocently.

"I heard through the grapevine that you were having trouble filling your order for them. You know we still talk,"

Christof said.

"The last thing I heard them tell you was not to let the door hit you in the ass on the way out," Ruben replied.

"What people want you to see and what is true are two different things, my friend." Christof smiled cryptically.

"Don't I know it, FritzFolio." Ruben was rewarded by the frozen smile on Christof's face. It was gone in a flash. "By the way, genius move to name your shell company after your dog. Like no one would ever figure that out."

"So you've been picking up the breadcrumbs I left for you. And they brought you here to me. See, you're a smart guy. Smart enough to know when you've been beaten." Christof's poker face was back in place. "I just took your stock away, and now you'll renege on the ConStead deal and it will revert to me. See how all that works? You can learn a lot if you come to work here." The smug look on his face would have changed Ruben's mind even if he had come looking for a job. Guys like Christof overplayed their hands, the cockiness overriding their natural advantages. They always turned the screw once more than necessary.

"Better recheck your order, Brandt. Read the fine print or you're liable to make an expensive mistake." Ruben grinned. Christof's face paled, and Ruben knew he hit the mark. Time to leave and let him figure out the details on his own. "Let's stop running into each other, okay?" Ruben turned to walk out the door.

"It's too bad your girlfriend is having so much trouble finding a new job," Christof said, freezing Ruben in his tracks. He turned to look at Christof.

"You must be referring to the lucky break of figuring out what kind of guy you were before signing on the dotted line. Anyone would be relieved to dodge that bullet," Ruben said, wondering where this was going.

"Did she tell you her boss Jack and I were at boarding school together? We lost touch for a bit, but I was sure to reconnect with him last week, to catch up on what we're doing. He was so surprised to hear about the way Ivy tried to sleep her way into my company. Tacky if you ask me. But of course I took her up on a sampling of the goods. Mmmm." Ruben felt the fog coming on, an anger like he'd never known. His skin flushed all over, hot and cold at the same time, and he was acutely aware of his fists clenching at his sides. He could have killed Christof with his bare hands.

Rage was an emotion Ruben didn't like but appreciated. In the moment, it would get him through this. He just had to channel it, to find the way to hurt Christof the most. A fist wouldn't do it because they were in Germany, Christof's country, and Ruben didn't like his odds dealing with the police as a foreigner when he didn't speak the language. He had to focus the rage somewhere else, a soft spot that would feel the pain more deeply than a punch to the face.

"Now I know you're lying, because women like that don't go for men like you. Stop pretending you're anything other than a vulture, Christof. We can all smell the garbage on you," Ruben spat. "You'll never be your father. You think he talks like this to his competitors to get respect? Nope. He doesn't have to. That must kill you, knowing you'll never live up to his reputation." Ruben watched Christof's face turn red, his fingers clenching the fabric of his sweater while his arms were casually crossed. The guy was trying hard to remain cool, but the details gave him away.

"Why don't you ask your little princess how tight she held onto my cock? That woman has a grip, Ruben. I'll be replaying that memory for years." The twisted grin on Christof's face reminded Ruben of a funhouse mirror at the circus, vaguely human but distorted from reality. He didn't know if his rage morphed his vision or if Christof was truly that warped. The longer he looked at him, the funnier he thought it was. This pathetic piece of crap was someone he thought of as a competitor? Even remotely equal? If that was ever true, those days were gone. For the first time, Ruben saw the man cowering inside the shell, an overgrown bully who accidentally found a victim who'd fight back.

Ruben chuckled, softly at first, and then progressed to a full-on laugh. Tears started gathering at his eyes and he put his hands on his knees to stabilize himself. The release of tension flowed from him, and he saw Christof for what he really was. He bullied for attention because he didn't have another way to get it. People dismissed him as his rich father's spoiled son, and they were right. The stupid clown grin on his face was the only way he had of looking evil. Christof's face went from red to a shade of purple. This was not a man used to losing.

"Did you practice that look by studying the Joker on Batman or something? If you're going to be a bad guy, at least try to be original. Get a signature move, a catchphrase, or something. Maybe wear a certain kind of hat. But don't imitate the bad guys who've gone before, because you don't have the stones for it," Ruben said, trying to control his laughter.

"Get out," Christof said, teeth clenched. "Get the hell out of my office. And don't ever come back here again."

"Nice doing business with you, Christof." Ruben laughed as he walked out the door.

CHAPTER THIRTY-THREE

"I've really mucked it up, Lil," Ivy said. Seriously, I'm gonna be crashing at Rose's old house in Arizona soon if I don't clear my name and figure out a way to pay the bills."

"You always find a way out, Ivy. I've known you all my life, and if anyone can get out of a tight scrape, it's you. It's like your weird superpower or something," Lily said. "Tell me what's up."

Ivy stretched out on her couch, phone cradled against her shoulder, as she updated Lily on her status. "I think Ruben and I are okay, but I still don't see a way for us to be together. My days at the Embassy are numbered, and if I don't find another job soon, they'll send me back to the US."

"You aren't giving this enough time, Ivy. It's not like you can find a great job at the snap of your fingers. Remember how that worked out last time?" Lily asked.

"Ugh. Don't remind me. I wish I'd never heard of Christof Brandt. He almost ruined everything. And he still might ruin my career." Ivy put her feet up in the air, the happy color of green on her toes reminding her of leprechauns and luck. She could certainly use some right now. "Do you remember Ben, the guy who went to the club with us that night?"

"The nerdy thin guy?" Lily asked.

"Yes, he's the one. He cultivates that image, you know. Says it lands him more dates being the quirky guy. See, this is why my dating life has been in the toilet for so long. I never branded myself appropriately. That's what all the cool kids are doing these days." Ivy laughed.

"Yeah, imagine us just stupidly trying to be ourselves," Lily said.

"Not working out so well, is it?" Ivy said.

"I don't know. You landed Ruben by being a smart-mouthed bitch, which is pretty much your base personality. And I found Kan just by dancing. Though I don't know if I'll ever see him again." Lily sighed.

"If the guy could find you at a hotel you weren't even registered at to deliver a drawing, I have a feeling you'll see him again," Ivy said. "So, about Ben. He's helping me find a new job. Doing all the research and helping me prep for interviews. Says he only wants me to take him with me when I go. My right-hand man. What do you think about that?" Ivy asked.

"Well, it sure wouldn't hurt. You have a tendency to, uh, run over people a little. Having someone to give you perspective is a good thing," Lily ventured.

"That's a nice way of putting it!" Ivy laughed. "Ben got me a meeting with my old boss Sylvia. She's got her own consulting company, and it would be a good fit to work there. But she's got some reservations about me, and I guess I don't blame her. Apparently I'm too independent and selfish."

"Tell me something I don't know," Lily said.

"Hey, guilty as charged. I'm beginning to see how I might possibly have let it get out of hand. I'm not going to turn into Mother Theresa overnight, but this whole experience has taught me a lot. I'm willing to prove myself again. I've got no choice," Ivy said.

"My goodness! Did you hear that, everyone? Ivy Cross is having a moment of personal growth!" Lily cooed. "Good for you. This can't be easy, and I'm proud of you for sucking it up and learning from it. You're going to make it through this just fine."

"So what's up with you? How are you going to spend your time off?" Ivy asked. Lily's job at Doctors Without Borders usually worked in three-month contracts. She then took extended time off in between to make up for being constantly on call when on assignment. Ivy hoped she'd do some traveling in Europe so they'd see each other again, but sometimes Lily ventured off on her own, emerging weeks later with a tan, a tattoo, or a vague story about motorcycle rides across the desert. She was a free spirit, but only when she was between jobs. When she was on assignment, she was all business, singularly focused on caring for her patients.

"Still thinking about that one. First I'm going to help Violet find a new apartment in New York. The place she's in now is just a temp. And then who knows? I'm taking a few months off this time, so we'll see what happens," Lily said, vague as usual about her plans. Ivy knew something bad must have happened at her last gig for her to take so much time off now. *The kind of things she must see.*

"Well, I might be able to offer you an empty apartment in London," Ivy said.

"No thanks, girl. London is too civilized for a woman like me," Lily replied. "Don't worry about it, Ivy. You're going to be fine. You will make it through this, just like you always do. And you might even come out a better person." She paused, waiting to deliver the final blow. "But I wouldn't count on it."

Her laugh was like music to Ivy's ears, a reminder of their long history together and how she could always count on her for the straight truth.

CHAPTER THIRTY-FOUR

"I'm going to be working part of the time in London going forward," Ruben announced to his senior team as they neared the starting line of the race. It was Wednesday, a local holiday in Madrid to celebrate Fiesta Nacional de España. The wall in the reception area of his company held team pictures from previous years at the race, Team Alegre Data arm in arm at the finish line of the 10K for a local children's charity.

"You're joking, right?" Tomas stared at Ruben as if trying to work out the angle of the joke he was playing on them. "We need you in Madrid. The clients in London don't need your handholding."

"Not a joke. I'm doing it for personal reasons, and it won't change anything. Except for the fact that you won't get to see my handsome face every day. I'll post headshots around the office so you won't get lonely, Tomas." Ruben grinned and nudged him in the side with his elbow as they found their spots.

Most of Ruben's team members were runners or cyclists, and he felt like an imposter donning the Spandex running gear with the pinned on number when his last run was this time last year. Ruben preferred a grueling workout with a trainer in a gym, a way to sweat out his aggressions by hating on a guy who practically tortured him for pay. There were probably some subconscious masochistic tendencies there that needed to be explored, but he wasn't willing to go down that rabbit hole —unless Ivy was, of course.

He heard Tomas talking, but he missed what he said.

"Earth to Ruben." Tomas snapped his fingers in front of his face, drawing him back into the moment. "You must have skipped your coffee this morning. You're thinking and acting crazy today."

"My head is clear for the first time ever," Ruben responded with a smile. Pilar was right. He wanted Ivy to make all the sacrifices. But once he arrived in London and showed her he was serious, she'd know their relationship was real. He wasn't going anywhere. Ruben didn't want to call it a happily ever after because that sounded too boring for people like them. But it would be exciting.

The runners were set and the announcements started. The conversation would have to resume at the finish line. Ruben was usually humming with energy, a trait people often commented on, and surrounded by all these runners today, Ruben felt a little bit incognito. They were amped up just like he was on a regular day.

As the starter pistol fired, he began a slow pace, waiting for the crowd to thin out so he could find his rhythm. He saw an opening ahead and wove his way through, finally able to hit his stride. The steady beat of his feet and heart were the soundtrack to his brain's activity, a replay of his conversation with Pilar and Alejandro.

What have I done for Ivy lately? The song lyrics were planted in his head on a loop, echoing Pilar's words. He had to show Ivy he was willing to compromise if they were going to be together. She hadn't mentioned Christof again, and it felt like they were moving toward a truce. Telling her he was coming to London would be another step forward.

As he ran through his beloved Madrid, Ruben wondered if Ivy would like it here. Surely she would come for a visit if he made London his part-time home? They had so much to talk about, but one thing he knew was that she wasn't going to slip away from him again.

The runners raced around the final bend, the finish line with bananas and water and cookies just ahead. Ruben ran through with a small group of people, hardly breaking a sweat. He walked over to the refreshments table and took a cookie and some water, waiting for his team to show up. Tomas barreled through the finish line with a flushed face, followed soon by Rodrigo and Evelina, slow and steady.

They picked up their swag bags with T-shirts and protein bars and walked down the street to a cafe, the air becoming crisp as their bodies cooled down. Ruben zipped up his jacket. They found a table inside and ordered their coffees and tostadas with tomato, olive oil, and salt, the standard midmorning meal in much of Spain.

"So what's this talk about you going to London part time? You know that's not going to work. We need you here, Ruben." Tomas's opinion was clear. Rodrigo and Evelina were more patient in their responses, waiting for an explanation of this decision.

"I have a personal situation that requires my attention, and this is the only way. You will still have the same access to me that you always do," Ruben said.

The barista brought their coffees over, pouring the hot milk into the cups right at the table. Normally Ruben drank espresso, but after a workout he could indulge in a sweeter *cafe con leche*, complete with a full packet of sugar.

Silence reigned for a moment as everyone doctored their coffees. Then Evelina spoke. "It's not us that we're worried about, Ruben. What about our customers here who are used to interacting with you directly? Or the new business we're recruiting? You know deals are made in person in Madrid. You can't phone it in." Evelina's logic was sound, and Ruben knew it would be a problem. But he didn't see another way.

"This is the perfect time for each of you to step up and become more integral in some of these relationships," Ruben said.

"Let me get this straight. You're going to London to give your little boss some action and this is good for us because we're getting more responsibility?" Tomas was angry, and he wasn't hiding it. "Ruben, you act like the ConStead deal is setting us up for a lifetime of profits. We've already had one major problem with Lars, and if you were in London then we wouldn't have had time to work out a solution before he screwed us over. The deal hasn't even started yet and you've already had to save it once. What makes you think you can leave now?" He gripped the side of the table with his hands. "This is a bad idea."

"Drop it a level, Tomas, before you say something you'll regret. This is the woman I'm spending the rest of my life with, and you'll show her the same kind of respect I'd show to your family," Ruben said, his voice an eerie calm.

"You're right. I'm sorry. I shouldn't have said that. But the point still stands that this company cannot run without the CEO living in Madrid. It just won't be as successful, and we risk losing clients and missing out on new opportunities if you're not here." Tomas was trying hard to dial back his anger, Ruben knew, but it was hard for him to put the hammer back down once he'd started hitting with it.

"I'm going, and we'll adjust. I didn't bring this up as a point of discussion. I am the CEO, and this is my decision." Even in a best-case scenario he'd work with them another few years before they went out on their own. And he wouldn't risk Ivy for a few years of camaraderie at work.

"Nice to know we're still a team," Tomas said. The waitress came over with their tostadas, and when she set them on the table, Tomas asked her to take a photo of them with his phone.

When she handed it back to him, he stood and threw a few Euros on the table. "This is the real team photo for today, isn't it? The day Ruben told us all how much he valued our contributions to the company." Tomas picked up his jacket and stormed out of the coffee shop.

The silence was deafening. Rodrigo and Evelina looked down at the table, faces unreadable. The other people in the cafe looked over, wondering what the drama was about.

"He's not wrong, you know," Evelina ventured. "And you're not wrong, either. We all deserve a life. But when you make big decisions like that without even listening to our opinions, well..." She held up her hands and looked at Rodrigo, who also shrugged.

"It's a lot to take in, *jefe*. The extra work isn't the problem. It's that you might decide to go to London permanently, or make another big decision without consulting us. This isn't the Ruben we know, the one who worked with us. This guy is more unpredictable, and that makes us all a little nervous."

Ruben looked at the two of them, the more reasonable people in his company. He expected a negative response from the moody but brilliant Tomas, but not from these two. They were steady, unflappable workers.

If he made this sacrifice for Ivy, would he also be sacrificing his company?

"This is a new era for the company, and it means change. You're not going to like everything I do, but you should trust that I'm doing it for the right reasons," Ruben said, hoping that was true.

CHAPTER THIRTY-FIVE

"Trust has to be earned, Ivy," Sylvia said. "My gut can lead me, but my brain is where I make my final decisions. I like you, and I want to offer you a job, but first you'll have to prove yourself."

Ivy bit back her tongue. She was forty-two years old and had twenty years of experience, and Sylvia wanted her to prove herself?

"In what way?" Ivy asked, trying to stay neutral.

"We're starting off with some grunt work, the true behind-the-scenes work that doesn't get noticed. I have two Spanish clients now, and I need you to interface with them and do the research and legwork. That means working the phones and digging through stacks of documents. Not glamorous at all."

Ivy cocked her head as Sylvia spoke, the wheels already turning.

"Show me you're paying attention to what's going on around you and you know how to work with a team and you'll go places with me. Keep working your own agenda and you'll be out on your ear. I can't make it plainer than that, Ivy. I need to know you've got the company's interests in mind, not just yours."

"How many Spanish clients do you have?" Ivy asked.

"Right now I have two, but if things go well with them, I think I can land the biggest department store chain in Spain. The connections are there. I just need to show some big wins first." Sylvia's eyes narrowed in concentration. "Why do you ask?"

"I can do the grunt work, no problem. But what if I did it in Madrid and gave your business the presence it needs to attract major clients?" Ivy leaned forward, pulling a notebook out of her purse and placing it on Sylvia's desk.

"How do you propose to do that?" Sylvia put her elbows on the desk and looked down at Ivy's notebook.

"First we'd need to do a press release about opening shop in Madrid and touting the strong connections we have with business and government all over Europe. Some testimonials from people we've worked with would be great." Ivy scribbled furiously. "Then we'd start networking with business journalists in Spain, commenting on the news and generally making ourselves known." Ivy stuck her pen in the corner of her mouth as she thought. "I could start a column about international business for Spanish companies. We could set it up as a subscription service and start building our sales funnel that way. Maybe it grows enough to get picked up by a major news site."

The mood was electric, the first magical moments after the birth of a great idea, when possibilities rained down and problems were far away on the horizon. Ivy hadn't felt the rush of a great business idea in years. Her head couldn't contain all the ideas erupting inside. As Ivy wrote, Sylvia's smile grew.

"You'd move to Madrid to make a project like this work?" Sylvia asked, her focus on the horizon instead of the rain. "This wouldn't be a short-term assignment, Ivy. If we commit to this, you're going for years, not months."

"I wouldn't have brought it up if I wasn't willing to do it. I'll be your grunt to prove myself, Sylvia. But I'll also be your first outpost, laying the groundwork so you can grow across Europe in the coming years. If my method works in Spain, you can use it in every country in Europe." Ivy's heart beat double time, the solution to her work issue and her personal life sitting right in front of her. She could go to Spain, create her dream job, move mountains for Sylvia, and have her heart's desire with Ruben.

All the turmoil and trauma of the last few weeks would be worth it if Sylvia said yes. Ivy had to remind herself to breathe.

"You are excited about this now, but I can't help but worry that you'll change your mind. What kind of guarantee do I have?" Sylvia asked.

"All I want is a chance to build something great. And when I say that, I don't just mean business. I'm ready to give my all in a way I've never been before, in both work and love. Madrid holds both of those options for me, and if you send me there, not only will it change your business, it will change my life. And I can't think of a more loyal employee than one who credits her boss for making her love possible." Ivy gripped her pen so tight her knuckles turned white. *Please, please, please say yes.* "Your guarantee is love, Sylvia."

"You surprise me, Ivy Cross. I wouldn't have pegged you as the romantic sort." She chuckled and shook her head. "Then again, I wouldn't have pegged me as the romantic sort before, either, and now I'm getting married." Sylvia picked up Ivy's notebook and scanned her notes. "I have a good feeling about this," she said, looking over her reading glasses at Ivy. "A very good feeling."

Ivy's whole body unclenched at once, the relief washing over her. "So that's a yes?"

"Yes, Ivy. You are now the head of our Spanish division," Sylvia said with a smile. "Try not to let it get to your head, especially since you have no employees or an office yet."

Ivy breathed a sigh of relief. "You won't be disappointed, Sylvia. I promise. But about my staff, I have an idea."

"Don't go diva on me, Ivy. You're pushing your luck," Sylvia warned.

"It's not that at all, Sylvia. I'd like to take Ben with me. If your plan is to expand, it will be a perfect time to train someone now to take this show on the road," Ivy ventured.

"He's smart, capable, and willing to learn. He'd be an asset to your company, and I'll make sure he learns what he needs to know." She thought of Ben's pink-haired friend. "Maybe you'll decide to open up shop in Germany one day. You know he speaks German, right?"

"Ben? I had no idea you were close with any of the support staff at the Embassy, or that you'd go to bat for them. You surprised me again, Ivy. In a good way," Sylvia said. "Send me his résumé and I'll check it out. If it's all good, he can come, too. I'd like to see more of that kind of thinking, Ivy."

"Oh, I've got big plans for Madrid already, Sylvia. You have no idea," Ivy said. "This is going to be the best decision you've ever made."

# # #

"This calls for a celebration! I'm coming to London soon. How about an insanely expensive dinner followed by an entire weekend in a fancy hotel room with just room service?" Ruben asked, already imagining Ivy's vibrant red hair spread out on the white Egyptian cotton sheets.

"Don't plan your trip yet, Ruben. I may have to do a bit of travel first. Let me get sorted and then we'll plan a visit." Ivy brushed him off, and warning bells sounded in his head.

"Oh, already the big shot and taking road trips? I hope you'll make time for me in your busy calendar. Maybe I should get your assistant's number?" Ruben teased. He couldn't help but feel a little rejected. The first thing he wanted to do when he won the ConStead deal was to celebrate with Ivy. Why didn't she want the same with him?

"You know I'll always have time for you," Ivy said.

"Just not right now," Ruben countered. This conversation was going south, not at all how he pictured a congratulatory call about her new job. But Pilar was right; he needed to meet her halfway. "So tell me what you'll be doing."

"I'll be working with clients in Europe on growth strategies based on economic indicators. That probably sounds really boring to you, but it's what I'm good at. And I'm lucky to find such a good job after the mess with Christof." Ivy sighed, and Ruben knew the last weeks had been hard on her. But he was planning on moving part-time to London to be with her. It's not like he hadn't made sacrifices. Though he had to admit his sacrifices were still theoretical, given that he hadn't told her he was coming to London or found a flat yet. But the scene with his team at the race was still swirling in his head, making him wonder if he'd rushed into this. Ivy's cool manner on the phone wasn't helping.

"I don't think we'll be hearing from Christof again," Ruben said, smiling. He waited for her to ask what he meant, but she didn't.

"I'm sorry to sound so distracted, Ruben, but I'm so close

to sorting this all out and just have to concentrate to get there. I really do want to see you, and we will very soon. I promise." Ivy's tone was reassuring, and since he was looking for anything to hold on to, he took it.

"Okay, Ivy. I'll trust you on this." Ruben frowned. She was pulling away from him, and he didn't know if it was because she didn't think she needed him now that her career problems were fixed or that she didn't believe he would do his part to make their relationship work. Or maybe she was just stressed out with the new job with Sylvia. He didn't know, couldn't guess, and she wasn't talking about it. They said goodbye and he was left feeling unsettled.

Ruben was good at analyzing problems, but with Ivy he just didn't see any clear answers. And he was becoming less sure about the decision to move to London part time. Maybe he should have waited to announce to his team until after he talked to Ivy.

He turned his chair back to the door when he heard a knock and saw Tomas standing there. They hadn't spoken since the race, and Ruben knew this first conversation would be difficult. But he also knew Tomas would come around. They'd worked together too long.

"Sore from the race?" Ruben asked, lobbing an easy greeting to set the tone of the meeting.

"No, but I'm still sore from our conversation. I can't work this way, Ruben. You've shut me out, and it will only get worse if you're not here." Tomas leaned on the doorframe, arms crossed.

"Come in. We'll talk about it," Ruben said, motioning to the small sitting area in his office.

"There is no reason to talk after you've already made your decision, Ruben. I just stopped by to tell you I'm resigning. You'll have the official letter by end of the week." Tomas turned and walked away without another word, but it wouldn't have mattered if he stayed. Ruben knew he couldn't talk him out of it. Tomas needed stability to function at his peak, and Ruben took that away. Theirs was always a delicate balance, and now he'd stepped off the seesaw and let Tomas crash down.

Without Tomas in Madrid, it would be impossible to spend half his time in London. Or any time, for that matter. Going halfway to meet Ivy was going to cost him a lot more than he thought, and her distance on the phone earlier set off alarm bells.

CHAPTER THIRTY-SIX

"How was work today, hon?" Ivy teased Ben as he slid into the booth at the restaurant, suit jacket draped over his arm and messenger bag on his shoulder.

"Hopefully, not as good as yours. Tell me how the meeting with Sylvia went," Ben said, loosening his tie and flagging down the waitress. "I'll have a pint of London Pride," he said, indicating his favorite draft beer. "And a plate of chips," he added.

Ivy raised an eyebrow as the waitress walked away. "That's your dinner, a plate of fries?"

"For your information, that's my appetizer. You're taking me somewhere much nicer for dinner," Ben said.

They were at The Stuck Pig, a pub near the Embassy where employees often went after work to unwind. The pub was typical—dark wood interior, red pleather upholstered booths, and a barman and waitresses who wore jeans and took no guff from customers. The Stuck Pig was not a place for tourists, and that's why Ivy liked it.

"What makes you think I'm taking you to dinner, cheapo?" Ivy asked, a smile curling on her lips.

"Because I think Sylvia offered you a job today. And I hope that means one for me, too. Spill it, sister," Ben commanded.

"Thanks to my new assistant, we have a job." Ivy beamed at Ben, glad to finally share the news. She didn't want to do it over the phone, hoping to enjoy his reaction in person. She wasn't disappointed.

"High-five, Ivy! I knew you could do it." Ben's beer arrived at the table, and he raised his glass. "To our hot new future together!" Ben drank and then added, "But not in that way, just in case you're getting ideas. Ewww."

Ivy started to reply when she saw Ben's expression change. He was facing the door, so someone interesting must have just walked in. She didn't have to wait long to find out who it was.

"Ben, Ivy." Jack nodded his head at the two of them. "I was told I could find you here." There was no good reason for a guy like Jack to be in a pub like this. "Am I interrupting a celebration?"

"What brings you here, Jack? Ben is off the clock, and you've sent me on an indefinite vacation. I don't see a reason why we should be talking right now." Ivy wanted to knock the smug look off his face.

"I'd like to remind you that you have clauses in your contracts regarding your security clearance and your ability to work for other agencies," Jack said. "You can't just take what you've learned here and offer it on the open market."

"You think I'm flaunting my analysis skills in front of other suitors? What kind of woman do you think I am?" Ivy asked, hand on her chest. "I don't know where you're getting your information, Jack, but you should get better sources." Jack was blowing smoke, but even though he couldn't make it hold up, he could get her security clearance put on hold during an investigation.

"My source is impeccable. You must have really done something to piss him off, because he's putting a lot of pressure on me to do something. You make enemies a lot faster than you make friends," Jack said. Ivy could see that he wasn't really into this, but she also knew he'd follow through anyway if it suited his long-term interests. She was not going to miss working for such a tool.

"You frat boys really do stick together, don't you? Funny thing about Christof is that he has no real friends. You know that, and I know that. He burns every bridge he crosses, and he'll burn yours, too. Better make sure you're in your ivory tower when it happens or you'll never be able to reach it again." Ivy smirked and Jack crossed his arms over his chest.

"I don't have to like everything I do in this job, but it doesn't mean I won't do what I have to. Watch your step." Jack looked at Ben, too. "Both of you." The look he gave Ben was one of regret, and Ivy wondered how far his interest in Ben had gone.

They watched him walk away in silence, waiting for the squeak of the door closing to resume their conversation.

"We should have invited him to join us, you know. Get him rip-roaring drunk, and then when he passed out, shave off one of his eyebrows." Ben grinned. "I'm really pissed we didn't think of that while he was still here."

The waitress returned with a plate of fries, and Ben squeezed a glob of the ubiquitous HP Sauce all over them.

"You're an American, Ben. You eat your fries with ketchup," she scolded.

"Hey, if we're going to be staying in London, I should blend in with the locals, don't you think?" Ben shoved a few fries in his mouth, brown sauce hanging tight to the edge of his lip.

"About that," Ivy began.

# # #

"Is this because of your boyfriend?" Ben asked. The plate of fries was empty in front of him.

"Does it matter? You can work for me, or you can work for Jack."

"Well, when you put it that way," Ben said thoughtfully, never bothering to finish the sentence as he took a swig of beer.

Ivy hoped Ben wouldn't bail on her. As much as she resisted his help at first, she'd grown to depend on him. Starting over in Madrid without him wouldn't be nearly so interesting. Well, at least not when it came to work.

Starting over in Madrid in every other respect sounded like a dream come true. Ivy couldn't believe it. The sequence of events that first destroyed her life then gave her everything she was looking for—a life with Ruben, a career in the private sector, and a chance to make a name for herself. At least it was everything she wanted until Jack walked in and made his threats. Ivy shook her head to clear the unwelcome intrusion. Jack might be able to cause some disruption, but even he wouldn't put himself so far out on a limb for Christof unless it was a sure thing, and pushing her on a non-compete agreement that had already been vetted by Sylvia's lawyer was not a sure thing. Jack was a politician through and through.

The thought jolted her.

Why would Jack bother with such a low-level problem like this? Ivy thought of Joanna Savage and Sylvia Pusey and all the other smart executives she knew who looked for cause and effect so much better than she did. It was time for her to start honing her skills.

"Why does a man like Jack waste his time asking around as to where we might be, driving over to a pub he'd otherwise never be caught dead in, and make vague threats to an employee who has no secrets of his and won't even be working there much longer? There is no personal or professional reason for Jack to do this." Ivy sounded out the problem. "Why is he hounding me?"

"The threat was to both of us, remember? And my job wasn't in jeopardy until today. What about this new Ivy, the one who is less self-centered and works like a team?" Ben frowned at her. "Or have you forgotten about your new heart, Tin Woman?"

"Ben, this is no time for games. Think about it. Why would Jack possibly go out on a limb for Christof when he has nothing to gain from hounding us?"

"What can Christof offer a career politician like Jack?" Ben pursed his lips as he sorted the puzzle pieces in his mind.

"Jack is getting ready to return to the US next year, and rumor is he's going to run for office. He's doing this dirty work for Christof in exchange for some kind of political favor!" Ivy hit the table hard, attracting the attention of waitress. "I wonder what he's offering him."

"Money. Has to be money. What else could he offer?"

When the waitress came over, Ivy ordered a curry.

"Do you eat anything else, woman?" Ben asked. He then

held up two fingers to the waitress, doubling the order.

"Hey, if we're moving to Madrid, we have to enjoy the best of England before we go. I might have curry every day until then," Ivy said.

"You'd eat like that while trying to woo your new man? Believe me, you don't want to risk the after-effects of that much curry with your clothes off," Ben smirked. Ivy hid her smile with her hand, remembering just how well a night of curry and love turned out for her in the past. Ben looked horrified. "You are one sick woman. I am never going to get these images out of my head."

"Hey, you brought it up, not me." She took a sip of wine. "Now let's get back to business. Christof found out what Jack wants and is now pulling the strings. We have to figure out a way to counteract that."

"How about Sylvia? She's been a surprise so far, and if she's part of our new team, she needs to know about it," Ben offered.

Ivy turned the idea over in her mind. She wasn't quite comfortable with it, but that's how real growth felt, right? Socrates nodded in her head, reminding her to build the new. This was where the trust began. Her days of flying solo were over.

# # #

"I was worried you'd rescind the offer, actually," Ivy said.

"I don't back down from a challenge, Ivy. I want you in Madrid, and Jack can kiss my ass if he thinks he can hold up progress just to squeeze a few pounds out of an old boarding school buddy. What is he, in the nineteenth century or something?" Sylvia was irritated, but Ivy was glad to know it wasn't at her. "Let's take care of this right now." Sylvia picked up the phone and dialed from memory. She must have a direct line to him, because she didn't go through the switchboard or his assistant. "Jack, what is this nonsense about pestering Ivy over her clearance?" Sylvia demanded. She put him on speakerphone and then put her finger to her lips. Ivy nodded in understanding.

"Sylvia, nice to hear from you. How's the new business?" Jack asked.

"Better than you expected, I'm sure. And if you piss me off about my new employee, I'll have to remind you just how good I am at getting what I want." Sylvia was like a bulldog.

"Sylvia, I'm just protecting the interests of the US government, making sure that her clearance is in order before she goes out to the private sector. There's nothing personal here." Jack's voice was soothing, as if he were talking to a belligerent child. From Sylvia's expression, that was the wrong move.

"What a noble idea, Jack. As a US citizen myself, I'd want

to make sure that nothing was being done to compromise our government, either. Say, finding out that a senior member at the Embassy was letting a foreign national dictate employment practices in return for a hefty political contribution from his father's investment bank." Sylvia laughed. "Boy, you know how sensitive people are about banks these days. I'd be surprised if anyone with that kind of shadow could get far in his first Senate race, no matter how good his track record was before. Especially if those pesky journalists started following the money trail to see if he'd done it before. Gotta love that First Amendment, right, Jack?"

Ivy's hand went up to her mouth, holding in her laugh. Sylvia was good, and not only that, this was all impromptu. Ivy had only been in her office ten minutes, spilling the story and crossing her fingers the job didn't get yanked out from under her. Instead, Sylvia surprised her by cutting Jack off at the knees. Maybe Ivy should have been more trusting of other people all along. It was certainly working out for her now.

"Sylvia, there's really no need for either of us to waste taxpayer money on frivolous investigations. It does no one any good, does it?" Jack paused, waiting for Sylvia to reassure him. When she didn't, he continued with a little less confidence than before. "You know that an investigation wouldn't stop her from going to work for you, and it probably wouldn't even last very long. She'll be in the clear in just a few months. Let's say you allow this to happen and I get my donation. Maybe I can send a few choice contracts your way?" Jack offered.

Ivy didn't know what to think. Sylvia was shrewd and her

company was new. Would she offer Ivy up as the sacrificial lamb for some plum assignments? Ivy wouldn't blame her if she did. What if this whole thing backfired on her?

"Jack, we've known each other a long time, haven't we?" Sylvia's voice was friendly, nostalgic even.

"Too long to let a petty problem like this interfere with our relationship," Jack said, voice as smooth as butter.

The bile in Ivy's throat threatened to escape. Sylvia's success was forged on her relationships, including the one with Jack. Ivy was a probationary employee with baggage. It didn't take a genius to see which side she'd take.

"I have no intention of letting that happen, Jack."

"I knew you'd see reason, Sylvia. There is no reason we can't both get a little something out of this unfortunate Ivy Cross situation."

"Glad you see it my way, Jack. What I'm getting is a new employee with a security clearance and absolutely no further interference from you. In addition, you'll make a public statement thanking her for her years of service and congratulating her on the new position in my company." Sylvia winked at Ivy as she said it.

"And what am I getting out of this arrangement?" Jack asked, his buttery tone gone.

"I'm allowing you to save yourself, which is more than you

deserve." Sylvia paused a moment to let him consider her words. "I record all my phone meetings, as I've clearly stated to you before, both when we worked together and the one conversation we had before now. This is not unknown to you, and still you chose to offer me a bribe with government money so you could start a false campaign against a loyal employee in order to take campaign financing from a foreigner. Do I have my facts straight?"

"Sylvia, I think you've misinterpreted what I've said," Jack hastily replied.

"There is no interpretation necessary, Jack. It is all recorded, easily played back right now in front of us or later in front of a judge. Or maybe the ambassador." Sylvia held firm and Ivy was in awe of her self-control.

"Dammit, Sylvia! This is how the world of government works, and if you don't know that by now, then your whole career has been wasted." Jack was probably spitting into the phone as he spoke, his fury growing the more Sylvia held her ground.

"Jack, Jack, Jack," Sylvia sighed. "This is how you might play ball, but you're in the big leagues now. You can either choose to play by the new rules, or you can put your bat and ball between your legs and scurry back to the farm league. But you will not be investigating my employee now or in the future. Is that clear?"

"You can't win with this kind of bullying, Sylvia. It is

unladylike," Jack sneered.

"Then it's a good thing I decided to be a CEO instead. I'm going now, Jack, but if I get one whiff of you tormenting Ivy again, I'm going far and wide with this. Your own mother will stop buying you birthday presents before I'm done. Don't mess with me, Jack, now or ever again." Sylvia ended the call and looked over at Ivy.

"You are incredible, Sylvia. Thank you for sticking up for me," Ivy said.

"You have no idea how long I've been waiting to do something like that," Sylvia said with a grin. "We're a team now, and I will always act like it. I expect you to, as well," Sylvia replied.

Ivy reached into her bag and brought out a small cardboard box. She lifted the lid and turned it around to face Sylvia. Inside were two giant strawberry cupcakes from her favorite bakery.

"To celebrate," Ivy said, picking up one of the cupcakes.

"You expected this to go well, I take it?" Sylvia asked.

"I figured with cupcakes it could go either way. If we won, we'd celebrate together. If you booted me, I'd eat both of them before I got to the elevator." Ivy smiled and took a bite, smearing icing all the way up to her nose.

CHAPTER THIRTY-SEVEN

Ivy locked her apartment door and walked next door to Mrs. B's, trolley bag behind her. She knocked on the door. Mrs. B opened the door while wiping her hands on a dishtowel.

"Off already, are you? Well, you have a good trip, dear. And don't worry about your plants and mail. I'll take care of all that until you decide what to do next." Mrs. B was in her usual apron, hair perfectly coiffed, and smelling a little bit like cookies. "You must be so excited! Madrid sounds very exotic to me."

"Thanks so much for helping me out, Mrs. B. I really appreciate it. This is happening so fast." Ivy wondered if her new next-door neighbor would be so friendly.

"Dear, you never ask for a thing! I'm so happy to be able to help you. And when you come back maybe you'll remember to bring me a little box of those chocolates you shared? I did love them so." Mrs. B's cheeks turned pink at her request, which made Ivy laugh.

"No problem at all. I'm sure I can sneak a box into my

luggage for you. And if I'm gone too long, I'll pop one in the mail so you don't have to wait." Ivy reached out to hug her, the first time she'd ever done so. Mrs. B stiffened momentarily, unused to physical contact with her neighbor, then warmly returned the hug.

"Now you take care, dear. Don't worry about a thing here. Go off and have a wonderful adventure!" Mrs. B held the dishtowel to her chest as if it was a handkerchief and she was going to dab her eyes at any moment.

As she gave her final wave and turned away, Ivy thought back to her recurring fantasy of escape. Back then it was the dramatic exit with her resignation, a direct route to the airport, and jetting off to places unknown, sipping champagne and laughing without a care in the world.

Reality was flying to Madrid, a city she'd never even visited, to start a new job and a new life with a man she loved —even though she couldn't tell him that yet. She was bringing a ton of baggage and an assistant, and she was flying business class.

Would it change the outcome of her fantasy? Make it better or worse? Her nerves got the better of her, and while she waited for a taxi, she sent a message to her friends.

Ivy_Cross: Just locked up my place. Leaving for Madrid. Wish me luck!

RoseGarden: Buena suerte! (Better start practicing your Spanish.)

VioletStackDesign: We want a pic when you land in Madrid!

LilyL: KAN IS IN NYC!

Daisy_Eats: Is Kan a new food?

Ivy_Cross: Only if you like tall, dark, and handsome.

Daisy_Eats: I'm confused, but happy for you anyway, Ivy. And Lily, I guess.

LilyL: More info later. But I'm meeting Kan tonight. Love you!

Ivy_Cross: Ruben doesn't know I'm coming, FYI.

RoseGarden: What????

Ivy_Cross: I thought it would be nice to surprise him.

VioletStackDesign: Do men like it when you show up at the door with suitcases?

Ivy_Cross: I'm not crazy, Vi. I have a hotel.

VioletStackDesign: Risky move, but totally you.

RoseGarden: Keep us posted. We want a blow by blow.

Daisy_Eats: I don't think we want that, Rose.

VioletStackDesign: Speak for yourself, Daisy. I'm in a sexual drought right now.

Ivy_Cross: Okay, okay! I'll give you details later. Right now, heading to Heathrow. Love you all!

As the cab pulled up to the curb, Ivy put her phone in her pocket and settled into the back of the cab. These big black London cabs were the first clue that life would be different when she arrived ten years ago. Every time she got in one, she flashed to that moment at the airport when she was too nervous to try the Tube to get into London and paid a fortune for a cab, back when she couldn't afford such a luxury. Now she was as accustomed to this city as any native-born person. Would she feel the same way about Madrid over time? What would be her first impression after landing at the airport? So many questions swirling in her head, and she had no one to talk to about it. Ben was still working at the Embassy, his final day still three weeks away. But then he'd be joining her in Madrid, and together they'd build up Sylvia's company into something strong.

It took an hour to get to Heathrow, and along the way Ivy looked out the window, wondering what Ruben would say when she arrived. He said he wanted them to be together, but it was one thing to have a girlfriend in London and another to have her in the same city. Maybe he said he wanted it before because he knew it could never happen? The doubts crept in, combining with her excitement to produce a distinct nausea. Ivy had the overwhelming urge to throw up in this nice black taxicab.

She looked out on the highway and knew they couldn't pull off, so she pursed her lips and breathed through her mouth for a little while. The cabbie looked at her through his rearview mirror. "Everything okay back there?"

"Just a little nervous about my trip, that's all. It will pass." She smiled weakly, hoping he'd take that as a clue to leave her alone, but no such luck. He decided to open up.

"I hate flying, too. Give me a car any day, a train if I have to, but don't put me in a metal tube in the sky," he said. "But you must have taken a long flight from the US to get here."

"I live in London. Well, I lived in London for ten years," Ivy corrected herself. "I'm moving to Madrid now for work, and I'm just a little nervous about it."

"Sunny Spain! I took a vacation there once with the wife. You can't beat the weather," he reasoned, as if that were the answer to all problems. When she didn't answer, he continued, "You speaka da Spanish?" he asked.

"*Sí, hablo español*," Ivy said.

"See, you'll do fine. Nothing to worry about," he said with a bright smile, happy to have solved her problem. He pulled the cab to the departures curb at the airport and helped her with her bag. As she counted out her money to pay him, the cabbie motioned up to the gray sky. "London is sad to see you go, but you'll have a sunny welcome in Spain. Good luck to you." As he drove off, Ivy stood at the curb with her hand gripping the handle of her suitcase. A deep, cleansing breath was interrupted by a passing bus, the exhaust intruding on her Zen moment. Ivy turned on her heel and walked into the airport, ready to find out if Ruben meant what he said and if she could say it back to him.

# # #

This is where I'm going to live for the foreseeable future, Ivy thought as the cab drove her farther into the city of Madrid. The buildings started out as boxes that could be in any city near any airport, but as they ventured closer to the center the architecture took on a more regal and historic flavor. The streets were smaller, parking almost comical with tiny spaces surrounded by stanchions. How could anyone negotiate such a space?

People walked the sidewalks with purpose, fashionable in their skinny jeans and scarves. The economist in her noticed the many different mom-and-pop shops and cafes scattered within the bigger-name chains. She imagined sitting outside to have coffee or a glass of wine, a rare treat in London but an everyday thing in this city.

She asked the cabdriver to drive her through Malasaña on the way to her hotel near the Plaza Mayor. This was Ruben's neighborhood, and she wanted to see if he was reflected in it.

Would the neighborhood be brash and witty like him? Stylish and funny? Smart and intense?

"Tell me about Malasaña," Ivy asked the cab driver in Spanish.

"This is like SoHo or Greenwich Village in New York City," he replied.

"You've been to New York?" Ivy asked.

"*Sí*, drove a cab there for fifteen years." He adjusted his cap and winked. "Don't you know the cab drivers in New York all come from somewhere else?"

"Now you sound like a New Yorker," Ivy replied with a laugh.

"This neighborhood is like a little town within Madrid. You've got your butcher, your cafes, restaurants, and bars, plus lots of little vintage shops. That's all the rage now. But you're also really close to the main shopping street in Madrid. If you have some money, this is a pretty nice place to live." He shook his head. "Twenty years ago no one came here. Twenty years from now it will probably be too expensive for regular people to live in."

Ivy looked out at the small plazas within the neighborhood, filled with people sitting around small tables enjoying coffee and small cups of beer. Other people walked their dogs, carried backpacks to and from work and school, and stood on corners talking to friends. In London there were lots of people out going places, but in her own neighborhood, it was pretty quiet. This neighborhood seemed to be teeming, even at the siesta hour of four o'clock.

Would she meet her friends for coffee in the afternoons on one of these plazas? Take dance lessons at the local studio? Buy her clothes from the trendy shops? Ivy found it hard to picture herself here, living such an outdoor life after her years in London. She wondered which street was Ruben's, whether he had a large or small flat and whether it came with a terrace. He'd told her he used to live in Salamanca, the ritziest neighborhood in Madrid, but since it was filled with old people and families, he decided to get a little grittier in Malasaña. Now she could see what he meant.

"Want to see it again?" the cabdriver asked.

"That's it?" Ivy replied.

"Central Madrid is a pretty small place. This isn't New York," he said. *Or London.* The cabbie turned down Calle Fuencarral, a main shopping street, and headed toward her hotel.

Ivy worked everything out up until this point of her plan, and now she had to figure out how to tell Ruben she was here, for good.

Oh, and that she loved him.

CHAPTER THIRTY-EIGHT

Ruben paced in his office, trying to figure out a solution for his company and his personal life. Tomas leaving was a big blow to the company and to him personally, and he knew word would get out as to why. Would they consider him a weak leader, being led around by his heart? Or worse yet, his dick?

Ruben prided himself on running a family-like organization. And he knew he blew that when he made such a big decision without even asking for feedback. But he was going to have to disappoint one part of his life to make the other happy. There was just no way around it, and he was tired of disappointing Ivy. He had to show his commitment to this relationship or it wasn't going to work. How could he say, "I love you" and not even want to be together half the time?

Still, Ruben found the practice of being in love a lot more difficult than the feeling of being in love. It still bothered him that Ivy hadn't told him she loved him. Ruben tried not to be juvenile about it, knowing it wasn't a tit-for-tat statement. He wanted her to say it when she was ready. But couldn't she hurry up? He was already disrupting his business with plans to be with her, and she couldn't even tell him if she was serious.

Tonight he'd call her and have a more serious conversation. No more of this playful banter. She had a job now, and he'd made the decision to be in London part time. They needed to discuss the logistics of their relationship and get some things sorted. Then he'd feel better about this.

He sat down at his desk to start thinking about the second problem—Tomas. How could he repair that relationship and get him to stay? If he had to replace that position, there was no way in hell he could spend half his time in London. Why had he rushed into that decision without even pretending to ask for input?

As his mind searched for solutions to his problems, his phone buzzed.

"*Hola*," Ivy said.

"You told me when we first met that your Spanish was so good it would break my heart, but that I'd never be lucky enough to hear it," Ruben replied. "What's the occasion?"

"*Viernes*," Ivy replied, saying the Spanish word for Friday. "TGIF, if you need a translation."

"There are so many things I need translation services for, Ivy Cross. The main one being you." Ruben didn't know if now was the time to have this conversation or not, but he was diving in anyway. Maybe Ivy could help him come up with a solution for Tomas. Or tell him she loved him. Or have phone sex. At this point, any of the three would turn his day around.

"What's so hard to understand about me?" Ivy teased. "You want me. I want you. When we're together, nothing else matters. The only thing we need to work out is how to be together."

"Simple as that?" Ruben asked.

"Simple as that," she confirmed.

"I'm coming to London. To live. Well, at least part time. I told you I loved you, Ivy, and I meant it. This is how I'll show you. I'm coming to London and hope that you'll try to spend some time in Madrid, too. We can make this work." The words spilled out of Ruben's mouth, and he was pretty sure he'd just shot down the chance of phone sex. Two options left.

"I like a man of action, Ruben," Ivy said, silent on the specifics of his plan.

"I'd hoped you'd more than like it," Ruben said, frustrated with her coy manner. There was a time and place for it, and this wasn't it. But then again, she was riding high on the new job and had no idea he'd just suffered a huge loss at work. Maybe he should tell her. "I'm sorry I'm being so short with you. It's been a tough day. My team did not like the news I was moving part time to London, and one of them quit." Ruben felt good sharing the stress, not having to pretend it was all okay, even if it did dampen the mood for phone sex.

"Oh, Ruben! Why didn't you tell me first?" Ivy exclaimed.

Ruben's stomach lurched, hoping she wasn't about to say what he thought she was going to say. If this call was about her staying in London and keeping their relationship as a casual fling whenever he was in town, he was not going to be happy. In fact, he might just board a plane tonight to tell her about it.

"I wanted to surprise you," he offered, playing down the stress of the decision and how every business bone in his body rebelled at him for it.

"Surprises are—unpredictable," she said slowly.

"That's why they call it a surprise, Ivy. Are you unhappy that I'm coming to London?"

"Well, yes. I'm very unhappy you're coming to London. And when you arrive, I won't be able to see you," Ivy said.

Ruben clenched his phone so tight it almost cracked.

"Dammit, Ivy! You said you needed time, and I've given it to you. You said I needed to show commitment, and I am. You can't keep jerking me around like this!" He felt the flush of anger on his cheeks and spreading throughout his body. What a fool he'd been to think he'd ever tame her.

"Shhhh," she said, as if calming a small child. "It will be all right, I promise."

He was at the tipping point, knowing this conversation was either the beginning of a great life together or the start of the downfall. He didn't want to consider which one it might be and how powerless he was to control it. *Screw being powerless.* The anger in his voice was palpable, and he knew it. "Ivy, we are not going to continue like this. The crazy train stops now."

"Turn around," she whispered. Ruben stood still, every hair on his body at attention. He felt himself growing hard at her words. *She's going to drive me crazy.*

He slowly turned from the window to the door of his office. There she was, leaning against the doorframe, phone against her ear. She closed the door with her black stiletto shoes, the click of the door as audible as an earthquake in the silence of the room.

"I wanted you to hear me say it in person, Ruben," Ivy said, walking toward him with the phone still against her ear. "To know without a doubt, by looking into my face, that I was telling you the truth. That what I had to say was the foundation we could build our lives on. I love you, Ruben Alegre. And I will do what it takes for us to be together," she breathed into the phone. He couldn't believe she was there, in the flesh, not only in Madrid but in his office.

Ruben wasted no time rushing to her, grabbing her so tightly he worried he'd break her. She dropped her phone to the floor and put her arms around his waist.

"This is the part where you kiss me," she said.

"Always bossing me around. I'll kiss you when I'm ready," he scolded. "A surprise trip to Madrid does not forgive your delay in proclaiming your love to me. Most women do it within five minutes, and it astonishes me it took you this long."

"Then before you kiss me, perhaps I should tell you this isn't a surprise trip," Ivy said.

Ruben was confused.

"I think I'd remember if you told me you were taking a trip to Madrid," Ruben said. "I would have slept for twenty-four hours beforehand to be ready for you," he teased.

"I didn't tell you because I didn't know how you'd react," Ivy said, tracing the buttons on his shirt. "You see, I'm not here on a trip. I'm being transferred to Madrid for my new job."

Ruben's face froze, wondering if this was some kind of joke. Ivy, living in Madrid? Working in Madrid? Available for Tuesday night dinner, Saturday bike rides, and meeting his friends?

"Ivy, don't joke with me like that. You know I want you here more than anything, and I'm willing to come to London for you," he said.

"I know you are, Ruben. But this is how it played out. I have a great new job centered in Madrid. You live here. I speak Spanish. You speak English. We love each other. If this is going to happen, it's going to happen here," Ivy said.

Ruben's heart exploded. He couldn't believe she did this for him, for them.

"It's going to happen right now," he growled. Ruben pulled

her lips to his, claiming her as his other half. He wanted to be with her, in her, beside her, and on her now and every day going forward. He explored her mouth with his tongue like it was the first time they'd ever kissed. She was all new to him, a fully open version with nooks and crannies to explore, dark corners now filled with light. All those parts of Ivy that used to be closed to him were available, and he wanted to know every one by touch, by scent, and by heart.

Without another word, they quietly but vigorously celebrated Ivy's inaugural visit to Madrid on the couch in his office. After the tension of the past few weeks, the drama, the misunderstandings—it was finally over. They were together in a way they never thought possible, and their bodies yearned to celebrate.

In the past few weeks they'd gone against distance, Christof, the US government, his company, and their own stubborn personalities to make their love work. If they'd done this much just to be together, imagine how good they'd be in everyday life in Madrid with no roadblocks.

"Let's go celebrate," Ruben said, lifting her up as he stood. I promised you a great dinner and nice sheets, and I happen to have both at my apartment."

"Are you going to make me have sex on the coffee table as punishment? Because if you did, I wouldn't blame you," Ivy teased, biting his neck before standing in front of him to dress.

"Before we're done, we'll have sex on every surface in my apartment," Ruben said, pulling his pants on. His grin was interrupted by a knock.

Ivy giggled, pulling on the last of her clothes.

"*Momento!*" Ruben called out, zipping his pants. He crossed to the door to answer, and there stood Tomas with the resignation letter in hand.

They stood staring at each other for a few seconds before Tomas broke eye contact and looked at the ground. He shuffled his feet before raising his head. "This is weird. It feels like I'm saying goodbye to family."

"It's because you are."

"Families don't treat each other this way," Tomas replied.

"Then your family isn't like mine. We say stupid stuff all the time, but we always know who's team we're one. Sometimes, we just need to be reminded."

"Are you reminding me, then?" Tomas's jaw clenched.

"No, you reminded me. And I'm sorry it took me so long to realize it. Don't go, Tomas. We can work this out," Ruben said.

"You can't tell me we'll work it out when you make decisions without even consulting me. I'm supposed to be your right hand, and you kept me in the dark."

"I'm not always good at the family stuff, but that's why we work so well together. I push us to the edge, and you keep us from falling over. This time I just went a little too far. Will you stay if I stay?" Ruben asked.

"Ruben, it's not about the decision, it's that you did it without talking to me. How can I trust you if you don't trust me?" Tomas replied.

"You're right. I didn't tell you about my situation because I didn't want to hear the reasons why I shouldn't do it. I thought if I cut you out of the decision, it would change the situation. I was wrong." Ruben squeezed him on the shoulder. "C'mon, Tomas. Stay with me. We've got big things ahead of us."

Tomas took a step back, surprised by his response. "What changed?"

"Everything," Ruben said, looking over at Ivy. "Everything."

Tomas looked inside the door at Ivy sitting on the couch. She waved and smiled. Tomas awkwardly returned the wave before looking back at Ruben.

"I don't want to know what just happened, but if you're staying, I'm staying. But I can't have you making decisions like that without talking to me," Tomas said, face full of relief.

"You're my second in command, Tomas, and I don't want to lose you." Ruben held out his hand to shake, and Tomas took a step back.

"No offense man, but I think I know what that hand has been doing." He grinned, stepping forward into a giant bro hug.

Ruben hugged him back, red face hidden.

"See you tomorrow?" Ruben asked.

"Yeah, see you tomorrow." Tomas smiled as Ruben ripped up the resignation letter and let the pieces fall to the floor.

Ruben turned back to Ivy as Tomas walked away, shrugging his shoulders and spreading his arms to the side as if to say, "Can you believe that?" And he couldn't.

"Aw, that was so cute, the way you two made up," Ivy said, arms stretched along the back of the couch.

"Just wait until you see the way you and I make up. I might have lied to Tomas. There's a good chance I'll be calling in sick tomorrow," Ruben said. He hummed a few bars of "American Woman," strumming his air guitar as he danced his way back to the couch, back to Ivy, and forward into a life he'd never imagined possible.

# # #

Ivy_Cross: I'm in Madrid, in love, and in business. What more could a girl want?

Daisy_Eats: Wine! Have you tried the Albariño yet? Divine.

RoseGarden: Daze, how can you think of wine at a time like this?!

Daisy_Eats: It's my job! And plus, it goes with sex and love.

Ivy_Cross: That it does, my dear.

VioletStackDesign: Another one of Ivy's adventures has a happy ending.

Ivy_Cross: But no casualties this time. Progress!

LilyL: I'd call Christof a casualty.

Ivy_Cross: Yes, but he did it to himself.

RoseGarden: Will you invite him to the wedding?

Ivy_Cross: Do we look like the marrying type? Let's talk about yours.

RoseGarden: Fair point. I expect you all in Australia in six months.

Daisy_Eats: Wouldn't miss it. You'll have shiraz, right?

VioletStackDesign: Ignore her, Rose. We'll all be there. And we finally get to meet Ruben and Mateo.

Daisy_Eats: Does this mean we all have to find Spanish lovers now? Just checking the rules.

LilyL: Not me! I'm bringing Kan.

Daisy_Eats: Where is he from?

LilyL: No idea. And isn't that the best part?

WHAT HAPPENS NEXT?

Wondering what happens to Ivy and Ruben next? You can download their epilogue for free at BetsyTalbot.com/ivy-ending. While you're there, be sure to check out the weekly episodes of The Quickie Romance Podcast, where you'll hear excerpts of great romance books narrated by me, along with a little behind-the-scenes info I've discovered from the author.

NEXT IN THE SERIES

Did you like Ivy and Ruben's story? The two of them would love it if you'd leave a review wherever you bought this book. And don't miss Book Three in The Late Bloomers Series: Tiger Lily. The mysterious warrior-artist Kan has enthralled the logical doctor Lily. She's reeling from a tough assignment in Africa, witness to atrocities that would shatter most people. Can Kan teach her to follow her life's work without breaking her spirit? Coming January 2016!

Get behind-the-scenes info, short stories, early review copies, pictures from research trips, and publication announcements when you sign up at BetsyTalbot.com. Late Bloomers get the first and best of everything!

ACKNOWLEDGEMENTS

I don't just write about Late Bloomers; I have them in my life! And it is because of these wonderful women (and a few good men) that my books make it to your hands.

My thanks to the village it takes to produce a work a fiction.

Alison Cornford-Matheson and Andrew Matheson loaned me their RV in the northwest coast of Spain to finish this story in peace and quiet. Even smarter, they didn't allow me to drive it anywhere.

My writing group and fellow indie authors, most of whom I know online: you are too numerous to list and too generous to be believed. I am humbled by your continued support and encouragement.

My beta readers are the best in the world, and their enthusiasm for this project and detailed feedback made Ivy's story far more exciting. Big thanks to Claire Ashman, Erika Banks, Roxane Baxter, Kaycee Bowen, Carol Carver, Alison Cornford-Matheson, Gale Cushenberry, Teresa D'Aurizio, Carole Dillard, Carrie Fannin, Pat Fordyce, Pauline Frost, Cinta García-Stone, Wynne Gavin, Sarah Glashagel, Michelle Goerdel, Julie Gover, Vindella Heath-Williams, Sue Jochens, Trena Johnson, Joan Kerr, Tricia Krohn, Betsy Maples, Mary Kay Martin, Cheryl Moran, Lynn OConnor, Lori Osterberg, Sandra Pisarski, Jackie Purkess, Leah Rhea, Grace Rodrigues,

Trisha Rogers, ReAnn Scott, Vanessa Shapiro, Carol Sloan, Carol Smith, Shawn Tuttle, Ruth Vahle, Diana Van der Velden, Margaret Walton, Jan Wenzel, Tracy Wood, Lori Wostl, and Patricia ZelmEmmart.

Above and beyond the call of duty honors go to Paula Russell Weiss, Mary Gebhart, and Lynne Mullan. I owe you ladies copious amounts of wine.

Danijela Mijailovic provided me with beautiful covers for the entire Late Bloomers Series. Her creativity has put a great face on my stories.

My proofreading team: Amanda, Tracy, Mary, and Diane. You taught me so much this time around! I promise to be better on book three.

Last but certainly not least, I thank my business, life, and crime partner, Warren Talbot. As with everything good in my life, this would not have happened without you—or have been as much fun. Thank you for making me stick to my deadlines and keeping the coffee and wine flowing. I don't deserve you, and I hope you never figure that out.

HOW THIS SERIES CAME TO BE

In 2010, my husband Warren and I sold everything we owned to travel the world. The decision was not a light one; we both had good jobs, a nice house, and good life. But after my younger brother and a good friend both had brushes with death at the age of 35, I began to look at life in a different way. After two years of planning, we set off on our adventure, never realizing how completely it would change our lives. (You can read more about that at my website at BetsyTalbot.com.)

In January 2013 we rented a house in Morocco for a month with another couple who writes and works mostly online like we do. After cooking a tasty tagine, pouring cocktails, and turning on some music, we sat on cozy couches and talked about what we wanted to accomplish in the coming year.

I talked about romance books, how writers I knew were having huge success with these stories but none of them had characters I could relate to. The main characters were in their twenties or thirties, a stage I'd already passed and didn't long to return to. The future was ahead, and I wanted to imagine more of what that would look like.

The four of us agreed that the market was big enough for all kinds of books, so we dared each other to write one quirky romance that didn't fall into the norm and to publish it within a year.

I've always wanted to write about interesting women,

strong friendships, and hot love affairs. And my life has been about travel for so long that's it's like breathing. Mixing all those things together with a few cocktails gave me the start to a five-book series.

Much of what I write is drawn from the bits and pieces of real women I know, real places I've been, and real experiences I've had or been told about first-hand. They are as real as they can be, with a heavy dash of fiction to dress them up.

Thank you for reading this second book in The Late Bloomers Series. And if you want to know more about the writing process for a romance (at least mine), you can check out the "How I Became a Romance Writer" series on my website at BetsyTalbot.com.

Next up is Tiger Lily, a bohemian doctor who is recovering from a painful divorce and navigating a stressful job with Doctors Without Borders. I hope you'll come back to read her story and find out what happens when she gets to know the mysterious warrior-poet Kan.

I can't wait to write what she tells me.

Happy reading,

Betsy Talbot

Galicia, Spain

August 3, 2015